Whither Thou Goest

Sisters Held Captive by America's Pioneer Serial Killers

Robert G. Huffstutler

Published by BNS Publishing House, 2024.

I0635914

This is a work of historical fiction. Although it is based on real people and events, liberties have been taken for literary effect.

WHITHER THOU GOEST

First edition. June 1, 2024.

Copyright © 2024 Robert G. Huffstutler.

ISBN: 979-8989091010 (Print)

ISBN: 979-8989091003 (Digital)

Written by Robert G. Huffstutler.

A special thanks to my lovely wife for what she has done. I am a better writer and a better man because of her.

WHITHER THOU GOEST

Doing chores—most folks consider it a rite of passage for every young boy and girl. Some children fight it. Others accept it as part of growing up. Johnny faced his rite of passage with glee. When told what he would do, Johnny jumped around the cabin chanting, "Feed the chickens. I'm gonna feed the chickens."

His older sisters, Susan and Betsy, laughed at Johnny's misplaced excitement about him doing his first chore. What began as jumping quickly turned into a quirky chicken dance that caught Pa off guard. Pa sprayed his drink across the table to avoid choking. Even Mama, expecting another baby, found it difficult to scold her husband for his mess, since she too, laughed at her son's antics.

As bedtime neared, everyone heard Pa tell one of his tales. That time, they heard a story about pirates chasing after a pot of gold. A new twist to the story had a young boy capturing a chicken so he could feed the starving heroes. Afterwards, Mama tucked in her children and kissed them goodnight. As sleep overcame them, Johnny thought of that day as a good day. Oh, if only his next day lived up to its promise.

PART ONE - Chapter One: The Battle at Robert's Folly

On a typical farm, one would hear the familiar crowing from a rooster as the first rays of daylight rose above the horizon. Things happened differently at the Roberts' farm.

The General, a muscular, statuesque, and regal-looking rooster with a persnickety disposition chose when everyone should rise and shine. The fowl's inner clock, not the light of day, led the rooster to break forth with his peculiar call. It began as a low, raspy "cock-a-doo". Then after a pause, the "dle-doo" screeched out as if someone had scraped their fingernails across a small slate board, the type children used in a classroom.

The bird's ungodly and incessant call could be heard almost any time during the day or night, but never, never at dawn. Nobody could make The General stop, nobody except for their dog Samson. His deep bark could make The General stop. The family dog and the rooster had faced each other before, and Samson always won.

John and Anne immediately regretted giving the children permission to name the rooster. The Roberts Family had an illustration of the newly formed country's first president above the fireplace. Betsy had noticed a distinct similarity between The General's beak and Washington's nose. John and Anne knew they had lost the debate at that point. Luckily, for both rooster and president, John and Anne nixed calling the bird by the name *Washington*.

The General satisfied everyone since the rooster strutted like one. Giving pet status to "that damn bird," as John often complained, confounded the parents. Anne once thought of serving him up for a Sunday dinner but quickly dropped the idea. How could she say to her children, "Eat up. We're having The General for dinner." Besides, with such a mean temper, she doubted The General would taste delicious. The bird had found his niche in the world.

The family never understood why the rooster acted strangely until a traveler stopped by for a bite of food and a place to rest. Upon spotting the yellow-necked rooster, the man enthused, "That there's an English Gamecock. He's a fightin' bird." The man, an avid gambler who made a living betting on cockfights, went on and on about what a fine specimen of a rooster they had.

The talk of entering The General in a cockfight or two appealed to John. It reminded him of an earlier life, a life he often missed. The traveler offered to buy the rooster, for a good price too. However, since the children considered The General as a pet, Anne would not hear of it.

Owning a farm, even a farm, took hard, backbreaking work. John hated it. Anne, on the other hand, felt very comfortable living a rural life in the Swannanoa Valley. Their home wasn't far from the Black Mountain range in western North Carolina. Farming flowed in Anne's veins and their tiny farm made her happy.

John once talked of going back home to Wilmington now that the War for Independence had finished. He dropped the idea when Anne nearly broke down in tears. She loved their home and vowed to live there for the rest of her life.

When they first bought the land, the couple had some concerns about whether they had enough flatland to build all that needed building. A gully washer blew through almost as soon as they stopped the wagon. Like so many dreamers before them and many dreamers who would come afterward, John and Anne snuggled up and gazed out at their property from the back of the wagon. There, beneath the lightning, thunder, and rain, the two planned out the perfect homestead to complement their promising future. Oh sure, the land had hills, lots of them. However, amid the waves of water rolling down the hillsides, they found an island with enough space for everything they needed to build.

The work needed to create Anne's dream farm didn't bother John so much. The monotony did. Through the years not much changed in their lives—except when some crisis, always bad, drove them further into debt. Every morning of every day, of every month, of every year, John rose from his bed before dawn. It didn't matter how healthy or sick he felt, what weather conditions he faced, or what else needed his attention, he had to work. Time never stretched far enough to do what needed doing.

Early on, they thought of hiring someone to help get the farm up and running, even though they could scarcely afford it. However, in a land where one-seventh of its people lived as slaves, hiring help most likely meant hiring a slave- or one of slavery's second cousins- an indentured servant.

Anne, an indentured servant herself, ran away and married after completing only part of her multi-year obligation. The authorities would have returned her to her owner if she were ever caught. She never wanted a life where others controlled what she did, where she went, or how she behaved. How could she do that to another living soul? No, as a couple they decided to stay away from owning another person to do their work for them. The idea of hiring help never came up again.

WHITHER THOU GOEST

MILKING THE COW STOOD atop the list of things John needed to do that day. He made his way to what one would generously call a barn. The Roberts family, always short of cash, did what they could when they built it. Other expenses were more pressing, but the cow and team of horses needed a dry spot during the winter. John had built it out of scraps of lumber, leftover nails, hinges, and whatnot. Truth be told, it looked more like an oversized lean-to than a barn.

On his way back, John shooed away the cat, Millie, before placing the bucket of milk on the porch for his wife to retrieve. The feral cat had shown up one day begging for milk and piqued John's interest. He squirted a stream of milk from the cow's teat into a depression in the ground. The cat devoured the milk in seconds. Ever since then, John shared a little milk with his new companion. She gave him someone to talk to while everybody else still slept.

To the chickens' disappointment, John chose to change his daily routine that morning. He grabbed an axe and began splitting wood.

According to a self-proclaimed local farming expert, John needed to cut up to forty cords a year to have enough wood for cooking and to heat up a fire in the winter. Thanks to a large stand of evergreens and deciduous trees, his woodpile, halfway down the small incline on the east side of the cabin, never lacked for wood. Still, the cumbersome task of chopping down and splitting wood remained an exhausting chore and John spent a good portion of the day at the woodpile.

The family treasured their own personal forest; for hidden between the trees ran a brook with a small waterfall. The brook apparently came from an underground stream located beneath a nearby hill. In the middle, a small pool of fresh-flowing water gave them a place to bathe and frolic whenever the weather cooperated. The tiny brook eventually dumped into a creek which fed into the French Broad River.

After splitting the wood, John turned toward the chicken coop, located west of the cabin. The coop, a rather elaborate affair, stood out as the finest building on the farm. It was built before their cabin and served as their initial shelter. Their first child, Susan, was born there.

When John and Anne started farming, they depended on Anne's expertise since she alone knew anything about farming. Anne designed and supervised the building of a chicken coop. Unfortunately for them but fortunately for the chickens, Anne's recollection of how one built a coop depended on her childhood memories; and to a young child everything seems larger than reality.

With Anne in charge, the coop grew and grew and grew. It took some neighborly help from a couple of men from the Davidson clan to complete the building. Anne took a perverse pride in the chicken coop's name when the men called it, "Roberts' Folly". Curious travelers went out of their way to see it after hearing of the Folly. To Anne, her coop stood as her masterpiece, not a folly at all.

John pulled a bag of feed from the specially designed storage bin. The bag weighed at least twenty pounds. At last, the flock of birds believed their hunger would soon disappear. John raised the bag high for all the chickens to see. The birds took one step forward, and in unison raised their heads high. They stared blankly at the farmer. This amused John as he carried the bag of feed back to the cabin.

He said to himself, "Dumb clucks!" and placed the bag on the porch for his son. He noticed a popped-up nail on the porch and made a mental note of its location. He decided he would get to that later as he entered the cabin for breakfast.

SOMETIME LATER, LITTLE Johnny jumped out of bed realizing time had passed him by. A full-blown morning, not dawn, awaited him. He overslept and already regretted his error. The cacophonous rumble from the chicken coop made the lad move faster. Johnny slipped on his pants and clamored down the ladder from the loft he shared with his sisters.

Mama, anticipating a quick getaway, said, "Eat your breakfast" before the boy could reach the door.

As expected, Johnny whined, and for his effort, he heard a more adamant, "Eat!"

Dejected, Johnny sat and ate as quickly as possible. Anne's anxious son got up from the table. She instructed him that Pa left him a bag of feed on the porch. Johnny opened the door; a good-sized dog of no particular breed entered.

Seeing Samson enter with his tail wagging reminded Anne to give one final command, "Oh, and tie up Samson to the tree out back. I don't want him spookin' the chickens."

She stared at her son when he pleaded, "Mama!"

Giving up, Johnny turned to his four-legged companion and said, "Come on Thamthon."

"S...S...S...Samson" came the correction from the voice now behind him.

Johnny turned back to his mother one last time, and with a big, impish grin said, "Come on BOY." Off they went before hearing anything else.

The time for Johnny to face his challenge finally arrived. The bravado he showed the night before now waned in the light of day, especially since his pa had already left to do his own chores, and his ma relegated Samson to behind the cabin. Johnny felt lonely.

The lad wrapped his arms around the bag and heaved. Nothing moved. Again, still nothing. Johnny tugged and pulled, pulled and tugged, until the bag finally gave way. Ever so slowly, the boy maneuvered the burlap bag to the edge of the rickety porch. As he pulled one more time, the bag snagged on the nail. The boy ended up falling backward and landing on the ground. So too, did the bag.

What's fun about this? the boy wondered. Like all young boys, he felt duty-bound to make his chore fun. Johnny recalled his pa's story from the night before, and that's all it took to create a new storyline. No longer did he carry a bag to feed the chickens. Instead, he protected a bag of gold doubloons from a band of marauding pirates. For Johnny, he had found a worthy reason for pulling the heavy bag. With renewed vigor, he yanked hard. The bag seemed lighter. That's all the proof he needed to continue surging forward.

Johnny lopped off the head of one, then another imaginary pirate. Swinging to the left and then to the right, with the bag in tow, he grew in confidence. Johnny had become a master at head lopping and he didn't even need a sword.

The General greeted him when he reached the chicken coop. The rooster turned his head, and with one watchful eye studied the lad. The lad studied the rooster.

Was the General really a pirate in disguise? Johnny contemplated. He slowly started to open the gate. At that point, The General flapped his wings, flew up, and for just a second looked right into Johnny's eyes before landing again. Startled, Johnny somersaulted backward, inadvertently pulling the gate open behind him.

"Cock-a-doo...dle-doo" screeched The General, and the Battle at Robert's Folly began. Wave after wave of white-feathered fowl streamed through the partially opened gate. First in line came the matriarchal hens. One did not trifle with those battled-tested birds. Following closely came the fleet of younger hens. The young chicks brought up the rear. Those yellow balls of fluff continuously bumped into things, rolled over, and popped right back up again.

Johnny's heart dropped when he looked back to see where they were headed. A wide path of gold, not doubloons but bird feed stretched back to where his adventure began. Johnny never realized that the nail that snagged the burlap bag on the porch tore open a sizable hole in the bag.

He whirled about and dove toward a nearby hen. The hen, suspecting danger, made one of those now-you-see-me, now-you-don't ninety-degree turns chickens do but people don't. Johnny ended up spitting out dirt and bird feed. The hen pecked him on the cheek just to see if he tasted edible. He didn't. Johnny tried again, and again, and each time met the same result. Johnny hated the pecking. Instead of catching the birds, he became quite adept at entertaining the flock. An uproar of cackling, similar to the thunderous laughter heard in a theater, occurred every time they felt the boy thud. They never had entertainment with their meal before.

As the bird in charge, The General strutted back and forth, crowing his cock-a-doo...dle doo while watching the battle unfold.

If humans understood chicken talk, someone might have heard The General's taunt and believed he said, "Who's the dumb cluck now?"

Johnny knew that eventually somebody would take notice of all the noise coming from the chickens. He assumed correctly.

As Betsy came around the corner of the cabin and saw the chaos, she yelled, "Johnny, whatcha' doin'?"

An exasperated, "I don't know!" came back in reply. Betsy, always the leader of the three children, flew into action after dropping the vegetables her mama had planned to use as part of the evening meal. She waved a cloth above her head. Betsy's effort made the chickens scatter, but it didn't force the flock back into the fenced-in area. At least now Johnny had a partner, one he gratefully appreciated.

Johnny prayed to no one in particular, "Oh please, don't let Mama know! Please, please, don't let Mama know! Just then, Mama opened the cabin door and stepped out onto the porch, her favorite place for snapping peas and husking corn.

Anne saw a panoramic view of the area and imagined what had transpired. She turned to Susan, her eldest daughter who stood behind her, and said, "Go get Samson. He's tied up out back." Susan ran off. Anne looked at Johnny. Johnny would not look back. Humiliated, with his arms covering his head, he laid like a fallen soldier. A large white hen came by and pecked him as if to confirm it.

Susan ran as quickly as she could around the side of the cabin and almost as quickly slowed to a cautious walk when she saw Samson. Live animals made her nervous. Susan preferred them either in a pot or on a plate. To her way of thinking an animal should come with a pot; the bigger the animal, the bigger the pot. Living on a farm and disliking animals created a strange dichotomy she could never adequately explain.

After a stretch of barking, yelping, and whining, Samson had finally called it quits. He couldn't fathom how anybody would tie him up when something so important took place. He renewed his plea for freedom once Susan appeared. Samson tugged at the rope again. Susan appreciated that the dog didn't pay a great deal of attention to her. Instead of untying the rope from around Samson's neck, she loosened the rope at the base of the tree. Samson shot forward with the rope dragging behind him. He didn't know what he should do, but he knew a mission awaited him.

Susan rejoined the fray by guarding the side of the cabin not already covered by Betsy. She deployed a unique strategy for stopping the forward progress of any bird. She would gain ground by taking a couple of steps, and with a fluttering of her fingers in a repeated outward motion, capture the critter's attention.

Then, as if talking to a person, Susan would nervously say, "Shoo, you chickens, shoo." Surprisingly enough, her approach worked.

When Samson appeared, Johnny felt invigorated. He watched how the dog scampered back and forth, herding the birds toward each other. He then followed his canine friend's lead. Unfortunately for Johnny, and anyone else in the family, nobody could do what Samson did. Every chicken who met Samson face-to-face encountered a bark, or a growl, or a flash of his long canines. The incentive to retreat became more popular by the minute for The General's army.

Anne worried about the loss of income her family would face if any of the chickens escaped. She waved her apron at the flock. Her effort showed a measure of success at turning them back toward the chicken coop.

She told both Susan and Betsy, "Do like this," confident she was doing the right thing. She moved out away from the cabin. The mother and her daughters waved their aprons, so they fluttered in the wind. With a bit of imagination, a person could believe they watched a Man-of-War with its sails at full mast about to bring reinforcements to the battle.

A hen broke away, then another, and another. Anne noticed the birds and moved to intercept. So too, did Samson. The rope around the dog's neck dragged behind him like a snake slithering in the grass. It spooked the three hens and they dispersed. Anne moved left. Samson moved right. Samson abruptly changed direction in response to the erratic moves of his prey. Then it happened. Down came Samson and Anne with a thud. The dog had wrapped the rope around Anne's legs and the two lay tangled in a heap. Samson's loud yelping captured everybody's attention in a hurry.

With Anne between him and the ground, Samson felt awkward, especially when the rope bound him and Mrs. together. The rope tightened each time he made a spasmodic move. Looking for traction, all four of Samson's legs kicked high into the air. He thrashed about, but terra firma evaded him. He wasn't hurt. He felt trapped and out of control, unable to complete his mission. Anne could do little, what with Samson on her back and her face in the dirt. She struggled to free herself but the weight of Samson, and the weight of the child inside her stifled her efforts. Even with both daughters coming to her aid, things didn't improve much. The tangled rope had wrapped too tightly around her and the dog.

Betsy finally asked, "Should we cut the rope?" Anne reluctantly nodded her head. Susan jumped up to fetch a knife her mama recently used while cooking. Unable to reach the rope herself, Anne told Susan, "Slide the knife sideways under the rope and then turn the blade up away from me." She told Betsy, "Keep Samson still as best you can."

Susan lacked experience at sawing. She slowly drew the sharp utensil up and down across the thick twine. She made little progress at first, especially when Samson tried to twist away. His sudden jerking caused her to pierce her mother's skin more than once. The knife slipped out of Susan's hands, and when she tried to grab it, she carved out a triangular-shaped chunk of flesh. Anne urged Susan to continue even though she felt considerable pain. The tears welling up in Susan's eyes made seeing where she cut even more difficult.

The task successfully diverted the two girls' attention away from the more pressing concern Anne had, and for that Anne gave thanks. It started when she fell- a small twinge deep within her. She felt this sensation before when she went into labor with her other children. However, this time she knew something wasn't right. Every time the sensation reappeared it lasted longer and increased in intensity. They shared a collective sigh when the twine finally snapped. Samson scampered off to renew his task of herding the chickens.

"Now, can you two help me to my bed?" asked Anne. It took a herculean effort to get Anne on her feet again, to reach the cabin, and to maneuver her into bed. Before going inside, Susan looked back at Johnny and stuck out her tongue. She kicked the door shut behind her. It left Johnny and Samson alone to finish what they started. Johnny knew he wasn't welcome.

Samson, back on the battlefield, turned the chickens toward the coop. Things proceeded much faster. Finally, Johnny shut the gate, and let out a "Phew!" Samson and the boy went searching for any stray birds that might have escaped. They found one large hen stuck in the brush under a clump of nearby trees. Johnny brought it back to the coop and opened the gate. He plopped the bird down. Adding a swift kick of dust at the bird helped soothe his bruised ego. The General, seeing the gate open once again, moved forward. The rooster stopped cold when he heard Samson's low growl.

Hearing the cabin door open, Johnny turned to see Susan and then Betsy leaving. Betsy paused and said, "Bye, Mama." She then shut the door behind her.

Johnny came to them and asked, "Where you goin'?"

"To bring Pa his lunch," replied Betsy.

"Can I come?" Johnny asked.

"No!" retorted Susan. "You're in trouble. Ma wants you to stay on the porch."

Dejected, Johnny groused, "Aw!" He kicked the dirt as the two girls ran off with a basket in tow.

All alone again for the second time that day, Johnny sat on the porch with his legs crossed. His head rested on his two fists which pressed against the sides of his face. Johnny reflected on what had transpired. After just a bit of time elapsed, an unbearable period for a boy his age, Johnny stood. He had reached a conclusion of some kind and readied himself to act upon it.

Without an inkling of doubt or fear, he walked off the porch in direct defiance of his mama's wishes. He didn't care. He willingly accepted whatever punishment he might receive. He had something to say, and he wanted the world to hear it.

At about twenty feet away from the porch he stopped. He brushed off his clothes as well as possible, wiped away much of the grime on his face, and licked down the cowlick at the back of his head. He wanted nothing to distract him, nor did he want anybody else to miss hearing what he had to say. Johnny turned toward the cabin and stood tall.

With what he had experienced. the now more serious Johnny placed the blame for it all squarely on his tiny shoulders. He raised his head and said a serious and heartfelt, "I'm thorry."

Had Anne known, she would have burst with pride over her son's apology. He didn't avoid responsibility, or shift the blame to someone or something else, nor did he need prodding to apologize. He exhibited a level of maturity many adults never grasped. She would have forgiven him.

Too bad—nobody heard him.

Chapter Two: Best Laid Plans

"**D**amn!" What John planned to complete that day failed again. The small, metal wedge that held his axe in place on top of its handle fell out. Both the axe and the wedge flew off and disappeared. More and more, minor frustrations like this irritated John beyond what they should have. John threw down the handle and looked about for the two missing parts. He couldn't find either.

His temper flared. John felt an irrepressible urge to inflict pain on someone or something as a way to punish whoever or whatever made things go wrong. This time he blamed the handle. He lifted a sizable rock to punish it.

He had allowed his emotions to overwhelm his ability to think and act rationally. Thankfully, and just in time too, John realized the stupidity of his idea. He twisted to his side at the last moment so the large stone, already breaking free from his grasp, would miss its mark. The stone did miss the handle. It landed on his foot instead. Without knowing it, John successfully punished the one who caused things to fail.

John howled in pain and rattled off a row of expletives. Each successive curse added more color to his core complaint of the uselessness of clearing rocks from a field when all that appeared to be growing were rocks. John's questioning of his original idea of buying land grew louder with each passing day.

John and Anne had scraped together enough money to buy a piece of land. They'd planned to grow tobacco on it as a cash crop. If all worked as they hoped, it would help pay the bills; and maybe, just maybe they could buy a few nice things now and then. John found a parcel of land that they could afford. The field, strewn with large rocks and a good trek away from the farm, didn't quite match what they desired. Still, it sidled up to a stream of fresh water, and they didn't go deep into debt paying for it.

Night after night John would come home after clearing rocks all day, and would say something such as, "That land will be good for growing something, if it would only stop growing rocks." Anne, always supportive, would offer her husband a sympathetic smile.

John's foot throbbed, his back ached, and he needed a break. He hobbled over to the nearby creek, gingerly pulled off his boots and socks, and inspected his foot.

"Thank God," he said after seeing no major damage to his foot. He expected some bruising, but the biggest bruise affected his ego.

"Ah," he sighed when he dipped his feet in the creek. He enjoyed wiggling his toes into the water's muddy bottom. He cautiously checked to see if any prying eyes lurked about. Seeing none, John reached under a large rock that jutted out from the creek bed and pulled out a bottle. He took a swig and closed his eyes, hoping to find some relief. Instead, he dreamt a dream that he had dreamt many times before. A dream that plagued him for most of his life.

Chapter Three: John's Dream

What today we would call Post Traumatic Stress, to John seemed like an oft-repeated dream he could not shake. He often found himself back in battle, terrified and fighting for his life.

"Friend, it looks like you need company. May I?" The man sat without permission.

"Name's Remy, Remy Bonpasse, and you'd be?"

John hesitated for a second then said, "John Roberts."

"Well, Jean Robert," Remy spoke with a mutilated French accent and called John Roberts, *Dzon Rŏ'ber.* Remy often called people by the French version of their name or some bastardized interpretation that he himself concocted. He was largely French, part Indian, and part frontiersman, which made for colorful conversation.

"Care for some comfort?" He offered John a swig from a half-consumed bottle.

Taking a drink, John asked, "Comfort, is that what you call it?" John handed the bottle back.

"Oui? Wouldn't you?"

"I guess so," replied John.

Over the next couple hours, and through a couple bottles of "comfort", Remy slowly pulled family history and personal stories out of John. His casual nature made John feel at ease. The liquid courage helped, too. John always found it hard to make friends. Acquaintances yes, but friends, not so much. This time seemed different. He appreciated the camaraderie. It felt as if he had found a long-lost friend, or an older brother he'd never known.

"How about family, Dzon Rober?" asked Remy.

"I have a wife. We've been married for almost..." John paused and made a "huh" sound slightly to himself once he tallied up how long he had a wife.

"Going on twenty-four months now."

John continued, "She's the most beautiful woman you'll ever see. She has hair as black as coal, and her eyes are a color of blue like you'd see in a cool lake."

"Ooh-la-la" responded Remy. He shook his hand up and down to double note John's choice of women.

"We have a baby girl, too. She's got my looks, though."

To tease John, Remy said, "Too bad." John snorted in agreement.

'Her name is Susan, but I call her 'Doodles'. You know Cock-a-doodle..."

"Doo?" Remy finished the phrase, and then in a more inquisitive tone asked, "Pourquoi?...um...Why?"

"Because she was born in the chicken coop," John replied.

Remy took a moment to look behind him. John twisted around to see, also. Nothing of interest grabbed his attention, John turned back to Remy and gave his new friend a questioning look.

Remy good-naturedly responded, "Lookin' for feathers. Is she a..." Remy, at a loss for the word chicken inserted its French counterpart "le poulet?" instead.

John unsure what "le poulet" meant responded hesitantly, "Uh, I don't know."

Remy then flapped his arms like a chicken and sounded out, "Baaawk, bawk, bawk. Bawk!"

Immediately, John chimed in, "Chicken." He now understood his new friend's question.

Remy appreciated that the two could communicate with each other despite the occasional misunderstandings.

He responded with a relieved, "Oui."

"Oh! No! no!.no! no! I don't think so," John responded with a serious tone in his voice, as well as an expressionless look on his face. Remy didn't know how to react to John's response. John snickered, and when the snicker developed into a full-blown laugh, Remy joined in the merriment.

On and on it went. The more they talked the closer their friendship grew.

The next day, "Dzon Rō'ber" rang out throughout the campsite. John immediately recognized the voice as that of Remy's. He waved for his new friend to join him. John had just cleaned his long rifle and safely packed away the lead balls he would use in the upcoming battle. A small fire offered some warmth against the autumn chill.

"My grandpapa, he'd be French you know. Grandpapa, he used to say, 'When you talk to a man about somethin' majeur, always bring a bottle.' Here." Remy handed John a bottle and kept another for himself.

"Sounds like your grandpapa was a smart man," commented John.

"He be refined," said Remy, as he accented the "re" of "refined".

John asked, "What's so major?" Remy described a disturbing dream he'd had.

"Mon Dieu. It jest don't feel right to me. Like it's my time to..." Remy finished his explanation by sliding his finger across his neck, while at the same time he made a ratcheting noise.

The two men agreed to tell the family of the opposite person about his demise if either one might pass away. Neither man thought about what to do if both perished.

Once relieved, Remy asked, "Why do you fight, Dzon Rober'?" John pondered a moment. He then told a story about his father's quest for power and control. John's animosity and disappointment poured out as he told of the persecution of some men of the cloth, all because they belonged to a church other than the Church of England. John blamed his father, the Reverend Jebediah Roberts, a local leader of the Anglican Church, for instigating the persecution. Because of his father, freedom of religion and the right to speak your peace without fear of being arrested topped John's list of reasons to fight.

Remy listened closely, leaned in toward John, and asked, "Dzon, are you fightin' for a new nation or are you fightin' against your papa? Dangerous to be fightin' a personal war," Remy declared.

John stared at the fire, looking for answers among the embers.

Recognizing the importance of a man's private time, Remy slowly started to slip away. John stopped him.

"How about you?" John looked at his friend and waited for a reply.

"Moi?" Remy replied with a smile on his face. "My family's part French you know, so, when possible, we Frenchies like to câlisser une volée les goddons. You would say, Give the Redcoats a piece of hell."

"That's it? That's your reason?" asked a surprised John.

"Does one need better? To vengeance!" Remy proclaimed.

"Vengeance!" replied John. They clicked bottles and toasted the night away.

On the day of the battle, Remy jawed away most of the way up the mountain, even when making a sound could spoil the best of plans. Fortunately, a steady rain muffled their approach. They walked alongside a group of volunteer soldiers fighting for freedom. As they neared the top of King's Mountain, hoping to surprise the Loyalists, the soldiers heard Remy spouting off.

"Mustn't be much of a king if this be his mountain and all. Not much of a mountain." King's Mountain actually derived its name from the King family, local residents in the area, not King George. Soon afterward, word filtered back through the lines to stay quiet.

Remy, using what he called his hushed voice but still louder than anyone else's said, "Sorry, Colonel." He continued with nary a pause or change in volume.

"Now, if you want to see mountains, you need come out to where I'm from."

"Damn it, man! Will you be quiet?" whispered a nearby soldier, a fierce-looking man- mentally preparing himself for battle. Remy put his finger to his lips, acknowledging he would stop talking, then lightly jabbed John in the side to get John's attention.

He nodded toward the angry man, and then whispered, "We'll talk later."

John and Remy found a fallen tree to hide behind and readied themselves to kill or to die. Once the Patriots encircled the completely surprised Loyalists, their leader, Colonel McDonald yelled, "Fire!" The shooting began.

King George's troops held the high ground, an important advantage but also their only advantage. The number of wounded or dead soldiers on top of the mountain grew faster than those who shot at them. With the exception of Major Patrick Ferguson, the commanding officer of the loyalists, every soldier who fought at King's Mountain called America home.

John looked to his left and watched in amazement as the enemy fixed bayonets to their Brown Bess muskets. In a crisp line, the trained soldiers, dressed in their bright red uniforms, charged down the hill toward the patriots.

Unwilling to give up, the patriots retreated down the mountainside out of reach of the Loyalists. Standing behind trees, they aimed their long rifles and fired. When the British forces returned to the top of the hill, the patriots then returned to their original position. The strategic maneuver happened repeatedly, like an absurd minuet.

The patriot's long rifles could shoot farther and had greater accuracy than the British muskets. John worried about their defensive position. He wondered if lying on the ground behind a fallen tree would adequately protect them if the enemy, standing directly in front of them, chose to fix bayonets and charge.

He pointed to an ongoing attack on their left and asked Remy, "What happens if they charge like that here? Can you get up fast enough?"

"Sacré bleu! I can run like a jackrabbit when I hafta', but I ain't gonna' move when I don't need to. You can get your head blowed off that way." John tried to put the possibility of a bayonet charge out of his mind.

John and Remy fell into a pattern as the battle increased in intensity. While one shot, the other reloaded. With Remy covering the left flank and John covering the right, they felt they had a pretty good chance of surviving.

While reloading, Remy chimed up saying, "Like shootin' turkeys at a turkey shoot." "Oui, like shootin' Tur..."

A musket ball punched a hole about an inch in diameter as it entered just below Remy's left eye. It exited by cracking open the back of his skull as if someone cracked an egg for breakfast.

It took John a complete cycle of firing, reloading, and firing again before he asked, "What did you say?" John swung all the way around to look at Remy when he didn't hear a response.

Being a preacher's son, he had seen death before when attending numerous funerals. He had even faced death as a boy when his mother died. However, never, never before had he seen one man wreak such violence on another man. It sickened him.

John stared at Remy's body for what seemed the longest time. Somehow, the thrust of the bullet repositioned Remy so it looked as though he sat relaxing against the tree trunk without a care in the world. John couldn't understand. Why should Remy die? John turned to his religious upbringing. One particular Biblical passage jumped out at him, "O death, where is thy sting? O grave, where is thy victory?" It felt like a hollow phrase from a hollow God.

Did Remy have it right? Could all the fighting and dying wrap around some lofty dream of a new county? Remy believed there could be a different purpose, something far less pure. Did he know something that others didn't? At that moment, John knew his new friend lay dead, and something needed doing about it before his heart broke. He turned and fired. He would do the stinging and hope he'd not get stung. Vengeance!

With the fighting complete and the Patriots winning the day, John longed to get away from that God-forsaken place—a land others would later call "hallowed ground." He longed to be in the arms of his wife again, to make love again. He wanted to wipe away the memory of Remy's death, and John's taking the life of others out of vengeance. This memory refused to fade away. It burrowed deep into his mind and would haunt him forever.

Just as he could not force his mind to leave it all behind, he couldn't physically leave either. Close to three hundred bodies needed to be put underground. Scores of wounded needed tending to, and over five hundred prisoners needed watching. Tensions ran high as they moved the prisoners.

Like a pot boiling over when placed over a fire too long, emotions boiled over against the Loyalists. A kangaroo court convened and soon thereafter, scores of those on the losing side found themselves in line for hanging. Nine soldiers' bodies laid out on the ground before the travesty came to a halt. Their lives or deaths depended solely on the reason they gave for siding with England. This too would someday haunt John in another way.

Fulfilling the promise John made to Remy challenged him. He had promised to notify Remy's family. He felt weary- weary from loneliness, anguish, and guilt over surviving when Remy didn't. He felt physically fatigued, too. Hunger, lack of sleep, and autumn's falling temperatures wore him down. John continued his journey, for a vow was sacrosanct. One couldn't ignore a vow.

It turned out that visiting Remy's family at White's Fort provided the only bright moment from those days. At that place, later called Knoxville, he envisioned a future that better fit what he wanted for himself and his family.

When Anne opened the door that night, she found a broken man. It took most of the winter to restore him physically. She could do little to help him emotionally. No longer did John act as good-naturedly as he did when they first married. The new John grew irritated at the smallest of things. His mind sometimes drifted off to some far-off place. John's tendency to fall into a state of melancholy worried her most of all.

JOHN'S DREAM ENDED abruptly when he heard the sound of a flock of birds flapping their wings to escape some perceived danger. He knew who approached when he heard the high-pitched giggling.

He placed the bottle back under the rock and thought to himself, "It's time to talk to Anne about moving out west again."

Chapter Four: By the Side of the Creek

The girls slowed to a leisurely walk when they could no longer see Johnny and he couldn't see them. They hardly spoke a word but somehow broke into spontaneous laughter at the same moment remembering Johnny's antics. They felt some foreboding that someone would get a whuppin,' but they felt relieved that the punishment would most likely be for Johnny and not them.

"Don't go tellin' Pa 'bout what went on today, you hear?" Betsy warned.

"Why not? He'll hear 'bout it sooner or later," quipped Susan in response.

"Uh-huh, but not from either of us he won't. Johnny was jest tryin' to do what Pa wanted him to do," Betsy replied.

Betsy expected her sister to embrace her advice. Susan really wanted to tattle on her brother. She knew she shouldn't, but in some convoluted way she thought tattling on Johnny would put her in good stead with her pa. It would make her feel more secure. Susan worried that Betsy would tell about how she accidentally cut her ma. After all, if she tattled on Johnny... They both felt the tension as they walked side by side.

Betsy broke the silence, "I won't tell Pa about you cuttin' Ma neither." Susan hugged her sister. Both sisters knew they would have to worry about the knife incident later.

"Do you think she's alright?" Susan asked.

"Hope so," Betsy responded.

"Me too," added Susan.

Anxious to change the subject, Betsy said, "Race you."

Susan complained, "That's not fair. I'm carryin' the basket."

"So," teased Betsy, and off she ran. Susan gave chase. Betsy reached a clearing first. Susan caught up.

Betsy chose to ignore her sister's complaint about the fairness of the race and declared, "I win." She then stuck her tongue out at Susan. Susan did likewise. They giggled at the silliness of it all.

Betsy took the basket away from Susan as she said, "Gimme." She marched up the final hill before they reached their pa. Susan stayed put.

Noticing that Susan hesitated, Betsy walked back to her sister and asked, "What's wrong?" No response. Betsy knew that Susan and her pa didn't get along. Susan always needed encouraging. She reached out and took her sister's hand, "Come on." Susan reluctantly followed her sister until they found their father sitting by the side of the creek.

"Hi, Pa. We brought you lunch," Betsy explained. Susan said nothing. She took the basket from her sister and set the food out on a flat rock beneath a large tree.

"She made cornbread for you," exclaimed Betsy, while pointing with her head toward Susan.

Betsy whispered to Susan, "Tell him."

Susan finally spoke up, "Mama taught me how today."

John knew he ought to say something positive. He responded with a bit too much zeal. "Wonderful! I love cornbread. Thank you, Doodles." He cringed the second that last word came out of his mouth. What little self-esteem Susan acquired from his comment quickly evaporated when she heard the detestable nickname.

Susan once asked her mother how she got the nickname "Doodles." Anne had that special talk to her daughter and explained that she was born in the chicken coop. The easily embarrassed thirteen-year-old grew even more embarrassed.

Betsy watched her sister wilt, so she pushed the conversation in another direction. Betsy asked, "Why you soakin' your feet?" John went on to tell of his foolhardy escapade. He made a special note of his own stupidity hoping somehow it would make up for the calling Susan, "Doodles." John then asked the girls to help find the missing parts of the tools. Both girls, already barefoot, started looking. Susan searched in the creek while Betsy looked around the tree.

Betsy yelled out, "Found it." She found the axe. They never found the wedge. Her pa then asked Betsy for the rope she used as a belt. He foolishly thought he might tie the axe to the handle somehow and still keep working.

Susan, enjoying the water swirling around her feet, stayed in the creek. She noticed something shimmering beneath a rock and picked it up. "What's this?" she asked as she held up a bottle.

Immediately embarrassed, John yelled, "Susan!" which startled the girl. Susan naturally let go, and the bottle fell from her hands. It broke open once it hit a rock.

Susan's clumsiness drove John's patience beyond its flashpoint. He had only brought that one bottle.

John moved with surprising quickness despite having put only one boot back on. He pounced on Susan. The second he reached her, he angrily yelled right into her face.

"You stupid girl! Why can't you leave things alone that aren't yours?" John shook the girl like a rag doll. Susan, too afraid to resist, took the abuse.

Betsy protested, "Pa, stop it!"

John continued, "Stupid girl." He then slapped Susan.

Betsy would not accept any more of that. She stepped in the water, and grabbed her pa's arm while yelling back, "Stop it, Pa. I'll tell Ma." Betsy's threat tempered John's anger. He let Susan go and left her standing in the creek with tears rolling down her cheeks.

After his anger subsided, he felt guilty over how he had mistreated his first-born daughter. Words failed him. Instead of apologizing and repairing his relationship with Susan and Betsy, he tried tying the axe to the handle.

Betsy pulled Susan from the creek and said, "We gotta get back. Ma's feelin' poorly." She waited for a response from her father. Hearing none she continued, "Ma's feelin' poorly. She wants you to come back soon, too." John still didn't respond. "Pa?" John finally nodded his head but showed no signs of leaving so the girls went on ahead.

When the sisters were out of sight of their father, Betsy asked, "Are you alright?" She paused for Susan to regain her composure.

A weak smile appeared on Susan's face when Betsy said, "Come on. Let's pick some blackberries for Ma. It'll make her happy."

Chapter Five: The Noises Within

Once Johnny spoke his peace he returned to the porch and waited for his mama to open the door. He knew he would get punished. He just didn't know what form that punishment would take.

Time hung still as Johnny waited. First, he fidgeted. Next, he roughhoused with Samson. Finally, with nothing else to do, he grew drowsy. Samson laid his head on Johnny's lap and occasionally looked up to see if they could leave yet.

The boy scrambled off the porch and lost his balance when he heard the blood-curdling scream coming from inside the cabin. Samson followed right behind.

"Mama?" he squeaked out... Nothing.

Johnny cleared his throat. He once again asked, louder this time, "Mama?" Still nothing!

Johnny knew others would expect him to do something, so he nervously walked toward the cabin and stepped back onto the porch. When he placed his hand on the door handle. He heard an agonized groan from inside the cabin. Johnny had heard enough. He scurried away from the door.

When will somebody come back? Johnny thought to himself and could not stop his body from shaking. Seeing Johnny so upset, Samson considered it best to bark and keep barking for as long as it took.

"Listen," said Susan. She heard it first. She lightly touched Betsy's arm when Betsy responded.

"What are you..." asked Betsy.

"Shh... Hear it?" They both waited quietly. Susan heard the distant sound of barking again.

"That's Samson. Come on. Something's wrong."

They raced forward, not knowing what to expect. As they came running down the hill, both girls spotted Johnny standing a good distance away from the cabin. He stood still, staring at the door. Susan rushed past her little brother. Betsy stopped by Johnny, dropped the basket, and knelt by him. He looked really scared. It frightened her.

"Johnny, what's wrong?" He could not talk. He could only point. Betsy put her hands on Johnny's face, and turned his head toward her so they could see each other eye to eye.

"You gotta' get Pa. Do you hear me?" Betsy said with intensity. Johnny violently shook his head.

She spoke again, this time louder and with a great deal of firmness.

"Get Pa! He's at the creek near the big tree. Go!" Betsy shoved her brother forward to get him going. It worked. Johnny took off. Samson needed urging as well. With all that barking, the dog had a parched throat. He'd spotted all the blackberries that fell out of the basket when Betsy dropped it. Samson knew they belonged to him.

Betsy pointed toward the boy running away and said, "Go, Samson, Go!" Ever loyal, Samson chased after Johnny. Betsy then turned and ran toward the cabin. To her amazement she saw that Susan had stopped just outside the cabin.

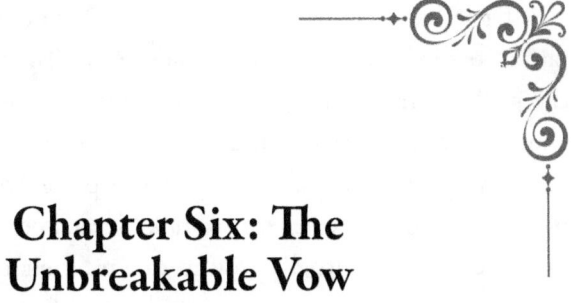

Chapter Six: The Unbreakable Vow

B etsy opened the door and entered. A sickly, sour smell gave her a moment's pause.

"Mama?" she quietly beckoned. Anne moaned. Betsy waved for her sister to come in. The smell in the cabin brought Susan up short as well. Susan had grown accustomed to the smells of baking in that cabin, but those pleasant memories evaporated when pushed aside by the odors that now filled the room.

Unless they sat in church or attended some other important event, most children, John and Anne's included, went without shoes and stockings during the summertime. Because of this, both felt the wetness beneath their feet when they stood by their ma. They dared not think about its origin. They knew it wasn't there earlier. They hadn't yet noticed the pool of blood slowly growing beneath Anne at the center of the bed.

"Mama, are you alright?" asked Betsy in hushed tones. She touched her mama's forehead. It roused Anne. Now, she lifted her arms, reaching out for her daughters. Both girls clasped one of Anne's hands in theirs.

"The baby's gone," Anne stated as tears welled up, rolled off her cheeks and landed on the pillow beneath her. The wet chicken feathers inside the pillow added their peculiar smell to the room. What their mama said confused both girls.

If the baby's gone, where did it go? they wondered. Seconds passed before what Anne said made sense. The room erupted with the girl's crying. Even during Anne's darkest hour, she soothed her daughters as well as she could.

"There, there. The child's in a better place. She's in heaven now." It took most of Anne's energy to talk. Susan and Betsy's initial shock over the death eventually wound down. Their reaction to the loss slowly switched from wailing to sniffling and whimpering.

Anne yearned for her husband's return. She longed to be in his arms again. She also wondered about her son.

"Where's Johnny?" she whispered.

"He went to get Pa," replied Betsy. Anne looked away and closed her eyes. Her lips quivered. Anne gathered her strength and said, "Tell Johnny it wasn't his fault."

Susan responded, "You can tell him when he gets back, Mama." Susan then looked at Betsy. What she saw disturbed her. Betsy took a place sitting on the side of the bed and held her mama's hand. Susan watched Betsy heave up and down and gasp for air in between the tears. The likelihood of her mother dying, and dying soon, finally sank in for Susan.

"Oh, Ma!" Susan choked, as she laid her head against her mother.

"Hush, child." Anne stroked Susan's hair, savoring the moment. Time passed. Anne knew things needed saying before time slipped away.

"Get the Bible," she requested. Betsy rose from her place on the bed. She went to a tall secretary where the Bible lay open on an angled lid. When she returned, Anne asked Betsy to read a passage from the Book of Ruth. Betsy found the verses, and haltingly read the scripture for everyone to hear.

"Turn again, my daughters, for whith...whith . . . "

Annie helped, "Whither. . . "

Betsy continued, "Whither thou goest I will go; and where thou lodg... lodgest, I will lodge." Anne reached out and placed her hand on Betsy's. Betsy knew she should stop. Silence filled the cabin. Finally, after taking several breaths, Anne said what they already knew. She took Susan and Betsy's hands and brought them together.

"You two gotta' promise me that you'll watch out for each other, just like in the Bible. Promise?" Both girls nodded that they would.

"No! I mean you gotta' really promise. You gotta' make a vow." With unusual strength, Anne tightly held their hands together as both looked at each other. Susan made her vow first.

Then Betsy spoke, "No matter what, no matter how dangerous, no matter how long, I will stand by your side. I will be there for you."

Anne added, "So help me God." The girls repeated the same.

The entire exchange exhausted Anne but she knew it needed saying. Anne felt their loyalty to each other would face challenges sometime in the future. The sisters would desperately need each other, and maybe, just maybe, a vow would sustain them even through the worst of times.

The girls looked at each other as their ma laid her head back and closed her eyes. Slowly, and with a lot of effort, Anne told Susan to fetch her brooch and her fancy hair-fork.

The hair-fork was an ornate comb used to hold a woman's hair back. Anne's hair-fork, a work of art made of silver, had two roses pounded into the top. John gave it to Anne as a wedding gift. Anne knew she should give it to Susan as an inheritance. It would shine for all to see against Susan's flowing red hair.

She bequeathed to Betsy a brooch that John gave her the day they ran off together. John always said the piece brought out the color in her eyes. Since Betsy inherited her blue eyes, she should have the brooch.

Satisfied she had done all she could, Anne Roberts, only thirty years of age, closed her eyes and waited for the inevitable. It didn't take long. In moments, she slipped away and joined her baby.

THROUGHOUT HER LIFETIME, Anne had remained the constant. Her will, applied lightly most of the time but forcefully when needed, was always applied with love. It held her family together, guiding them through some of the toughest of times in an unforgiving land. Now - someone else had to lead.

Chapter Seven: Fall from Grace

John, for the fourth time in his life, experienced a deep loss when someone close to him died- his mother, his mentor, his friend, and now his wife. He knew this loss would challenge him most of all. He doubted he could withstand the pain.

Death crossed over their cabin door at other times. Three infants, each one stillborn, laid peacefully at rest in the family gravesite beneath a large elm tree. Anne picked the land for the family graveyard because of its natural beauty, not for its practicality. Every time a new grave needed to be dug, it meant chopping through several roots from the nearby tree. Additionally, each grave needed to be dug deeply enough so the animals in the wild would not disturb the remains.

John had mourned the loss of each child but felt no lasting anguish because the bond between father and infant never flourished. His wife felt each loss more deeply.

Upon entering the cabin, John motioned for Susan and Betsy to wait outside. He could tell something had gone terribly wrong from the look on the face of each girl. When he slowly walked over to their bed where his wife lay perfectly still, he confirmed his worst fear. His eyes welled up with tears when he kissed her lips for the very last time.

Only a few hours had passed. He already missed her so. Her touch, her smiles, her caresses had gone away forever. The everlasting comfort he had assumed as rightfully his disappeared. He never imagined she would go first and surely not at such an early age.

Sometimes John felt that what others called love had utterly passed him by. Other times an annoying doubt led him to wonder if he had done the passing.

His love for his children often faltered. His lack of concern for his fellow man and his doubt about a Higher Being left him shallow. And now—the deep regret he had over not repeatedly showing and telling his wife how he truly loved her haunted him most of all. When love slipped away it left a hole in his heart that needed filling.

Little Johnny felt confused. His feelings of loneliness, confusion, and guilt over his mother's death would shape who he would become. When his pa brought Johnny to view what remained of his mama, all his memories became mixed up. He knew she had left that body. He didn't know what body she moved to, but he knew she didn't reside in the one he now saw. He would have nothing to do with kissing the corpse like all the others.

Already the shadows grew longer, and John knew that Anne's decomposing body would continue to do so with the summer heat. Her remains needed putting in the ground as soon as possible.

John gathered his children around him and explained what would happen. He vowed that he would watch over them, no matter what. Each child prayed that their pa's earnest promise would be as rock solid as their mother's love.

He sent them around behind the cabin to keep them busy while he wrapped Anne's body in a quilt. He tied a rope around the body to keep her tightly wrapped. John then lifted her body into his arms and lovingly brought her out as if he were carrying her across the threshold of a new home.

He took about twenty steps before falling to his knees. He tried standing but he couldn't. He tried to crawl on his knees while carrying his wife. That failed, too. John collapsed and lay with his head resting on her. He never felt so alone.

Coming from around the corner of the cabin, Betsy unexpectedly interrupted this extremely private and tender moment. She backed out of sight and watched. She watched until the weariness of the day made her drowsy.

Chapter Eight: John's Younger Days

The patrons at Charlie's House, a local drinking establishment first opened for business by the late Charles Dinwiddle, all enjoyed the presence of John Roberts. John, not yet a man, but definitely no longer a boy, felt at ease there. Few others his age received the type of welcome John received.

Because of his upbringing, John never felt comfortable around people his own age. He preferred those who preceded him in age, or those who followed behind by a great deal.

John lived a life as an only and lonely child. He felt abandoned by his parents. First, by his mother who died when he turned twelve, and then by his father, the Right Reverend Jebediah Roberts, who decided he had too little time and far too little interest in John's upbringing. Loftier matters concerned Reverend Roberts.

Thanks to the interest Charles Dinwiddle had toward young Master Roberts, things changed. Charles, known as a man of action, stepped in to do his part when he saw a wrong that needed correcting. Leaving John alone to grow up on his own without adult compassion and mature guidance was an unacceptable wrong he could not tolerate.

It took a bit of coaxing, and most likely an encouraging word from the governor (Charles' cousin) to the reverend to get things moving. It also took an exchange of some coins, not from the reverend to Dinwiddle, as one would expect, but from Dinwiddle to John's father just to ensure the wish came to fruition. John had acquired a mentor, one who acted more like a father than the one who sired him. John claimed the tavern as his second home.

Nobody asked outright why Charles did what he did, nor did the proprietor offer an answer. Both John's father and John's mentor stood above reproach in Wilmington. They had attained "pillar in the community" status a long time ago. The two disagreed about everything and vehemently argued their positions.

Despite all their differences, the two men always agreed on two topics.

First - neither would tolerate the mistreatment of John. If anybody mistreated the boy, the offender could expect some form of retribution.

Second - both men frowned on people prying into the family history of either man. An affront to one meant an affront to the other. Any man or woman who pried too closely could expect a considerable amount of woe.

Within a week, the lad did odd jobs around the establishment. He had a veracious interest in the things of the world. He also had a desire to learn more about the fairer sex. That's why he hung around after completing his chores- to listen to the men talk.

At first, John sat silently in the corner hearing the men speak of land management, animal husbandry, politics, taxes, the prospect of war, and sex—always about sex. Later as he grew older, he sat within the circle of patrons listening to heated discussions about, once again, the prospect of war.

Since Wilmington, North Carolina had an active Sons of Liberty group, that topic often opened the evening's discussion. Someone would ask what the group had done lately, and the jawboning began. The discussion quickly spread to politics and taxes. John occasionally joined the discussion when he felt comfortable enough to speak with some authority. When the conversation turned to women, John had no knowledge at all, so he never said a word. He never missed a word either.

Heady times - that's how John would later describe them. These conversations caused him to challenge the social mores he had accepted completely as a little boy. What his father spoke of from the pulpit on Sundays did not sound as absolute when someone spoke of them at Charlie's House every other day of the week. John began to question everything.

Along with John's questioning of what his father preached, John's lackadaisical attitude led him to shirk what his father willed of him. Once again, Mr. Dinwiddle stepped in. He would not put up with John's disrespect for his father and threatened to ban John from Charlie's House if he did not do as his father requested.

Over the next two years, a level of peace took hold, so both father and son could go about their daily lives.

The activities at the Robert's household boiled over again once a new stepmother and her brood of four moved into the parsonage. Clarissa Cox, a manipulative social climber, didn't waste time with her scheming. Soon after she arrived, the dinner discussions always worked their way around to sending John off to a boarding school, or a college preparatory school.

He bristled every time they talked about him as if he wasn't sitting at the table with them. No one felt more grateful for Charlie's House than John. It provided the sanctuary he sorely needed. He found his salvation there, albeit a different kind of salvation.

He continued to do the things his father requested and reading for the widow Pearson passed as one of the more palatable ones. Every Monday he would bring a book, newspaper, or anything else the widow desired. John didn't mind reading for the Widow for, although her vision failed her, she still had a keen mind and a dry sense of humor.

John knocked on the door and waited for someone to answer. The door opened, and for the first time in quite a while he lost his capacity to speak.

"Yes?" Anne questioned. John stood astounded by the incomparable beauty who stood before him. Anne often received unnerving responses like this and grew accustomed to them.

"May I help you?" the young woman asked.

"Oh...I'm sorry. I'm...My name is...I'm John Roberts, and I've come to read for Mrs. Pearson." Anne led John to the parlor where he waited for the Widow. John finished reading and then asked, "I have some free time later this week. Would you like me to stop by and read for you again?"

"If you wish. It's not necessary," she replied.

"It would be a pleasure," John stated.

"I'm sure it would. Anne—her name is Anne," the elderly woman responded with a smile.

"How did you know?" asked the surprised John.

"I may be blind but I'm not deaf," quipped the woman.

Thereafter, what began as a once-a-week event quickly turned into an every-other-day session. Mrs. Pearson requested John read more poems about love. She also had some pretext for requiring Anne to attend as well.

With the widow's tacit approval, a romance between John and Anne blossomed over the next few months. A furtive embrace here, a stolen kiss there, the two holding hands in the shadows, all exemplified John and Anne's love for each other. They tried to keep their love hidden from others. It bemused those who knew them well.

"John," one of the tavern's patrons called out. Luke, a regular, conversed with John quite often. John walked over to the gathering of men and made the appropriate salutations.

"John, we have a wager going and we need your help. You visit the widow Pearson do you not?" John nodded his head. He sensed danger lurking ahead somewhere the moment he heard Elsbeth Pearson's name.

"It was nice to see her back at the service after such a long time. Wouldn't you agree?" questioned the man. Again, John nodded.

"I saw she had a new servant with her," Luke stated in an inquiring manner.

"That's Anne," replied John. He regretted the moment her name escaped from his lips.

"Oh... Anne, is it?" One of the men in the crowd chimed in.

"Do you know her well?" Luke inquired. John felt a drop of sweat roll down his back.

"We talk in passing," John said. Another drop of perspiration journeyed down his spine, more quickly this time.

"I see." The inquisition continued. "We've taken turns trying to describe her. You see, the one with the best description wins a free pint. How would you describe her?" The man's question left John feeling trapped with no escape in sight. The men leaned in, anxious for a response.

"Me?" John asked. A smattering of, "Why sure, yes," and phrases like, "Of course," rose from the crowd.

"She's very pretty, especially with that long black hair of hers." John's answer led him to believe he had escaped whatever trap awaited him. The tension swelling in his shoulder blades subsided. Determined to win the real wager, Luke persisted.

"Come, John. You're a student of eloquent speeches and fine words. You can do better than that," urged the man. John never knew how easily he could fall for such a trap. Should he deny his love and preserve a safe and secure status among his friends, or should he declare his love and embark down an unknown path.

John took a swig from one of the nearby mugs of ale that sat on the table and began. "Anne is my love, my life's desire. She's a goddess. Her long, flowing hair is as black as coal. Her soft, smooth skin glistens like a coin. Her winsome smile calms the most savage of beasts, yet it stirs my heart. When she speaks, a choir of angels cries out with envy. However, it's her eyes, her lovely sparkling blue eyes that remind me of a cool, clear lake - a lake where I would love to swim forever. That's my Anne."

The room remained quiet for several seconds. Finally, one man grunted, another said, "Well, I'll be jiggered."

Luke held out his hand and said, "Pay up, gents. I think you heard your answer."

"What?" John asked. "I thought..."

Before John could continue, Luke proclaimed, "No, John. You were the wager. People wondered if you would ever tell anyone that you'd fallen in love," replied the happy and now more prosperous patron.

John left Charlie's House relieved, in fact, exhilarated. He wanted to tell the world about his love for Anne. He didn't need to. Within the week, the entire congregation of the church, as well as his circle of acquaintances, knew of John's proclamation. That also included the Reverend and his wife Clarissa. She finally had the reason she needed for putting her plan of action into play.

It took a little bit more than a month for Clarissa's plan to develop but when it did the results came out exactly as she hoped.

As usual, John stopped by the Pearson's place to read for the widow. Instead of reading what he originally planned, she gave him a letter.

Elsbeth asked, "Before anything else, would you read this please?" She could have had Anne read the letter, but she sensed that the letter concerned both of them, somehow. She thought the two of them should hear the news at the same time. She assumed correctly.

John sat down on a chair across from Mrs. Pearson while Anne sat next to her on the settee. John began:

DEAR AUNT ELSBETH,

I've recently learned that an unfortunate romantic relationship has developed between the son of Rev. Jebediah Roberts and my indentured servant, Anne Carpenter.

Furthermore, I understand that you have taken part in promoting this relationship. This union must cease immediately. I only authorized Anne to serve as your maid after you incessantly requested some assistance. I complied with your request against my better judgment.

I have some business to attend to in Charlestown at the end of this month, and I will stop by to visit you on the second of August. At that time, I will find someone more fitting to serve you. Please have Miss Carpenter ready to travel for she will return with me to the plantation.

Your Devoted Nephew,
Edward

JOHN WAS LIVID. ANNE, in deep despair, crumbled into his arms. They felt confused, at a loss about what to do. Elsbeth didn't waste time mincing her words.

She spat out a, "Damn it, that bastard! He wants you as his personal whore." Both John and Anne looked at Mrs. Pearson in shock, for they had never heard her say a cross word about anyone before.

The widow went on to describe how her nephew, obsessed over Anne's beauty, financially bankrupted Anne's family, forcing her parents to sell off Anne as an indentured servant. She explained how, after she and her late husband worked so hard to build a thriving plantation, her nephew by marriage, her closest male heir, automatically took legal control of two-thirds of her wealth when her husband died.

Of the third she retained; she negotiated a good portion of it away to him in exchange for Anne staying with her. Elsbeth expected that by doing so, she effectively kept Anne out of her nephew's grasp for the rest of the young girl's indentures. Anne still had four more years remaining.

Not three days later, John pounded on the door of the Pearson residence. He had an equally alarming story to tell of how his father and stepmother had enrolled him, against his will, into a college preparatory school for one year. After that, they prepared for him to study divinity at the seminary of the College of William and Mary. He was expected to move to Williamsburg, Virginia in September.

Elsbeth had the two lovers sit, and asked them straight out, "Do you love each other so much that you're willing to spend the rest of your lives together?" They gave the response she anticipated.

She went on to say, "Well then, we have some work to do."

The three then laid out a plan that would have John and Anne as husband and wife heading westward across to North Carolina before the second of August deadline. Elsbeth didn't trust her nephew, so the elopement was scheduled for the last week of July. This would protect them from any early surprise visit from Elsbeth's nephew.

The three worked tirelessly in preparation for the trip. John had to cut back on his time with Anne so he could maintain his other obligations and still do what he needed to do. He hated the idea of being away from Anne, but they could not afford to raise anybody's suspicions. Their plan's success depended on surprise.

Elsbeth agreed to bankroll their getaway. However, in order to do so, she needed to sell off some of her belongings. Out of all her possessions, and with a twinge of regret, the Widow Pearson sold off her jewelry. Thankfully, she found a buyer who had just as many reasons to keep the deal secret as she.

With ready cash available, Anne bought only the things they would need to get through the first leg of the trip. She felt that between the belongings the widow offered from her own house and what she bought they would have the needed supplies to get started. They could buy everything else along the way.

John had to acquire a wagon and a team of horses. They also needed a place to hide the wagon while loading it with provisions. He decided to have the horses delivered and hitched up, ready to go, as late as possible. That part of the plan concerned him the most.

John knew he couldn't do this all alone. After considerable discussions between the three, John approached Luke, the same man who upset John and Anne's secret in the first place. John had heard at one time that Luke Jeffers could magically get things done. Jeffers offered the use of his barn which was not far from the Widow's place. That solved the problem of where to store the wagon.

John never learned that Mr. Jeffers led the local Sons of Liberty and the barn served as the launching point for many of their attacks. Jeffers also knew of a man who, for the right price, would deliver the wagon all ready to go at a time of their choosing. It would cost them plenty. Mrs. Pearson happily paid.

John successfully carted off and packed everything he needed or wished to keep over the next couple of weeks with one exception, a brooch his mother willed to him when she died. He frantically looked everywhere but he still could not find it. John knew he had to confront his father over the brooch. He had no other option.

Holding a lantern in his hand, John pushed through the door to his stepmother and father's bedroom and demanded, "Where is it?"

The two in the bed slept soundly, so once again John demanded to know, "Where is it?"

Once Jebediah gathered his wits he bellowed, "How dare you enter this room unwelcomed. Now what is it that you want?"

"My mother's brooch, where is it?" John insisted. Jebediah rose from the bed dressed in a long nightshirt.

Perturbed, he responded, "I have it. Why do you want it?"

"It's mine. Mother gave it to me," John responded as the verbal jousting continued.

"She didn't have the legal right to give it to you," countered Jebediah.

"Are you leaving, running away with that trollop?" he asked. "You are, aren't you? You're not running away and paying for it with what's rightfully mine."

John, at the top of his lungs yelled, "But, it's not yours. It's mine. It's my inheritance."

Jebediah argued his strongest point, "Not according to the law. The rights and possessions of a wife or child are given only when the husband or father chooses to do so. You have no right to have it, or to run away at all for that matter, unless I say so."

John argued, "You may have the legal right, but why shouldn't a gift from a dying mother to her child be honored? Are not a person's final wishes sacred?"

Peeved at both father and son, Clarissa leapt from the bed. She wrapped herself in a blanket and opened her personal chest of treasures.

She threw the brooch at John and spat out, "There." The brooch fell at his feet. In disgust, believing she had dishonored his mother, John, charged toward Clarissa, ready to give her the back of his hand.

Jebediah yelled, "Stop!"

Then, with the calmest of voices, and barely above a whisper, he continued, "Stop, Son. There's the brooch. Take it." John reached down and retrieved it.

Jebediah continued, "Now leave! Go son! Go before something happens we both regret."

John locked eyes with his father. He knew more needed saying but didn't know what to say. He turned and walked out of the parsonage. He never looked back, not once.

John ran as fast as his legs would carry him. His mind raced even faster. He felt sure he had committed at least one of the over three hundred crimes that, according to British law, carried the punishment of hanging. John wondered if his father would report what just happened. He knew Clarissa would tell, but his father . . . he had doubts. Nonetheless, he and Anne needed to get on their way.

John rounded the corner of a nearby home and into Anne's arms. He asked, "Are we ready?"

Annie replied, "Just a minute." She pulled John to Mrs. Pearson who stood barely inside her home. Anne spoke up, "We worry about you, Ma'am."

"Don't, children. Nobody is going to bother with a blind, old widow. Besides, my name still carries some weight around the town," Elsbeth replied.

Anne continued, "But, what if they do . . . do something?" Mrs. Pearson grabbed the couple's hands in hers and squeezed.

"If so, then this tough old bitty has had a long life that's been full of joy, and what I do now will be well worth it." Elsbeth replied, assuring the two travelers. They said their goodbyes and climbed aboard the wagon.

John hoped for a more congenial setting for the next special moment, but conditions made that impossible. He shifted on the seat so he could face Anne.

Expecting to begin, Anne turned to him when they didn't and said, "What?"

"Will you marry me when we get the chance? Will you be my bride, and become Mrs. Anne..."

Having heard enough and knowing John's propensity for going on and on, she grabbed him and kissed him fervently. "Yes, now go," she urged him.

John opened his hand and showed Anne the treasured brooch. "It was my mother's. I want you to have it in honor of our engagement." Once again, fervor overwhelmed logic, and John received a long passionate kiss.

Elsbeth pleaded in a loud whisper, "Will you two please leave?"

John called out, "Hyah", and the hooves of the horses clopped along the cobblestone street in the middle of the night.

Chapter Nine: The Journey West

John and Anne didn't know exactly where their future would lead them. They only knew their "Promised Land" lay somewhere in the west. Unfortunately, their dream of starting a new homestead as quickly as possible far exceeded their reality. They had heard that on a good day a wagon could travel approximately twenty-five miles. When John and Anne started out, they had very few good days.

Crossing North Carolina meant going over one or more of the numerous Indian trading paths connecting one part of the colony to another. The Indians created a network of paths, not based on their own discovery, but by following whatever direction the buffalo took when journeying from one feeding place to the next. John and Anne wished that the buffalo would have followed a straight line and they would have walked straight east to west without making any turns.

The two ended up traveling more north and south than anything else. They also encountered paths that eventually became too narrow for a wagon. More than once the couple followed a path that looked promising, yet, in no time at all, they had to back up, turn around, and search for another path. They wasted a lot of time, effort, and resources during their first few days.

North Carolina burgeoned with an influx of immigrants from Europe. Many came down the Great Wagon Road looking for a new start. Wherever a path crossed a body of water, or two or more paths crossed each other, someone started a community. Most of them small, yet each town's greeting provided a welcome sight to John and Anne.

Even with all the frustrating moments, they both considered their journey an adventure. Anne learned how to drive a team of horses and shoot a rifle. John learned that what he accepted as the gospel truth about women from the men at Charlie's House didn't have a lot of truth to it. Most of what he gathered from the barroom tales amounted to little more than fairytales told by a patron to cover up his own inadequacies. Together they slowly learned to love, think, and act, as a couple.

With them still in the Wilmington region, days passed before they met anyone. Finally, they reached the small borough of Cross Creek, later known as Fayetteville. At Cross Creek, they heard about a map. The map showed all the trails in the colony a person could navigate. John took a keen interest in the map and finally had a general idea of where they headed.

He spent a good portion of an afternoon drawing a detailed copy of the map from the one located in town. Anne felt mildly perturbed with John for being so pedantic. She insisted that she could have completed a copy of the map in minutes. For John it took hours. Anne didn't want to start their first fight, so she returned to the wagon and straightened things out.

At Cross Creek, for the first time, people considered them as husband and wife. It amused them when someone would say "Will you and the Missus." this or "You and the Missus" that. The assumption led them to discuss and finally reach a decision about how they should go about getting married. Several barriers stood in the way.

Neither one felt satisfied with the idea of just living together and calling it a marriage. However, John found out that a marriage license cost thirty pounds, an exorbitant amount which they could ill afford. Furthermore, the wedding required that an Anglican minister perform the ceremony, and that the wedding must take place in an Anglican church. They both knew the danger connected with having a formal wedding in an Anglican Church. It would provide a trail for someone to follow, and neither looked forward to that.

ARRIVING AT SALEM, already a town of substance after only ten years of history, led to the first real disagreement between the two. John felt comfortable living a life surrounded by people. He immediately admired the town. Salem was a community built by Moravians, a religious sect of mainly German-speaking immigrants who adhered to a strict, Protestant code of behavior. It later became Winston-Salem after others built the town of Winston and the two communities merged. The residents of Salem developed a strong trading reputation on the Piedmont.

Anne cherished sleeping in a real bed as well as under a real roof. She also liked the town. However, she saw herself as the wife of a farmer just as her mother had been. Living in a town conflicted with her dream. John took the time to go out and purchase provisions for the journey ahead. The extra time gave John the chance to shop for a wedding present for his bride. He entered a finely decorated shop and knew he found the perfect place. There while talking to Johann Vogler, a local silversmith, John learned that the Moravian church owned everything. The church owned all the land and only church members could open businesses. The church even owned the slaves in and around the community.

John spent far more than he should have when he purchased a sterling silver hair-fork with two sculpted roses at the top. However, he wanted something special for this special occasion. He hoped Anne would like it.

John's adoration for the town evaporated when he realized a future for them there didn't exist since they weren't church members.

His disagreement with Anne disappeared too. He returned to Anne and let her know they would move on as she wished.

THE THIRD LEG OF THEIR journey brought them south to the small town of Charlotte. Later, when George Washington passed through the town, he called it "a trifling place." Those who named the town named it after King George's wife, Queen Charlotte. It had no more than five hundred residents. Most of them were immigrants from Scotland or Germany. Nobody knew that Charlotte would explode in size in 1799 when a twelve-year-old boy found a large rock to use as a doorstop. A jeweler who visited the boy's home recognized the rock as almost pure gold, thus starting the first gold rush in America. John and Anne would have had a different life had they stayed in Charlotte, but once again the festering argument of living in a town versus on a farm boiled to the top. They moved on.

While in Charlotte, John and Anne walked through the McCafferty General Store. The two noticed several postings about couples planning to wed.

John asked, "Excuse me, what are all these postings on the wall?"

The proprietor responded, "Those? Oh, those are people who plan to marry. It's called banning." He went on to describe how every week for three weeks, the couple needed to post their intent to marry, or make a declaration for three weeks at a church service about their plans. The couple could proceed with their wedding plans if nobody objected within that time frame. British law still forbade marriage ceremonies by religious ministers other than Anglicans, so a justice of the peace could perform ceremonies. At last! John and Anne found their solution. They married as soon as they possibly could. *If only we could decide where and how we want to live,* John thought.

The two continued their journey west. Since their finances ran short, they needed a minor miracle. They got it too. Just after leaving Charlotte, Anne noticed an envelope in a trunk full of kitchen goods. Someone had written on the envelope, "Open when you find home, not before."

They thought the contents of the envelope had some value, and it most likely came from the widow Pearson. "She must have had someone write the envelope for her," said John.

Stopping each other from opening the envelope before they found "home" challenged both of them. Their curiosity almost got the better of them. They kept each other on task and each day they gathered a greater understanding of what it took to live as a couple. Just as the widow Pearson desired, they realized that "home" meant a state of mind as much as a spot on a map. Mrs. Pearson's had wisely placed them in a situation where they had to work out their differences.

MOVING FURTHER AND further west required traveling on paths barely packed down by the weight of the wheels from other wagons. It also required crossing terrain where the peaks rose higher, and the valleys dipped lower. Anne had reached her limit. John would reach his soon. They drove on. They had to, but their team of horses were almost worn out.

The morning started quietly and stayed that way. Neither one said much as they climbed yet another steep hill. John stopped the wagon at the peak of a particularly high one. He pulled on the wagon's brake and, all alone, walked away. His action bewildered Anne. She watched him and wondered why. He gazed into the west for a few anguishing moments. At last, John called out, "Anne, come here." She reached his side and John put his arms around her.

"Look out there," John said while pointing to the far-off hills.

"Somewhere out there is our home." A breeze whipping over the mountaintop chilled her, so she pressed against him for warmth.

John continued, "I've been thinking... I can be a farmer, on one condition." Anne waited for the condition.

"We have to live fairly close to a town. We cannot live in the middle of nowhere." She squeezed John, knowing he was making a considerable sacrifice.

John went on to dream about where they would live. "We'll build us a fine cabin. It'll have a window, no, two windows."

Anne asked, "Can we have a porch in the front?"

"Hell's bells! We'll have it all the way across the front." John boasted.

"And a cellar?" asked Anne. "I need a cellar."

John questioned her dream, "A cellar, what for?"

"So I can store canned goods, Silly. I can't make you your favorite pies if I don't have canned fruit."

"Then I'll dig you the deepest gol-darn cellar in the county, and a stone fireplace with an oven to boot." John added.

The logjam had broken. The emotional wall they had been building between them finally crumbled. They spent close to an hour planning out the size and shape of their dream home. Anne imagined how she would decorate the inside, blue-checkered curtains of course. Later, when they built their first cabin, it fell short of most of their dreams. It did include, not the deepest gol-darn cellar in the county, but pretty close to it.

With the last barrier behind them, finding the right land only took a couple of days. They found a tract of land that met what they needed for starting a farm, including living relatively close to a market where they could sell their eggs. John and Anne had finally reached "home".

Full of high spirits, they entered Morristown, later renamed Ashville. They tracked down a local official by the name of Patton.

He informed them that the land had a previous owner and the land came with a price. Their hearts sank when they saw how much they needed to start their new life.

Both felt depressed. They would have left and headed further west if a late summer storm hadn't brewed up over the nearby mountaintops. It forced the couple to stay one more night instead of moving on. John and Anne opened the envelope that night. The letter did indeed come from Mrs. Pearson, and yes, it contained something of value. However, they didn't anticipate that it would contain so much. Neither one slept well for fear they might be robbed. The next day, with cash in hand, they started a new life as farmers.

A few months after they settled in, John and Anne wrote a letter to Mrs. Pearson. They expressed their eternal gratitude to her for her generous spirit and her wisdom. She was their guardian angel. When the Postmaster in Wilmington, North Carolina, received the letter he placed it off to the side in a bin titled, "Addressee Unknown."

Chapter Ten: By the Graveside

Whump... Whump... Whump. Betsy didn't know if the far-off sounds jarred her from a deep sleep or if she stirred due to the coolness of the night air. Frankly, she didn't care. She knew, for some reason, she hurt, and sleep deadened the pain. She wanted to stay that way.

Whump... Whump.

More awake this time. Suddenly the day's events roared back and so did her pain. She lifted her head and looked toward the source of the noise. Betsy noticed a path that creased the dusty land from the spot where her father fell atop her mother's remains to where he now stood. He had pulled the body to a large tree. Betsy watched her pa as he went about digging a hole in the family plot.

Whump... Whump... Whump.

Ever so slowly, the long shadows of the day disappeared into the dusk and the night. Betsy walked out to where her father dug. A full moon in the cloudless sky illuminated the ground and made it possible to work later than usual.

She squeaked, "Pa."

John said, "Hmm," in return. An uneasy silence permeated the family gravesite. Finally, John spoke up saying, "Watch your step." He then took a large swig from a nearby bottle.

After stepping back, she watched her pa stumble. She thought to herself, *I, should watch my step?* Especially after he nearly fell into the hole he'd just finished digging.

John spoke up, "Go get the lantern from the barn. The wind's picking up." Betsy refused to look at the body wrapped in the quilt and ran off. She anxiously did what her pa wanted. Doing anything, no matter how trivial, diverted her from dwelling on her loss. Betsy neared the barn. She could count on the one hand the number of times she had stayed out this late. She had never gone into the barn in the dark. She wished she already had the lantern instead of running to fetch it.

The light from the full moon helped her get in the door, but once inside- she moved about the barn with her hands out while feeling her way in front of her.

A dark shadow, off to the right and close to the ground, had to be the cow. Every so often the cow swished her tail or rustled about. That spooked Betsy. She also kept tripping over some round thing that clinked as it rolled into another round thing. They were some of her father's liquor bottles.

She wondered, *If this helps Pa stop his pain maybe it will stop my pain too.* Betsy sniffed the bottle. She even considered tasting what little remained, but a bitter odor caused her to put the bottle down. She would have to find another way to stop the pain.

Eventually she found the punched tin lantern hanging on the side of a post. Betsy ran back to her pa with the lantern in hand.

"No, no. You forgot to light it!" snarled John. While hearing her pa's rebuke, she happened to look down. John had moved the body. Her mother now lay underground. Betsy burst into a fountain of tears.

"Go on, tell your brother and sister to get ready, too." slurred John.

Betsy ran into the cabin, and called, "Susie."

Groggy at first, Susan responded, "What?" Just like Betsy, she had fallen asleep after the emotional strain of the day. Tiny whimpering and a high-pitched snore indicated the same had happened to Johnny.

"Get up and get dressed. Pa wants us there when he does the buryin'. Get Johnny ready too," Betsy said.

"I don't want to. Can't you take care of Johnny?" Susan complained.

"I can't. Pa wants his lantern right away," Betsy responded while lighting the lantern. She went for the door but at the last second, she returned. Betsy set the lantern down and retrieved the brooch her mother gave her. She pinned it on her dress. Betsy then went out the door with the lit lantern in her hand.

John said in an aggravated tone, "Took you long enough." Betsy knew that to say anything would lead to trouble, so she remained silent.

John asked, "Where are they? Let's start. We can't wait forever."

Momentarily losing his balance, John called out in a voice way too loud for such a somber occasion.

"Lord, we give to you..." He stopped.

In a much softer and business-like demeanor, he said to Betsy, "Hold the lantern higher." She did as she was told. That's when John noticed the brooch.

"What are you doing?" he asked. Betsy recognized her pa's foul mood, but she sensed that something new had raised his ire.

"What?" she asked cautiously.

John pointed to the brooch and said, "The brooch, why are you wearing it?"

"Mama gave it to me. She wanted me to have it. She gave Susan the..."

John interrupted Betsy before she could continue, "Oh, no she did not! Now, give it to me."

"It's mine. Mama gave it to me, so I'd remember," pleaded Betsy.

"Did you steal it?" he asked.

Hurt that he would ask such a question she responded, "No."

Slowly regaining composure, Betsy reframed her argument, "Mama gave me and Susie a keepsake when she died. She wanted us to have them."

"I don't care if it was her dying wish or not. It wasn't her right to. Women and children don't have rights. Men do. She needed my permission to give it to you," John replied while trying to sound formal.

"Your permission? That's not fair!" Betsy retorted.

"Fair or not, that's the way it is." John falsely believed he had gained the upper hand. He continued, "Give it back."

"May I have your permission to keep it?" asked Betsy. She already knew the answer, but she asked anyway, just in case.

"No," replied John. He grew more perturbed with each passing second.

Betsy pushed the argument further when she asked, "Why? Are you going to wear it?" Her last sarcastic question crossed the point of no return.

"No, and neither are you. Now give it to me!" John yelled. He stuck his hand out and waited. He had heard enough of Betsy's complaining. Father and daughter glared at each other for a very long time. Betsy finally unhooked the brooch and dropped it into his hand.

"Here," she grumbled. Her scowl spoke volumes. John turned and walked toward the cabin as he angrily called out, "Doodles!"

Betsy stood at the foot of the gravesite. She clasped her hands together and closed her eyes to pray. Her lips silently uttered a prayer that only she and God heard. She ended with a fervent, "Amen."

Pa wouldn't come back to fill the grave. Betsy knew it. He'd had too much to drink. So, she knelt down by the mound of dirt, rocks, and roots, and with only her hands she pushed the loose dirt into the hole. She had no other option, since John took the shovel with him when he sought out Susan.

Her pa's ranting, her sister's wailing, and the thud-like sounds of dirt pouring down on her mama made for a memory she doubted she could ever scratch from her mind. Then, with a lantern in one hand and a sturdy stick in the other, Betsy - cold, lonely, and scared, stood guard over her mother's earth-covered body.

In a time like that, a determined young woman needs a hero a protector to stand guard and make things safe. A hero came to her aid that night. Quietly, so he would not disturb the girl's stoic moment, Samson slowly moved to her side and sat.

He would stand guard and protect Betsy. No wild animal dared desecrate that hallowed ground, not with Betsy and her hero around. But John? It took less than a day for John to break his vow to his children.

Chapter Eleven:
Starting Over

Three years passed since Anne died. During that time, the dreams her mother had of building a thriving farm faded from sight. John loved his wife and accepted her dreams as his own while she lived. However, her dreams faded away once she died. John's new dreams took the family on a different journey.

John dreamt of starting over again, possibly even remarrying. He knew one thing for sure. He would live in a town the second time around, not out in the country. He missed the lifestyle he grew up with before he met Anne. He also missed the respect and camaraderie afforded him from the regulars at Charlie's House. He wanted something like that life again.

John knew starting over would take more money than he had, even if he sold the farm. He also knew he would have to work to earn a living. However, the prospect of starting over at the lowest rung of the economic ladder didn't appeal to him. Short of stealing, John needed a way to make a great deal of money within a minimal amount of time. He had no clue how to make fast money.

No ideas came to him until he once remembered a traveler who said, "That there's a fightin' bird!" From then on, John's scheme for getting rich came into focus. He would train the General to fight in cockfights, and he would wager on his bird to win, particularly when he could rig the fight.

John ignored the hoopla surrounding the first cockfight he ever attended. Instead, he paid close attention to how the fight progressed. That's all he did. He knew that most schemes to make money fail because too much depends on chance and not planning. Success requires preparation, not luck. At his second cockfight, he placed a small bet on "Feisty," a mid-sized Rhode-Island Red who looked promising. Feisty's opponent, a scraggly older-looking bird, didn't appear to have a chance of winning. John paid his debt when Feisty lay dead. He learned that a spry looking bird doesn't translate to a long-living rooster.

He saw that same scraggly old bird at the third cockfight he attended. Someone had named him "Rough and Ready." After that fight, John walked away with a tidy sum. He approached the bird's handler and said, "Excuse me, Sir. That's a fine lookin' bird you have there. I just won a nice sum of..." The man looked up at John as he put the bird in its cage and laughed.

"You're foolin' with me, right? Old Rough and Ready, a fine lookin' bird?" The man laughed a hearty laugh,

"Son, you best get yourself a pair of them Ben Franklin spectacles." The elderly man chuckled again, "Old Rough and Ready, a 'fine lookin' bird.'"

"How long have you been fighting him?" John distinctly felt that the man did not trust most people. He understood because he didn't like talking to folks either, especially to those who were wealthier than him.

It took all of John's winnings from the fight and a bit more to pay for a meal and quite a few drinks for the man. Only then did the man offer any of his expertise. John paid the price because he needed to know what this man knew.

The man answered with some coaxing, "I've been doin' this jest under a year now. Been in four fights. Why?" he asked cautiously.

"Sir, to be honest, I've got a rooster I want to fight." John told him about The General. The man discouraged John from fighting.

"Yur bird's too old," the man said, but John would not accept his advice. He really needed the money, and The General provided the only real option he had for making it.

Over a plate of sausages, the man talked about three different types of fights: bare heel, short spurs, and long spurs. Two of the types used cockspurs to increase the gore of the battle. In a bare heeled fight, the rooster's handler sharpened the bird's talons until they cut like a razor. A short spur fight used small metal blades about three quarters of an inch long. The handler would attach the cockspurs on a bird's legs with a leather strap. A long spur fight also strapped a cockspur to each of the rooster's legs, but instead of blades, they used actual knives that were out about two and a half inches long. More than one story traveled around the cockfighting circuit that once a bird's handler died by their own rooster's longspurs while strapping them on.

The man finally added, "If you be stuck on fightin' your bird, even if he's too old, then your best bet is havin' 'im fight bare heeled only. That's if he's as big and mean as you say he is."

"Why's that?" John asked.

"Cause when you add blades and knives, you lose your bird's size advantage. A younger, faster bird will win every time," the man explained.

He added, "You did say you had a big bird, right?"

"The biggest one in these parts, I reckon." John countered.

The man then offered a word of warning, "If you want to keep your bird alive, don't ever put 'im in the pit with cockspurs."

Chapter Twelve:
Learning by Doing

With Pa spending all his time attending to, promoting, and training the General, the rest of the farm gradually fell apart. Pa, not willing to give up the fast life of gambling and cockfighting, nor spending money that he desperately needed elsewhere, decided that Betsy, Susan and Johnny didn't need any more schooling.

The children had, for several years, made the trek to a private school up on Union Hill run by a schoolmaster by the name of Robert Henry. The girls enjoyed going to the school on the hill with other children, however, John suspected the girls would do nothing more than marry and raise a quiver of young'uns. He figured they wouldn't need too much of an education for that. They could read and write, and they could deal with numbers. What more did a woman need to learn?

John also wondered what to do about Johnny. He knew Johnny didn't do well in school, and he didn't like it either. Therefore, John considered an apprenticeship or something similar to it as an option for his boy.

One evening, while at the local pub, John met a trapper who had gone searching for a lad to train as his assistant. The two firmed up the idea of Johnny becoming a trapper's assistant. The man wanted to talk with the boy first. They scheduled to meet again for lunch on the day of the upcoming local fair. John kept the news about going to the fair a secret, at least for the time being.

Back at home, John needed the girls. He needed them to run the farm and do the chores he chose to ignore. Susan naturally gravitated to completing the chores in and around the house. That left Betsy to take over the work around the farm during the times when John would go away or fuss over The General.

John knew Betsy needed training. He just couldn't turn everything over to her without it. He figured HE had learned how. She could too.

He taught her how to look for diseases that could decimate a flock, how to fight off or discourage would-be attackers like hawks and coyotes, and how to negotiate a good price for the eggs as well as chickens they had already prepared for cooking. For the other farming skills, Betsy would pick them up either by watching her pa, or through her own experiences. Betsy learned on her own things such as how much to feed them and how to maintain a clean coop. She excelled at culling the flock of hens. Betsy found the art of candling eggs quite interesting. By slowly waving the light from a candle under the rounded side of an egg she could classify an egg as either a "yolker" or fertilized. She would take the yolkers and place them in the cold cellar to keep them from spoiling. Once a week, Betsy would gather all the yolkers and bring them to market. With the exception of the quitters, spoiled fertilized eggs, she would place the rest of the eggs back under the mother hens so they would incubate.

Betsy wondered if she would ever get use to plucking the feathers off chickens and eviscerating the birds. Betsy considered it a vile, disgusting chore she regularly had to do. She hoped nothing worse would come along.

Then there came the time her pa taught her how to chop off a chicken's head. John placed a meat cleaver in her hand and had her practice bringing the sharp tool directly down to the bloody stump. When he felt satisfied that she used the necessary force needed, he had her hold a vegetable in one hand while wielding the cleaver in the other. After practicing on an ear of corn she was ready to do damage to the birds.

Her time finally came. John showed her how to hold on to the chicken while she beheaded it. She let go the first couple of times. It caused the birds to be even more upset during the process. John said, "Now pick the bird up, and lay her on her side so the neck is flat on the stump. You got to be calm, so the hen stays calm."

How does someone remain calm when they're about to kill another living thing? she wondered.

She would never get used to killing chickens, and her stomach felt it would spew like some volcano she heard about in school Betsy wished she could sit in the
one-room schoolhouse once again.

"Now, bring the cleaver up above your head and hold it tight. Don't let go of it. You have to hold it tight," John coached. Betsy concentrated so hard, her head ached.

John gave his final instruction, "Now, on the count of three, bring the cleaver down quick and don't let go of it." Betsy's palms sweated profusely. She tried not to shake but she could not stop herself. She heard her pa say, "One, two, THREE!"

Betsy didn't know how she did it, but she did it. The bird's head fell off and out squirted some blood. When she lifted up the body by its legs, more blood poured out. As any young girl would do, she dropped the body.

The headless bird stumbled about, got up, and ran frantically around going in no particular direction at all. The bird would repeat the sequence of stumbling, getting up, and running about until its heart stopped pounding. The macabre chicken dance lasted close to a minute. It took Betsy about the same amount of time to frantically run toward the outhouse. No— beheading chickens— she would never get used to that.

Chapter Thirteen: The Fair

Betsy had just filled a bucket full of water to bring to the chickens when she noticed a two-person buggy working its way up the rutted road. It had recently rained, and traveling on the muddy route by farm wagon challenged the best of drivers. Using a town buggy was even more ridiculous. Betsy figured they must have some real important business to tend to if they came out in that thing. It stopped in front of their place. The two men in the buggy had a brief conversation. They then turned and came down the slight slope to the front of the cabin.

The driver tipped his three-cornered hat, "Good day, Ma'am." Betsy cautiously and quietly nodded her head. The other man impeccably dressed took a long time looking over Betsy from head to toe and then back up again. He tipped his hat after leering at her. It made Betsy feel uncomfortable.

"Is this the Roberts' homestead? John Roberts?" The man asked. Betsy answered, "Yes."

"Would you please fetch him for me?" She set the bucket of water on the porch and fetched her father.

As they came around the corner of the barn, John immediately recognized the man who had spoken to Betsy. He didn't recognize the second man. John told Betsy to make some tea. Curiosity got the better of her, so she eavesdropped on every snippet of their conversation while heading toward the cabin.

John greeted the men, "Afternoon, Tom, you're quite a distance from home. What brings you out to these parts?"

"That we are, John. That we are. John, this here's Jim, Gent..." Betsy heard very little else before she shut the door behind her. When she brought the tea out, the men had already gone.

Shortly after the men left, John asked Susan what she had planned to make for supper.

She said, "A meat pie, chicken meat pie." Her answer pleased him.

"Can you make that delicious peach cobbler you always make? Can you make it for tonight?" he asked.

Susan responded, "I can if there's any more canned peaches left."

"I'll check," John replied.

John brought up a can of peaches from the cellar. At dinnertime, Susan set the table. Next to the chicken pie, she placed a beautifully toasted peach cobbler. John had something important to tell his children, and he wanted an especially good meal for the occasion.

Johnny almost got away with not saying grace at the dinner table that night. Susan politely reminded him. He frowned. Johnny folded his hands in front of him and began.

"Dear Lord, thank you for the sun 'cause it makes things grow, for the moon 'cause it lets us sleep, for the air so we can breathe, the water 'cause we need to drink, this meal- to fill our bellies, and this yummy peach cobbler, 'cause I like sweets. Amen."

It was Johnny's usual prayer, but he added the extra, "'Cause I like sweets" phrase, just to make sure God did not forget about it the next time around.

Once Anne passed away, John changed a custom in the Robert's home. He discouraged lots of talking during meals. Talking always came afterwards. They finished that night's meal in record time, because everyone could hardly wait to hear the news.

He pushed himself away from the table when he finished eating and said, "I reckon you three have wondered all afternoon about what's going on." They all nodded their heads in agreement.

John began, "For a long time now, I've been thinking about us moving out to Tennessee, to a place called White's Fort. I'm tired of farming. I want to open an inn there." He went on to explain how fighting the General in cockfights made it possible for them to move. The children asked about the visitors who called on them that day. They heard about how fighting the General one last time at the fair in a couple of weeks would make a lot of money. Afterwards, they could move. The children all cheered when their pa promised he would stop fighting the General after that fight. They cheered even more when he told them that in a couple of weeks, they would all spend the day at the fair.

John told Johnny that a man wanted to meet the boy, and if all went well, Johnny would go out into the forest and trap instead of going to school. He told Susan about a baking competition he wanted her to enter since she had turned into such a fine cook.

And, to Betsy he said, "I suspect most of your friends from school will be there. It will be good to see them again, won't it?"

When they went to bed, each one visualized how that day would turn out. Susan saw herself proudly holding an apple strudel, her favorite desert, while someone pinned a blue ribbon on her dress. Johnny envisioned himself breaking away from the grasp of a stern looking schoolmaster. Betsy's vision had her holding hands with a cute blond-haired boy she used to sit next to in school. For John, instead of the recurring dream of death at King's Mountain, he dreamt of White's Fort, Tennessee.

The day of the fair could not come quickly enough for John and the children.

"Hurry up, Susie. We're gonna' miss everything," Johnny complained.

He, like everyone else, rushed to load all that he might possibly need in the wagon. John gathered all the essentials he would probably use for the fight and placed them in a worn-out carpet bag. The General was already sat safely crated in the back of the wagon, and he stuffed the bag next to him. John pulled the wagon around to the front of the cabin. He fiddled with a hefty money pouch while waiting for everybody to hop onboard. Johnny ran out of the cabin carrying a box containing cockspurs.

Johnny asked, while holding up the small box, "Pa, What about these?"

John replied, "We won't need them today." Johnny turned to put the spurs back when John stopped him. "Wait. Give them to me. I'll put them under the seat."

The night before, they had all agreed on when and where to meet at the end of the day and who would do what so they could get an early start in the morning. Johnny playfully teased Betsy for her excessive preening. At the same time, he thought the red ribbon in her hair looked pretty. Of course, he could never tell her that. Betsy wanted to look pretty for that special someone, just in case.

Almost forgetting, Betsy scampered to gather the eggs stored in the cold cellar. Those eggs, along with the fresh eggs she gathered from the chicken coop, filled two large baskets. John planned to drop off the eggs at the general store and have them credited to his account. At last, with the exception of Susan, they all sat ready to go.

Pa turned to Betsy and Johnny, and whispered, "On three, yell Susan. One, two, three..." Everybody yelled, "Susan!"

"I'm comin', I'm comin'," she replied. Susan held a fresh baked strudel in her hands. She exited the cabin and gave the wrapped cooking tin to Betsy to hold so she could go back and close the cabin door.

Once she hopped onto the back of the wagon, she heard her pa say, "Ooh, that smells wonderful." John then shook the reins and the wagon started rolling. As they rolled away, they all felt that something special, something significant would happen at the fair.

All three children jumped off the wagon the moment their pa pulled up to the livery stable that was strategically placed just outside of town. The deadline for the baking competition fast approached so the girls yelled, "Goodbye" as they hurried off. The stable man agreed to watch over the General for just a few pennies more. John then dropped off the baskets of eggs at the general store. They had freed themselves of any further obligations until lunchtime. Father and son headed toward the market. John didn't intend to buy anything at the market. He just wanted to look around. As the two walked through the outdoor bazaar, John spotted a peddler by the name of Peyton. The two had talked several times before and quite naturally started up a conversation once again. While they talked, Johnny kept eyeing a bag of marbles. Peyton casually mentioned having just returning from Tennessee, and possibility of starting up a new route out west.

John asked, "Did you have a chance to look around White's Fort?"

"Yep. Nice place. There's lots of people movin' out that way," the congenial man answered.

"Anybody build an inn out there yet?" John asked.

The peddler replied, "No, not yet. They sure could use one though. Why? You interested?"

"Could be," John replied, "Could be." The conversation stoked John's enthusiasm for moving to Tennessee even more. Peyton, always the observant one, a requirement if he wished to make sales, watched Johnny stare longingly at a bag of marbles. Johnny did not hear it, but Peyton broached the topic of the marbles with his pa.

"I can give you a good price for them," The peddler offered. He pointed with his head toward Johnny. Johnny rolled the marbles around with his fingers.

"How much?" John asked. He balked at the initial price, so the peddler countered with another offer.

"I'll throw in an extra shooter too. It's an alley." That closed the deal. Peyton, a magician as well as a peddler, hoped to close as many deals as possible and as early as possible. He had committed himself to putting on a magic show for the folks in the town. It surprised John that he so uncharacteristically bent to the will of whimsy, but hey, why not. John smiled when he saw Johnny looking over all the colorful clay marbles in the pouch along with the special shooter that he held in his hand.

As the two men parted company, the peddler said, "There's some boys playin' with marbles over yonder." He pointed with his head toward the games just as another customer came over and stole his attention.

Johnny and Pa sauntered over in the direction the peddler indicated. They came across a crowd playing Ring-taw, three separate games of Ring-taw in fact. Johnny took to the game quite naturally. His shots hit straight. They didn't glance off like so many shots made by the other boys. Quite a crowd of boys of all ages waited their turn with a shooter at the ready. Girls dared not show their faces here. They could play marbles with their brothers at home. Nobody had a problem with that. But here, not a chance.

An even larger crowd stood around the circle and peered down at the game from above - Men with old, creaky knees who dared not get down on the ground and act like boys again for fear they'd never get back up. These elderly onlookers, each a self-appointed strategist, felt called upon to offer useless advice to anyone foolish enough to listen. They found their joy in the game by wagering on the skills of one lad over the skills of another. That, and reminiscing about some thrilling victory or bemoaning that golden opportunity that once slipped away.

John joined in with all the betting as soon as Johnny started playing the game.

John, out of loyalty, usually wagered on his son, but not always. With the time leading up to lunch, John made numerous wagers. Whatever he used to decide when to bet seemed to work well. It had to be a good omen for things to come. He had already won enough to pay for the marbles, and the lunch.

In spite of Johnny's protest over leaving the game, father and son arrived at the pub with time to spare. The trapper arrived later. Their conversation gradually wound around to the trapper asking Johnny some questions. Like many other children his age, Johnny didn't have enough experience to have developed a firm opinion on many topics. Therefore, most answers Johnny gave consisted of a simple yes or no, and each answer always ended with a, "Sir." Then the trapper asked about school.

"Will ya be hankerin' for school once we git goin'?"

Johnny replied, "Nope! I can read already. I can write my name and I can count. I don't need no more schoolin'. Oh, I can put words to paper if I havta', too. Will ya need me to?" The trapper didn't think he'd need it but appreciated knowing the possibility existed.

After a few minutes where John and the trapper finalized things, the trapper told Johnny, "Be ready first thing Tuesday mornin'."

In one turn of an hourglass, the boy successfully escaped further schooling, something he detested, and joined the working class. The day had far exceeded anything he could imagine, and he had a bag of marbles to boot. The day had more in store. The cockfight remained.

Susan and Betsy reached the competitive bake-off with no time to spare. Susan quickly entered her apple strudel. She placed her strudel on the table alongside all the other entries. This competition did not come across as one of the more exciting of events, but, without a doubt, this event had the greatest aromas. The competition's judge, Robert Henry, the schoolmaster, had a difficult time keeping his stomach from rumbling, thanks to the luscious odors emanating from the epicurean delights. Both girls bit their fingernails down to the nubs while Mr. Henry tasted, re-tasted, and tasted yet again each entry. At least his rumblings disappeared. Determined to get it right, Mr. Henry bemused some of the onlookers when he ran around the table numerous times, first one way and then the other. When he announced the winners, he turned to Susan as the first person he recognized. She had won third place. He announced to everyone present that she was the youngest person ever to win a baking award. The award did not match her dream, but third place satisfied her.

Susan thought, *I could go home now. Nothing is going to top this today.*

Betsy had other ideas. They approach the jump rope competition. "Come on. Let's give it a try," she said, encouraging her sister. Susan, still receiving accolades from fellow bakers, chose to sit and watch instead.

"Well, I'm gonna." Betsy declared. She marched up and joined the line for the jump-roping competition. Three people, all of them younger, preceded Betsy. When her time came, Betsy, at the last moment, kicked off her shoes and jumped in barefooted. She hopped in beneath the twirling rope and started. The two rope twirlers and a few bystanders picked up a cautionary chant.

Little Miss Betsy, dressed in yella',
Went upstairs to kiss a fella.
Oh, she made a big mistake,
Wound up kissin'a mean old snake.
How many doctors did it take
Just to bring her back awake?

WHEN THE CHANT CONCLUDED, the rope whirled faster, much faster. Betsy lasted until the thirteenth swing of the rope. She then stumbled. She knew she would not win a prize. It didn't matter, for when she looked up she saw a cute blond-haired boy holding her shoes. Betsy's face lit up, and her heart jumped. Her dream had come true.

Betsy protested, but not too loudly, when the boy kept her shoes just out of reach. The boy figured that nobody could have too much fun teasing a pretty girl. He kept the shoes too, that is until Susan offered what remained of her award-winning dessert. She didn't object at all. To the contrary. Betsy's friend had a friend.

The two couples ran in the sack races, the three-legged races, and watched in amazement as the "Amazing Peyton" performed magical tricks. After eating barbequed turkey legs for lunch, the four whiled away the rest of the afternoon dancing the minuet to the sounds of a fiddle, a drum, and a fife.

The time came for the boys to say goodbye to Susan and Betsy. Somehow, the two couples separated from each other. Afterwards, Susan told Betsy she thought the boys planned it that way.

Betsy responded, "Of course they did, Silly."

The boy who tagged along with Susan left her standing alone before Betsy's friend left her. Susan then sought out Betsy. She found her sister partially hidden behind a large tree. Susan stepped up to Betsy just as Betsy and the blond boy kissed.

"Oh!" Susan exclaimed. Embarrassed, Susan turned and retreated until she stood a safe distance away from the couple. She then waited.

As far as kisses go, their kiss didn't reach the level of lip-smackin', let alone one of those amorous ones. It was just an any-day-of-the-week peck. So, what made that kiss special? Betsy had her first kiss, and every young lady should always remember her first kiss. She sure did.

As they walked back through the burgeoning town, the two sisters talked incessantly. No one could tell who had the most to say, or who could say it faster. They had so much energy that it felt like both had become spinning tops that had just been spun.

Both girls took off running as fast as possible when they spotted Johnny on the ground. He leaned against one of the wagon wheels and held his head.

Chapter Fourteen:
Betrayal

The grand opening of Gentleman Jim's surpassed everyone's expectations except for Gentleman Jim himself. His vision of what the future held for his new community far exceeded the vision of everyone else. As people in the area slowly learned, the man had an unparalleled dream; but he also had a voracious appetite to control everything of importance in the county. He desired a monarchy for his new land with him as the king and the place, "Gentleman Jim's," served as his own private castle.

Gentleman Jim left nothing to chance. His grand opening required perfection. That's why he hired one particular man to announce the cockfights at the outlandish, opening event. The announcer, a barrel-chested man, wasn't much to look at. However, when he spoke everyone stopped everything just to hear him. It didn't matter if he had something important to say or not. People likened his deep rich voice to what they imagined they would have heard when God spoke.

It had already been a long day when the announcer stepped up on a wooden box in front of the new cockpit and said, "Well folks, we've finally made it. We've reached the fight y'all have been waitin' for." He waited as a loud cheer lifted up from the crowd inside the packed hall.

"Gentleman Jim has gone to great lengths to bring you this fight. Thank you, Gentleman Jim. Stand up and wave to the folks. You're giving us quite a show." The inebriated crowd cheered loudly when Gentleman Jim stood and waved.

"That's Gentleman Jim folks. Y'all will get to know and like him as the days go by." Again, a cheer rose up from the crowd.

"This final bout pits The General, a local favorite in the county, a giant of a bird, a champion." The crowd cheered. "Some would even go so far as to call him a Goliath. Why this year alone, he successfully fought off five contenders." The announcer pointed to the second bird. "This goliath of a bird will face a newcomer to these parts. Folks, meet the Grim Reaper." A smattering of cheers quickly succumbed to the hail of boos and comments about the bird's name.

While pointing to each bird, the announcer said, "Will this Goliath finally fall to this David? Time will tell. Time will tell." He paused for a moment.

"Be sure to place your bets for two rounds of bare-heeled fighting. Each round will last fifteen minutes, and there will be a fifteen-minute break in between. So, join me as we count down from...ten, nine, eight..." The sound in the hall rose to an eardrum breaking level as the crowd picked up the count.

The opening round began with a flourish. Each handler swung their bird up over the circular fence and let go when the count reached zero. The General, trained to attack quickly, immediately pounced on the Grim Reaper. He made some damaging slashes to his opponent, but the Grim Reaper, a smaller and far faster bird, successfully broke free. From that point forward the Reaper used his speed advantage to avoid any further altercations with The General. It seemed as though he had no real interest in fighting at all. The onlookers grew restless. Many in the crowd, sensing The General's imminent victory, changed their bet or doubled down on their wagers. They wholeheartedly favored The General. Others in the crowd tossed derisive comments at the Grim Reaper. Some comments had a bit of wit to them and brought merriment to the crowd.

John appreciated that the Reaper and not The General took most of the crowd's displeasure. He convinced himself that The General would win. They would have to declare his bird the victor after watching the Grim Reaper's performance. Things were going as planned, but John didn't know that Gentleman Jim had planned better.

Nobody took the time to ask about the Grim Reaper's history, or who owned the bird. Nobody seemed to care, Gentleman Jim wasn't about to share with anybody that he owned the Grim Reaper. He bought the Reaper specifically for this event. People, in other parts of the state, recognized the Grim Reaper as a brutal killing machine. Just as John had trained The General to excel in bare-heeled fights, a master had trained the Grim Reaper to act docile in every fight that did not include cockspurs. Once someone attached spurs around his legs, the bird's superior speed, and overwhelming will to survive turned the Grim Reaper into a formidable adversary.

Just as nobody asked about the bird, nobody asked how somebody would resolve disagreements either. They all accepted the notion that the house would arbitrate all disputes. Therefore, Gentleman Jim made the rules. He also hired enough thugs to make sure nobody disagreed with him. Many a gambler felt suckered that day. No one felt more suckered than John.

With the first of the two rounds completed, John took some time to crack a joke or two with people in the audience. He then excused himself and told Johnny to give The General some water and a bite to eat. He also told Johnny to apply a salve on any of the General's wounds. John meandered back through the audience. He seemed pleased with how the fight was proceeding. Well-wishers who had successfully wagered on the General before, stopped John to say hello. It took a bit of time before John reached Gentleman Jim.

"John, your bird's done well so far. How may I help you?" the busy Gentleman Jim asked.

John answered him, "I want to increase my wager."

"Of course, how much of a bet do you wish to make?" the man asked.

"All I have, including what you offered me for entering The General," the buoyant John answered. He winked at Gentleman Jim since he was pretty sure of the outcome.

Gentleman Jim leaned in toward John so he could be heard above the noise of the crowd and said, "John, are you sure you want to do that?"

"Why not, The General's going to win isn't he?" John responded. He fully expected to win after the conversation they had two weeks earlier. John intently looked at the man to see if Gentleman Jim's behavior betrayed anything. A soft whisper deep within him caused him deep concern.

"Well, we certainly hope so, don't we?" Gentleman Jim winked back. That satisfied John.

When John agreed to the nefarious venture, he had made his decision based on two assumptions. First, Gentleman Jim had built an expensive hall for cockfighting and the man needed a rooster that people would pay to see fight, especially at a grand opening. Second, people made wagers when they felt confident they would have a good chance of winning. Gentleman Jim needed a large number of wagers since he'd planned to attach a fee to every wager made. The General's popularity and reliability as a fighting bird made him the obvious choice. Therefore, John entered into the agreement. He could not pass up this winning proposition.

John glossed over the all-important third part of the equation. If everyone bets on The General who wins, then who pays off the bets? Most likely, they would turn to Gentleman Jim to cover their bets. In no way would Gentleman Jim accept that solution. He had not come that far in life by playing fair.

Yes, Gentleman Jim needed The General to bring in the crowd, and yes, he needed The General to boost the number of wagers, but no, he needed The General to lose, not win. He needed The General to lose without question. He needed The General to die.

A second or two after John walked away from Gentleman Jim back toward the pit, Gentleman Jim signaled for one of his men. A man stepped forward, listened to his boss, and disappeared into the crowd. It didn't take long before a chant erupted—a chant of, "Longspurs, Longspurs, Longspurs," spread through the crowd. The chant reverberated inside the hall. The first round disappointed the crowd, and their thirst for blood needed quenching.

Surprised, John whirled around to stare at the crowd. He feared the worst. John looked over to the announcer who could only shrug his shoulders. John glanced over to the man who tended after the Grim Reaper. That man had already attached one of the deadly longspurs to his rooster.

The Grim Reaper's handler seemed prepared for this situation as if he knew beforehand that this change would happen. John hurried back to the old satchel he always brought along to each bout. He looked inside, and as he expected nothing inside the carpet bag resembling longspurs.

John heard the announcer declare, "I just got word. You need to use longspurs."

John complained. "That's unfair. I need more time. I don't have any here with me."

"I can give you ten minutes." the announcer declared. He then walked away.

"Johnny," his pa called. "Quick, get the longspurs. Look in the box under the wagon seat. Hurry!" Johnny hurried toward the exit. Nobody noticed that two of Gentleman Jim's thugs followed the boy.

Chapter Fifteen: A Warning Ignored

B etsy, winded from running as fast as she could, successfully wiggled her way past the money taker. She eventually worked through the crowd and reached her pa with only minutes to spare.

John, surprised to see his daughter and not Johnny, nervously asked, "Where's Johnny?"

"Somebody beat him up. Susan's with him now," Betsy replied with a loud voice so her pa heard her above the crowd.

John sounded alarmed, "What?"

"He said two men did it. Pa, Johnny told me to tell you they took the longspurs." John frantically looked for a way out of his dilemma. He spotted Gentleman Jim's two thugs enter, go to their boss, and place something shiny.in his hands,

Betsy added, "Johnny gave me these to give to you." She held out a pair of short spurs. They lacked the deadly effectiveness that longspurs provided, but they would have to do.

"Hurry, strap them around his legs. We don't have much time," John said as he held the struggling General as still as possible. Betsy strapped and tightened one cockspur to the rooster's leg with relative ease.

Just as predicted, The General fought against adding the second spur. He had only worn them once before. John heeded the old man's good advice to enter The General only in bare heeled fights. However, it also meant that if The General ever fought with cockspurs, he would likely fight wearing the uncomfortable spurs just as much as he'd fight the other bird.

Gentleman Jim had tricked John, and now the truth of the old man's warning became crystal clear. When Betsy strapped on the second spur, The General broke free from John's grasp. He repeatedly ripped Betsy's hands and arms with his own razor-sharp talons. She tried to ignore the pain. She had to, so much depended on what she did, not how she felt.

The announcer urged, "Hurry up. I can't wait any longer. I've already given you more time than I should."

"I know. Just one more minute, please," John pleaded. Betsy worked through the pain, both hers and The General's. She finally succeeded in setting the spur in place. She tied off one part, but the second part still needed tying. Then she heard it.

"Ten... nine... eight," The announcer yelled out above the raucous noise.

Her pa yelled, "Hurry." She ignored him.

"Seven... six," The impatient crowd picked up the chant.

Betsy's fingertips ached from the tension. She tied it at last, not as tightly as she hoped for. Betsy let go and pulled herself away.

"Four... three," With all his might, John swung The General over the fence and out above the cockpit.

"Two... ONE," John let The General fly.

The rooster soared higher than Betsy had ever seen before. In spite of his wounds, both old and new, The General still looked magnificent.

She never saw The General alive again.

Betsy could not watch the fight. She just couldn't. Instead, she turned away and, with her back pressed against the fence, slid down into a tight ball beside her pa. She covered her ears and eyes and waited.

Betsy felt something. It startled her. She tensed up expecting something sinister to happen. When she opened her eyes, she saw a cloth draped over her knees. An older, well-dressed gentleman, clearly a man of means, had watched her with great interest when she attached the spurs.

He took pity on her and mouthed, "For your hands." The older gentleman then returned to his front row seat to watch the rest of the fight. From that man's simple act of kindness, Betsy came to understand that a gentleman didn't need to proclaim himself as one- like Gentleman Jim. The man with the cloth could act like one without expecting something in return. Betsy hoped that one day she would find her own real gentleman.

Betsy watched as the crowd swayed to the left, then to the right, depending on where the birds struggled within the pit. How odd. People acted as if they wished to live or die like a rooster. With all the strained necks, people jumping up to get a better view, and individuals literally climbing all over the backs of others, it seemed as though everybody wished they fought and not just watched.

Still huddled on the ground against the fence, she turned to her pa. He too, danced about. Betsy quickly caught on that her pa imitated every move The General made. Both would attack, then pull back, feign a move to the right, then surge forward to the left. Whenever The General attacked, her pa would clench his fists. That's when she heard the fluttering.

It didn't take long to connect the fluttering sound to actual fighting. She hated the fluttering. It made her cover her ears. After one extended length of fluttering, Betsy saw her pa move slower and stop. She knew the battle had finished when her pa's arms collapsed down to his sides.

The bloodlust roar of the crowd rose high inside the hall, while at the same time, the squawks, screeches, and fluttering grew uneasily quiet from inside the pit. A simple cock-a-doodle-doo, not The General's distinctive crow, pierced through the den of gamblers.

Betsy looked over the crowd. *Why do they call this a sport? Why does one of God's creatures have to die just for someone's entertainment?* She saw faces glow red with enthusiasm and energy and knew each one had experienced something memorable. Yet not a soul cared that death, albeit the death of a crotchety old rooster, passed over the hall. It made her cry.

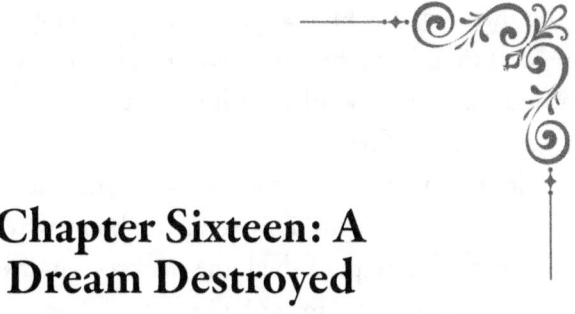

Chapter Sixteen: A Dream Destroyed

The crowd gradually cleared out, save for a few stragglers, who employees of Gentleman Jim escorted out. Only Gentleman Jim, his two accomplices, John and Betsy remained. Gentleman Jim walked toward John while holding a large, empty, burlap bag in his hand. Betsy stood by her pa when she saw the man draw closer. She could feel danger swirling about.

Gentleman Jim tossed the bag in Betsy's direction and with a great deal of disdain said, "Here, Missy, get your bird out of my pit." She looked to her pa for approval which he gave by nodding his head. Betsy crossed between the two men toward the pit's entrance. Betsy had worn her shoes all day at the fair and they hurt. She considered going into the pit barefoot to retrieve The General's body. She chose not to when she looked over the fence and saw that the sand was an odd shade of pink.

John Roberts bitterly complained saying, "How dare you." At the same time, Gentleman Jim nonchalantly walked back to his perch at the rear of the hall. Gentleman Jim knew he'd beaten John. Therefore, he approached the impending argument with great calm.

"How dare I what? May I call you, John?" Frustrated by the question, John waved his arm in annoyance.

"How dare I what, John?" John's name sounded more like a curse than a name whenever Gentleman Jim said it. John, angry over the situation, took a couple of aggressive steps toward Gentleman Jim.

The owner sat in his special chair. Two thugs stepped forward to protect their boss. John stopped when he saw the two. He walked to a point between Gentleman Jim, his thugs, and the exit. He could escape quickly if needed to.

John protested, "We had an agreement, and you broke it."

"John, you're right. I broke it. You know why? Because I can. It's MY place." More perturbed, the man rose and walked down to the cockpit. He gestured toward it.

"The pit's mine. I make the rules. I decide who wins and who loses, not you, I do." The more Gentleman Jim spoke, the more agitated he became. While speaking, Gentleman Jim took note of an unopened bottle of liquor. He took it, and tucked it under the arm of his elegant, gold, silk coat- the one he wore especially for the grand opening.

"What about my boy? Who beat him up?" John angrily asked.

"That? An unfortunate accident. It won't happen to the young'un' again. You have my word on that," Gentleman Jim replied. The boss turned and glared at the two men behind him. Gentleman Jim's comment came as close to an apology as John would ever receive.

"Your word? We had an agreement. You cheated me!" John argued.

Gentleman Jim responded, "Be careful who you call a cheat, John. How many fights did I hear your bird won this past year? Five, was it? How many times did you cheat? Two? Three? Five? Your bird started out too old to fight. It couldn't have won any of them without you cheating. So, don't go calling ME a cheat. Otherwise, I'm sure your neighbors would like to hear about how your bird really won." John, forced to face his own actions, stood silently.

"Do you know what the difference between us is, John?" Gentleman Jim asked. John grew tired of hearing his name bandied about.

"The difference is, I'm going to hell, and I know it... I'm alright with that 'cause while I'm here I get to live my life by my rules - nobody else's. You? You've got your feet in two worlds, and you're stuck."

The man pointed his thumb behind himself in Betsy's direction.

"You want them to think of you as a good man. No wait—you want EVERYONE to think of you as a good man, don't you? Well, you're like the rotten yolk inside an egg. You don't know it's rotten until the egg's cracked. When they crack your shell, and they will, they'll finally know how rotten you've become." John was a beaten man.

"It's time to pay up, John. It's time for you to pay up or else." Gentleman Jim's men stepped close and waited for the command. Seeing the two in the corner of his eye, John walked up to Gentleman Jim, and offered all he had with him.

"That's it?" the surprised man asked.

"That's all I have left," replied John. Gentleman Jim looked over to his men and contemplated his options.

Then, in a false gesture of magnanimity, the man put his arm around John's shoulder. While walking toward the exit, Gentlemen Jim said, "You know what John? For some strange reason I like you." A falsehood for sure, and they both knew it.

With no ambiguity in his voice, the man sternly finished, "I'll give you a week."

John called out, "Come on, Betsy." He then grabbed the full bottle of liquor out from under Gentleman Jim's coat. He turned and quickly left. John held in his hand what he considered his last measure of self-respect. The thugs moved toward the door to chase him.

"Leave him," the man said, "He won't be back." The two thugs left their boss standing alone.

Gentleman Jim said to himself, "Pathetic!"

After seeing Gentleman Jim break and humiliate her pa, send thugs to beat up her brother, and bring about The General's death, Betsy looked for revenge. She closed the gate behind her to the miniature coliseum of death and walked toward the door. Gentleman Jim, in his fine gold silk coat stood with his back to her. He didn't realize he had blocked her way to the exit.

Betsy held in her left hand the burlap bag this man had thrown to her for gathering The General's body. She reached in and covered her right hand with the blood of her family's pet. Betsy then came up behind the man and said, "Excuse me," as a way to ask the man to step aside. At the same time, she placed her bloodstained hand on the back of Gentleman Jim's silk coat. The coat, clearly an expensive work of art, soaked up Betsy's bloodstained handprint. The man turned toward Betsy, and after seeing her blood covered hands, he stepped back and said, "Watch it! Get away from me young lady, You're filthy." He then gave her an even wider path. She proudly walked past the man and smiled as she exited into the street. What she had done felt good. She felt justified in doing it.

John never said a word about it, but he paid for his daughter's blood-print. Oh, did he pay. Gentleman Jim's thugs made sure of that.

By the time she'd reached the wagon, stopping only to wash away the blood from her hands, her pa had taken a couple of swigs from the bottle he had stolen. He sat waiting, looking off into the distance, focusing on nothing.

In the back of the wagon, Susan held a wet cloth over the goose egg of a bump on Johnny's forehead. The two had already settled in for the ride home. Betsy jumped on, turned around, and dangled her feet off the back. She placed the burlap bag off to the side. In olden days, the time of castles, pageantry, and knights in shining armor, when a champion fell, they would carry him home to his final resting place on his shield. The General? He got a soiled burlap bag. Somehow, it didn't seem right.

John took the reins and clicked his tongue. The horses headed off on the long, silent ride home. The children fell asleep after the exhausting day.

Eventually, the horses stopped. Betsy looked up and saw their cabin off to the right. It looked dark and unoccupied. She wondered, *Why aren't we moving?* She twisted around to see what happened. She saw her brother and sister still asleep, but she saw nothing else.

Betsy called out from the back of the wagon, "Pa? Pa, we're home." Susan started to stir. Her pa said nothing. Frustrated, Betsy hopped off the back of the wagon and marched to the front. What she saw surprised her. The horses, all on their own had stopped in front of the cabin and waited patiently. They had traveled this route many times before and needed no guidance. Betsy looked at her snoring pa, curled up on the seat, and surmised he'd had too much to drink. She found the empty bottle on the wagon's floorboard.

Once she applied the brake, Betsy returned to the back of the wagon and shook Susan until her sister got up. Susan then woke up Johnny and the two disappeared into the cabin. Betsy returned to her pa. She tugged his sleeve, and said, "Pa, we're home." In response, he muttered something she couldn't understand. She then walked over to one of the horses, grabbed its collar, and slowly pulled the team and wagon down to the barn.

Her pa startled and then mumbled, "Bed them down. You can..." The rest of his unintelligible mumbling faded away. Having no choice in the matter, Betsy wearily accepted yet another chore that had once belonged to her pa.

Chapter Seventeen: The Funeral

Early next morning, even before someone milked the cow, Susan, Betsy, and Johnny stood by a small hole off in the corner of the family gravesite. They had come to give The General a proper burial. They figured that early morning best fit burying him, especially since that rooster never figured out the concept of dawn.

Johnny turned toward Samson, gave a short whistle, and said, "Come here, boy." Samson joined the ceremony.

Betsy asked her brother and sister, "Anybody want to say somethin'?"

"He's a bird," Johnny responded, a little put out by Betsy's question.

"Stop that," rebuked Betsy.

Johnny argued back, "Well he is...or was.'

"I know he was just a rooster, but he wasn't like them others. He was special, a pet."

Susan added her opinion, "No, Bets, you go ahead." Betsy nodded in agreement and stepped closer to the hole they dug for the General. She placed the smelly, burlap bag in the hole and started her somber eulogy.

"Lord, this here's the General. He was kinda like a pet around the place. He sure could cock-a doodle-do. You probably heard him at some strange times." Johnny snickered at Betsy's comments. His snickering caused Susan to snicker as well. Her snickering started small, but it quickly grew into full laughter.

"Stop it you two," Betsy reprimanded her siblings; but by then Johnny and Susan couldn't help themselves.

Betsy, slightly miffed, started again, trying to ignore them.

"Anyways, Lord, they dun' him wrong. He deserved better." As she said the next sentence, she too came down with a case of the giggles.

"Since he never figured out when to wake people, he shoulda' had one more chance to cock-a-doodle-do," Betsy did an excellent imitation of the General's peculiar call. All three children laughed themselves silly. Samson started barking. His barking came across as Samson's tribute to his old adversary. Susan, holding the shovel, picked up a load of dirt and dropped it in the hole.

"Wait," Johnny said. He rifled thru his pockets looking for something. He finally found it. Johnny had, at some point in the morning, taken off the cockspurs. He dropped the pair of blood-splattered weapons on the bag. Looking at them lying there on the burlap had a sobering effect on all three children. Another shovel of dirt covered up the spurs.

PART TWO - Chapter One: Two Brothers from Hell

Two horses, one bigger than the other, stood quietly tied to a half-broken-down fence. The bigger horse occasionally strained its long neck to reach for a tuft of grass. An evil-sounding laugh erupted from within the cabin, a cabin that had once appeared neat and well-kept. It looked more like a ramshackle hovel lately. Anyone who entered it had to squat down, because the roof over the porch at one end hung low. The skeleton of their mama's favorite, high-backed, rocking chair kept the roof from collapsing altogether.

Years passed since John lost his dream to move to Tennessee. He no longer showed interest in the place they lived and did even less to keep it going. That left Susan, Betsy, and Johnny to do the things that needed to get done. In fact, after the General debacle John pretty much lost interest in everything. At first, John drank to mourn the loss of his wife. Then he drank over the loss of his dream. Next, he drank over the loss of his children's adoration. He drank even more then. Finally, he drank because he needed it.

The number of visitors who stopped by for reasons such as finding shelter during a storm, recognizing a neighbor's generosity, or just to quench their thirst, dwindled to a handful each year. For some reason, an imaginary quarantine sign hung over their heads. It seemed as though the entire Roberts family had contracted a dreaded disease, and everyone knew about it but them.

Those who did visit looked far different from those who used to stop. The families hoping to make a fresh start out west, or neighbors dropping in just to say, "Good day" had all but disappeared. Instead, men traveling alone, or in pairs became their visitors. These visitors looked over their shoulder and worried that someone may have followed them. That behavior stood out as a common trait. The visitors who came this time looked and acted like all the others.

Neither Susan nor Betsy saw them arrive. They'd gone foraging for food. Foraging for something edible took up much of their time. It didn't matter whether they sifted through a picked over garden or traipsed through the nearby woods. It took time, and free time became a scarce commodity after Ma died. The family would have starved if Johnny had not found his good fortune.

After the trapper brought Johnny on as an assistant, he found Johnny's serious nature quite useful. The lad's determination to do what others expected of him pleased the man as well. Right from the beginning, Johnny's apprenticeship developed into a successful venture. Since the two trapped primarily for pelts, mostly beaver pelts, and not for the meat, Johnny often brought the meat home for the family. The family tasted a variety of wild animal meats over the three years that followed, thanks to Johnny.

To keep their business thriving when the beaver population neared extinction, Johnny and his boss had to trap further and further west. It also meant they repeatedly poached on Indian land. Johnny reassured his sisters and even his pa about the poaching. He always guaranteed that all would turn out well, but his family had their doubts. Every day someone kept a watch out for when he would reappear. They dreaded the day he wouldn't.

"Here he comes," Betsy squealed. She spotted him walking down a nearby hill. A wooden branch that Johnny used as a pole rested on his shoulder. It carried the carcasses of a pair of rabbits. The family and guests would have rabbit stew for that evening's meal.

With Johnny always away trapping, and pa- undependable, the chores Susan and Betsy completed often overwhelmed the two. They dreaded their futures. All they could see in store for them was abject failure.

Susan had grown into a quiet, reserved, young woman. She also had panic attacks of varying intensity. She preferred the solitude of cooking to the stress she felt when interacting with people. Much of her insecurity reached back to the doubts she had over her looks. With the exception of her thick, rich, red hair, Susan felt ugly. That only reinforced her insecurity. Susan looked a lot like her pa, not pretty, but not ugly either. She just felt ugly. John kept apologizing to Susan for her inheriting his looks. His apologies exacerbated her anxiety. Betsy inherited much of her mother's beauty. The combination of black hair and blue eyes grabbed people's attention.

Susan's insecurity also spilled over to how the siblings interacted. Contrary to typical family dynamics, Betsy's older sister and her younger brother looked to her for guidance and leadership. After their mother passed away, Betsy held the family together.

Betsy knew Johnny had to make an appearance in the cabin. She pulled him aside and warned him about the guests before he did.

Betsy said, "Something don't feel right."

Johnny, with immaturity, self-confidence and arrogance, boasted, "Everything will be fine. Besides, I'm ready if something does happen." He patted the sheathed knife that hung from his belt of rope. Johnny left the sisters and approached the cabin.

The door to the cabin swung open.

When John saw his son at the entrance, he called out, "Ah, Johnny, we were just talking about you." John then gushed over his son, and went on to give him an alcohol-inspired tribute. The conversation slowly wound around to Johnny's experiences as a trapper. Johnny's poaching on Cherokee land interested the Harpe

Brothers most of all. The boy shuffled back and forth on his feet just as any child would when forced to listen to parental boasting.

While standing there, John thought, *Sis, you're right. There's somethin' wrong with these two.*

"You must be good with a knife. Ain't that right, boy?" Wiley asked. Johnny noticed the fingers twitch on the knife's handle of the one they called Big Harpe.

Johnny thought about boasting but decided, what's the point?

Micajah Harpe, a formidable hulk of a man, stood close to, if not over six feet, four inches tall. He had that look and smell of a musty old tree about him. Big Harpe considered cleanliness to be a waste of time. Talking did not sit well with him, either. Oh sure, he could talk up a storm if the situation demanded it. Snarling–that's how he preferred to get along with others. He snarled.

Micajah took the empty bottle, tipped it upside down, and snarled, "I hope you got more."

"Why sure," replied John. The Roberts family sometimes went without food, but they always had an extra bottle or two tucked away, just in case.

Micajah demanded, "Boy, get us another bottle."

Micajah had grown accustomed to having his way. If things didn't go as he wished, he made sure those who failed him the first time never failed him a second. Few got to know this surly, evil-spirited man in his early to mid-twenties. Those who did knew they'd met one of Satan's disciples. People dropped the courtesy of calling him by his given name, Micajah, or Mickey, as his brother called him. They kept their distance, and that satisfied Big Harpe.

"Look in the storage bin," offered his pa. As Johnny headed for the door, his pa took a swipe at him with his foot, just to make sure the boy moved faster. John didn't know why he did that. He figured he was trying to impress his guests with a sophomoric prank, John missed. He leaned too far over in his chair and fell. The brothers laughed at John's embarrassing moment. It never occurred to them that they should ask about someone's well-being. They always just laughed at the discomfort of others.

Wiley, the younger by three years, had a difficult time speaking because he couldn't stop laughing.

He yelled out, "Bring two."

After sitting back down, John asked, "What brings you back this way?" He anxiously waited for his son to return.

"Have you ever been to Popcastle?" asked Wiley.

John said, "No, where is it?"

"It's an inn up north of here, up Kittrell way. We was collectin' a debt 'fore headin' out west," Wiley stated.

Micajah grew weary of the small talk right from the beginning. His interest remained focused on drinking from another bottle and how long it took Johnny to fetch it. Micajah turned his head toward the door. The door remained shut.

A few seconds later, Micajah looked at the door again, and once again, the door remained shut. He tried to engage himself into the conversation, as a way to mitigate his rising anger. The rapping of his knuckles a couple of times on the tabletop showed that his attempt at distraction had not worked.

"They had folks of all types comin' to see the cockfights they was havin'. When we was there, they done packed the inn to the gills, they did. Lots of 'em slept under the stars jest waitin' for the fights to get goin'," Wiley said.

This time, John casually looked up and noticed Big Harpe's discomfort. He chose to say nothing about it.

John had met the Harpe Brothers a little over a year ago at the local pub. They had shared drinks late into the night, and he invited them to visit the next time they came around. He didn't remember doing that, but he didn't remember a lot of things lately. He did remember how Big Harpe nearly beat a man to death over something trivial. John had forgotten what.

Micajah's temper rose to a new plateau when he picked up his tin cup and put it to his lips in search of something moist. When Big Harpe found the cup bone dry, he slammed the cup down on the table just to make sure everybody noticed his displeasure.

Wiley's narrative progressed from boring to irritating in Micajah's estimation, and he couldn't take it any longer.

He finally interrupted his brother and asked, "Did he get lost?"

John, not knowing for sure, surmised, "He's probably finding out when the food's ready."

Wiley started up again, "Had about sixty cock fights. We made good mon..."

Micajah vented, "He best be quick about it." Wiley poured what remained in the bottle into Mickey's cup to mollify him.

"I had a fighting bird once," exclaimed John. "The children called him The General."

"Who named him that?" Wiley asked. Wiley had no problem walking in the shadow of his big brother. Part of his responsibility as a second to Micajah meant carrying on conversations for the two of them.

John tried recalling who named the rooster and stated, "Betsy...I think...Yes, yes it was Betsy. She named him because the bird's beak looked a lot like Washington's."

"I always wondered if that man was a chicken," Wiley joked.

"Hey now," replied John. He added a forced laugh for affect.

Big Harpe held nothing against John. He simply knew his temper would soon overwhelm him and he couldn't do anything to control it, so why try. Wiley occasionally made an effort to divert his brother's ill temper by giving an encouraging look, or a nod of his head, anything to keep Big Harpe engaged instead of focusing on something that made him mad. With a supportive look from Wiley, Big Harpe asked, "What kind of bird was it?"

John replied, "A big English Gamecock."

"Shoulda' used a Rhode Island Red like Wiley there." Micajah offered. Wiley rose to his brother's prompting. While sliding his hands through his oily red hair, he jumped to his feet and pranced about like a chicken. A drink, or two, or three, always made playing the buffoon or acting up to his brother's expectations more palatable. Wiley's antics reminded John of his son's dance many years ago.

Within seconds of the cabin door opening, Micajah, not a bit cordial, said, "Took you long enough."

Johnny responded, "I was lookin' in on the stew." Big Harpe looked at John. John gestured as if saying, see. I told you so.

Micajah continued, "You shoulda' brought it in sooner." Micajah took the bottle from Johnny. Johnny considered responding. Out of the corner of his eye he noticed his pa slightly shake his head. The boy let the complaint pass. Johnny had no place to sit so he worked his way behind Wiley and his pa to the other end of the table. There, he leaned against the wall.

Chapter Two: Danger Lurks About

C hoosing the safe course of action is not always safe, not always wise. Sometimes danger lurks about just waiting for things to develop. John soon found that out.

Micajah's anger still grew. It usually did. He couldn't let it go. He had to utterly dominate whatever or whoever caused his discomfort before he could find relief. That's why Big Harpe asked, "Why this slop? Why don't you have something a man can drink, like whiskey?" He topped off his cup, put the cork back in the bottle and set it down at the end of the table.

Aware of Big Harpe's violent tendency, John cautiously proceeded, "I guess I just got a hankerin' for it."

Almost at the same time as his brother's comment, Little Harpe asked, "You fought in the war?"

Big Harpe muttered, "Waste of a drink if you ask me." John heard both statements but didn't know which statement offered him a way to not antagonize Micajah any more than necessary. John finally chose to answer Wiley's question.

John answered, "Not really, just for a couple of days."

"That's not true. Pa fought in the war. Didn't ya Pa?" offered Johnny.

Wiley's demeanor immediately turned sour. He pretended to be pleased when he responded to Johnny's comment by saying, "He did?" Wiley glanced over to his brother.

Big Harpe stopped his muttering and listened with keen interest, waiting to hear John's response.

Already suspecting they'd hear an answer the two brothers would find distasteful, Wiley asked with a bit of sarcasm, "So... Pa, what side did you fight on?" His question dripped with disdain.

John could tell the tension in the cabin rose again. His muscles twisted tighter with every question he had to answer. He wished the conversation would drift toward something more innocuous so his aching would cease.

It wasn't anything," John said. He tried to downplay his experiences, but his son would have nothing to do with changing the topic. The glory of going to war and fighting for a noble cause thrilled the boy.

"It was too. Tell 'em Pa. He fought at King's Mountain. Killed a man, too. Tell 'em, Pa," urged the boy.

Big Harpe followed up with a question, "What side?" His question had no inflection, no tone to it, but it jarred John into realizing he faced real danger ahead.

Again, the lad, anxious to praise his father, jumped in and replied, "The patriots of course."

"Did you stay for the hangins?" John's eyes widened. Nobody said a word about hangings. He wondered what was going on.

Excited to learn more about someone being hanged, Johnny asked, "Hangins, what hangins?"

John interrupted his son and responded, "Regretfully, they made us stay." John casually rose and grabbed the bottle at the end of the table.

He walked behind Little Harpe to where the high wooden secretary permanently sat. The piece of furniture stood about seven feet tall. Its top half had four shelves used for holding books and other collectable items someone would like to display. The family Bible, the same Bible Betsy read from the day their mother died, held a prominent place on the second shelf. The lower half of the homemade secretary consisted of a large wooden box with an angled lid on top of four nondescript legs. The box stored items not deemed worthy for showing. Fortunately for John, someone in the family had forgotten to close the lid.

Spotting the raised lid hatched an idea for John on how he could cope with his visitors. The likelihood of physically dealing with the Harpe Brothers grew with every passing moment. A loaded, two-barrel, dueling pistol lay hidden within the box. Each side of the pistol worked independently from the other side. A frozen trigger on one side rendered half the weapon useless. Therefore, a person could only shoot a single shot before the pistol needed reloading.

John successfully placed himself in a new spot between Little Harpe and the secretary. He did so without drawing any special attention to himself. His son stood close by - just on the other side of the secretary. John felt confident that he could reach his son if things continued to spiral out of control. John purposefully kept his hand on the bottle.

Johnny failed to recognize that the conversation had turned.

Out of ignorance he asked, "What hangins?"

John turned to his right and offered Wiley another drink saying, "You?"

Never one to turn down a free drink, Wiley gladly accepted the offer. John uncorked the bottle and emptied it into Wiley's tin cup. He made note of the fact that Wiley's reaction time had slowed quite a bit due to him drinking too much already. John nonchalantly switched the empty bottle from his right to his left hand and held it by the neck.

"What hangins?" pleaded Johnny.

While occasionally slurring a word here and there, Wiley responded, "A bunch of the king's men got strung up, just because they lost the battle...including ma's younger brother."

Big Harpe angrily interjected, "Damn near drove her crazy over it."

Determined not to be left out of the conversation, Wiley added, "Later, they done run us off our land, just cause we ain't 'Patriots." Wiley spat out the word patriot, "Done put her in her grave."

Johnny's eyes opened wide. He finally realized how dangerous the situation had become.

Big Harpe knew he was headin' for a fight and he had best get ready. He stood and stretched. He'd sat across from John and Wiley for far too long. He'd be ready if a fight broke out.

Big Harpe lived by the principle that it's always safer to land the first blow than to wait for the fight to come to you. One of his favorite strategies included taunting his opponent until the other man attacked. When the man attacked, usually driven by anger, the man would leave himself unprepared for a deadly counterattack. That was the strategy he used on Johnny.

Micajah taunted Johnny with a litany of embarrassing questions. He didn't care, not a whit, about the lad's sexual inexperience, or experiences he may have had. He just wanted a critical advantage.

Micajah asked, "So, boy, you still sleep in the loft with your sisters, right?"

"Yeah, when I'm home, why?" Johnny asked.

Micajah continued, "Do you take peeks under the blankets just to see what's different about them?" Johnny's face blushed red with embarrassment.

Johnny's pa stepped in and shouted, "Leave him be."

Big Harpe ignored the father's warning. Instead, he pulled his knife from its sheath.

Micajah knew that if he continued the boy would eventually charge. They always did. Micajah asked, "When you nuzzle up against your sister's breast do you dream of your mama?" Johnny exploded in anger just as Micajah expected.

Johnny took a single step before his father's empty wine bottle came crashing down on him. Good thing too, otherwise his next step would have been his last. John decided that if someone had to fight Big Harpe - he would, not his son.

Knocking out his own son surprised the brothers, and being surprised, Micajah and Wiley failed to react quickly enough to John's subsequent move.

John dropped what remained of the bottle and reached for the pistol. He then slid in behind Wiley and jammed the pistol's barrels against Wiley's right ear.

John had succeeded in gaining an advantage over a formidable adversary. Micajah had anticipated a knife fight, not a gunfight. He now reached for his rifle that leaned against the cabin wall.

"Don't do it," John warned. Micajah paused after hearing the warning.

Seldom had someone outwitted Big Harpe in a fight. It irritated him something fierce.

With a threatening tone in his voice Micajah uttered, "You're a dead man. You're all dead." John had no reason to doubt him. He mustered all the resources he had within him to stay as calm as possible.

John knew that if he showed the slightest amount of fear the fight would be over in seconds. His only hope depended on looking and acting composed. The ploy worked. Big Harpe chose not to kill them, at least not right away. They would talk instead.

John used his resonant voice, which he developed to emulate his preacher father. It was usually effective in dealing with difficult people. "So, you think we'll all be dead, and you'll just walk away? Then you should know this. You may be the one who survives, but you'll leave here all alone. Only one of you will leave this house."

Micajah wanted to strike and strike quickly, but the pistol served as a convincing deterrent. He waited silently. His silence convinced John to continue, "I don't want to die."

Micajah interrupted, "Then put down the pistol." Big Harpe's rejoinder made John chuckle.

Wiley shouted out, "He's bluffing, Mickey. You can see he's bluffing. Take him!"

With his left hand already around Wiley's neck, John tightened his grip,

John spoke once again, "I don't want to die. I don't want to kill you or Wiley either. You need Wiley to laugh at your peculiar sense of humor, to fetch what you can't fetch for yourself. You need him to back you up. If you two ever part ways, your bones will never find a resting place."

John wondered if Micajah had heard anything he said. He paused.

Micajah concluded, "Yer bluffing."

Like in poker, Big Harpe had called John's bluff and it forced him to prove otherwise. Without thinking, John quickly lifted the pistol and shot. The lead ball drilled into a beam in the ceiling above. John flinched for a moment, realizing that that was his only usable shot. He cursed his mistake but jammed the pistol back next to Wiley's ear. Wiley's ear rang from the sound of the explosion.

"Bluffing?" he quipped. John couldn't afford to show any change of emotion. He had to remain calm.

Micajah responded, "Dumb move, old man." Micajah felt something didn't fit, but he couldn't identify it.

John replied, "I don't think so."

Chapter Three: The Vow's Ultimate Challenge

With Betsy leading the way, both girls anxiously entered the cabin. It took both of them to carry the heavy pot of stew. Before Betsy could open her mouth and ask about the gunshot, Big Harpe yanked Susan away from the pot and swung her around so she became his human shield. The stew spilt everywhere. Samson came to the rescue to lick it up.

Things happened suddenly. Big Harpe put his knife to Susan's throat. He cupped his other large hand over her nose and mouth.

He menacingly whispered to Susan, "Be still or you die." And, for no apparent reason, he licked her ear. She cringed. Irritated by her rebuke, the behemoth of a man slowly squeezed her breath away. He wiggled his tongue past her earlobe once again. She dared not cringe a second time.

What made him do such a thing? Fortunately for John, he saw it. Unfortunately for him, he couldn't take advantage of it. Wiley stole that moment trying to break free. It took a sharp rap from John's pistol to the side of his head to stop him.

John, considering his options, thought, *Oh, if dealing with Betsy were that simple.* He knew he had to keep his "take charge" daughter out of the fight. If Betsy stepped in to free her sister, she would end up on the floor. Worse yet, John knew Susan would die if Betsy acted.

John wasted no time when he called, "Betsy," He called again, "Betsy." Out of the corner of his eye, he noticed his daughter look at him. He didn't dare look back for fear Micajah would do something rash.

"Saving our lives depends on you doing nothing, do you hear me? Saving our lives depends on..."

Betsy pleaded, "But Pa!"

John continued with his calm voice, "You have to trust me. Slide back out of the way and say nothing."

How can that be? Betsy wondered.

How can my doing nothing be helpful? What's wrong with me? If Johnny's still alive, I could tend to him. The man holding Susan, I could tear out his eyes. I can argue better than you can. I could at least, clean up the stew off the floor. OH, GOD! let me do SOMETHING!

Her pa knew exactly what went through her mind when he added, "You have to trust me. Trust me, you hear?"

With a piercing glare, she looked at her pa and thought, *Trust you, the man who has failed us day after day? I would just as soon trust the ones who plan to kill us than trust you. You brought them here. It's your fault, all of it. No more, Pa. Please don't let us down this time. Lord, help me?* Betsy slid back and stood by the fireplace. She grabbed the poking iron, just in case.

The bemused Micajah watched with great interest. He couldn't fathom why John didn't take a whip to his younguns like his pa did him. Hell, a beatin' or two on the Mrs. or the little ones was always a good thing. It let them know who was in charge. "Keep the whip close," he muttered under his breath to himself. "Always, always, keep the whip close."

Micajah also noticed something he hadn't seen before. The trigger on one side of John's pistol was broken. Big Harpe smiled. Micajah felt something he'd rarely felt before. His desire to wreak havoc upon John for the way he and Wiley were poorly treated disappeared. Instead, he wanted to see how such an amateur could get out of this predicament. He wanted to see where the fight would lead. He figured, even without Wiley, he could easily blot out the lives of these four if he had to. It wouldn't take much.

Micajah knew John would have to pay and pay dearly, especially for how he treated Wiley, but he'd make sure that John would live to see another day.

Micajah asked, "Well, what are you gonna do now?"

"Negotiate of course," responded John.

"Is that what we've been doin? I thought you was stallin'." Micajah laughed at John's foolish response. "Fair enough, let's negotiate. I never saw no one do this at a fight before."

"You don't want me to kill you, Right? So, what is it you's willin' to give up to save your sorry ass.?" Micajah asked.

John responded, "I won't kill Wiley."

After pointing to John's pistol, Micajah smiled when he said, "I know you won't. Your trigger's broke. You can't shoot no more."

Wiley exploded with pent up anger when he heard Micajah's news.

Wiley landed several punches before Micajah told him to quit. "Later," Micajah promised.

Big Harpe once again asked, "Now, what are you willing to give up?"

Expecting to die soon, the bewildered father could do little more than ramble on and on, wondering if he could save himself by sacrificing someone else. John remembered how Micajah acted toward Susan. He asked, "You fancy Susan, don't you?"

The question surprised Micajah.

He asked, "Is that what you're tradin? You would give up your daughter to save yourself?"

John looked at Susan and said, "Sorry Doodles." He turned back to Micajah and asked, "Do we have a deal?"

Both sisters screamed the moment they heard the offer. Susan began to sob. In between her sobs, she haltingly pleaded to anyone who would listen, "No! Please don't do this." Her plea wore on until she collapsed under the emotional strain.

Betsy wasted no time deciding what she should do. She came within inches of cracking open Wiley's head when she wielded the poking iron like a sword. Wiley wrestled the weapon out of her hands. She broke away from him and rushed to her sister's aid.

Micajah looked at John, and said, "She's a fighter. More than you, that's for sure."

Betsy yelled, "Pa!"

John responded, "Quiet child, I know what's best here. This is the best thing for everybody. Trust me."

Micajah erupted in laughter, "Trust you? The best thing for everybody?"

Wiley blurted, "You lie, old man. Everyone knows yer lyin'." He too started laughing.

While tending to her sister, Betsy gave her pa a look of pure hatred.

Big Harpe asked, "What makes you think I need to trade? I could kill you, all of you, exceptin' her. Then I'd ride away with her on my horse, and nobody'd be the wiser.

Betsy jumped into the argument, "She's not going with you."

"Quiet, woman. This is none of your doin'," retorted Micajah. He waved his knife in front of Betsy to drill home the point that he hated being interrupted. She kept quiet for once.

John replied, "That's true, but I suspect you need a place to hide every so often. We would be like kin, so the place would be yours to use whenever you needed it."

Big Harpe accepted John's offer of his daughter Susan. John traded away Susan like a horse or a piece of furniture to save his own life.

Betsy was dumbfounded. This stank. Betsy had questions that no one could or would answer.

Why did the Harpes have to come into our lives? Nobody wanted them here. Why Pa? Why can't you go back to being the way you used to be? Why can't you stop drinking? Other people have fathers who love, care for, and protect their families. Why can't you? Why did you welcome those men into our house? Why Pa? I hate you!

Betsy saved the most piercing questions for herself.

She remembered the promise she made to her mother. Even though I love my sister, will I willingly give up everything- even my life for her? Would she do the same for me? Does that even matter? Is what I'm about to do, done out of love or duty? Is this really my purpose in life, my fate?

Betsy whispered to herself the vow she'd memorized:

"No matter what, no matter how dangerous, no matter how long, I will stand by your side. I will be there for you. So help me God."

Ma, why did you make me promise? OH GOD! Why me.... Why this?

The two sisters made the same promise, and both knew its importance. As their world crumbled around them, Betsy dared not look at her sister any longer while trying to decide what to do. She looked down in sorrow and shame, instead.

After she finally reached a decision, in a soft, distant voice Betsy said, "I'm going with you."

"Huh?" questioned Wiley.

"You heard me. I'm going with her," Betsy said.

She couldn't back out on her promise. She couldn't break the promise to her dying mother and live with herself. She couldn't let her only sister travel through the depths of hell and not feel overwhelmed with guilt.

No. A vow stays with you. She'd learned that lesson from both her parents. She'd even seen the destructive results of breaking a vow. Betsy mourned how her pa failed to live by the same principles he taught.

Michajah asked, "What makes you think I want two women?"

"You will," replied Betsy. "You'll need me. I'm the one who'll make life interesting. It'll be a choice you won't regret."

"I forbid it," bellowed John. He made sure that everyone heard him.

"You forbid what?" questioned Betsy. She continued, "You trade away one daughter like she's chattel. She didn't want to be treated that way. Then you forbid another daughter to leave when she's willing? What do you forbid?"

Micajah started to talk, but Betsy cut him short.

"Quiet!" she yelled.

He grinned at John while thinking to himself, *She'll pay for that later.*

John stated sternly, "It's not your place to choose. I'm supposed to choose what's best for you. I'm your Pa."

"You're not my pa. You haven't been for years. You lost that right the night I buried Ma by myself." She continued, "You're just another drunkard waiting to choke to death on your own vomit."

Silence filled the room.

At long last, Betsy could restrain herself no more. A venomous voice, never heard from her before, rose up when she spat out three final words, "I despise you." The daughter glared at her father until he turned away.

Betsy knew she had to exert some control over her and Susan's future if they wished to stay alive.

She turned to Big Harpe and as politely as she could muster said, "Well, are we going or what?"

Betsy rose and helped her sister up. Betsy and Susan grabbed each other's hands and left the cabin for the last time. Susan followed Betsy's lead and refused to look back.

Betsy's "take charge" stance caught Wiley off guard. Without thinking, he responded, "Yes Ma'am."

Big Harpe spoke to his little brother before he followed Betsy and Susan out into the night.

Chapter Four:
Departure

The sound of a gunshot rang out inside the cabin. Shortly thereafter, Wiley emerged holding the pistol John had pulled on him earlier. He tossed it up to his brother who already sat atop his horse. Wiley said, "Nice pistol, half of it." Micajah half-chuckled in response.

Susan showed a look of anguish when she asked Betsy, "Did he kill him? Did he murder Pa?"

Overhearing Susan's question, Wiley responded as he climbed up on his mount, "Naw, just knicked him some. 'Spect he'll walk with a limp from now on, though." The brothers rode off at a leisurely pace. Walking behind them, Susan and Betsy hurried to keep up.

INSIDE THE CABIN, THE explosive sound of the lead ball leaving the pistol caused Johnny to stir. John, experiencing intense pain, reached over and pushed his son back down. He spoke with a faltering voice while doing so, "St... stay down...son.

I'm...I'm...I'm savin'...saving your li..." Both John and his son collapsed.

Chapter Five: Living
With the Indians

Prisons come in many shapes and forms. Some are large complexes, others, tiny cages made of bamboo stalks. The person who has all that one could ask for except independence would chuck it all for a chance at freedom. Prisons are not limited to a specific place either. For Betsy, her freedom depended on the consent of two brothers named Harpe and a promise she regretted making. For Susan, fear defined hers. It far exceeded any prison man could ever build.

"Whatdja' do that for?" the exasperated Betsy asked once she returned from chasing a ten-year-old Indian boy. The boy belonged to a family in the Chickamauga tribe, a dissident branch of the larger Cherokee nation.

"Why'd I do what?' responded Susan. She had allowed the boy to steal a fresh blackberry pie right out of her hands without any protest. She barely recalled doing it. Betsy, now pregnant, gave up the chase when she saw the boy jump across the muddy Beaver Creek.

The boy made it across the creek with ease. The hungry boy's theft took place in the small Indian town of Nickajack. The town sat on the land that eventually became part of Chattanooga. Nickajack, one of five Indian towns in the Chickamauga territory, had approximately fifty households.

Then again, who could blame the boy for stealing the pie? He often watched the warriors from Nickajack go off on raids and return with the spoils of war. He dreamed of one day bringing back stolen horses and scalps just like the others. His mother, having heard enough, kicked him out of the house when he complained about not going to the scalp dance.

Most of the men and older boys of Nickajack headed off to celebrate a recent, successful raid by their fellow warriors from Turkeytown. The highlight of the celebration included a dance where the women in the town danced while waving the scalps of victims on a stick.

"You let him steal the pie." Betsy had grown weary of Susan, always avoiding conflict and glared at her sister.

"So? I guess I didn't wanna' start a ruckus," Susan said. Susan had a good reason not to cause a ruckus. She, Betsy, and the brothers lived there as one of a few non-Indian households in Nickajack. The Indians called them Tories.

Tories, outcasts in their own country after the American Revolutionary War, faced pledging allegiance to a new country, or expulsion. Those who chose to leave, particularly the wealthier ones, most likely fled to England or somewhere else within the British Empire.

Many of those who originally called New England, or the middle states, home settled in New Brunswick, Nova Scotia, or Quebec. Others traveled to Florida to start anew. Still others journeyed west. Those who traveled west included Big and Little Harpe along with two women,

"Start a ruckus! What kind of ruckus do you think will happen when Mickey gets back?" asked Betsy.

Susan had not considered the long-term impact of her inaction. The makings of another panic attack rose up to incapacitate her. A racing heartbeat, a cold sweat, gasping for air, and a feeling of impending doom were the all-too-common symptoms Susan had to deal with most of her life.

Both Betsy and Susan knew explaining away the destroyed pie would fall to Betsy. Things like that always did. It did when Big Harpe had a desire for a pie in the first place. Susan was too afraid to explain that she didn't have the necessary ingredients, so she depended on Betsy to speak for her. Both sisters looked amazed when Micajah didn't explode at the news.

A couple of days later, Susan and Betsy were astonished when they heard a cow bellowing outside. The cow was ready to burst for need of milking. When they went out to investigate, they also found a bag of sugar, a bag of flour, a butter churn, and a pie tin.

The sisters never asked, and no one ever explained how the needed ingredients to make a pie wound up outside their door. Nonetheless, Susan knew she had no choice but to bake a pie.

The number of thefts in the Indian Territory, both large and small, had substantially increased since the arrival of the Harpe brothers.

Once the people of the tribe began talking among themselves, it didn't take long before they knew who to blame. Something needed doing, and it needed doing soon. Wiley caught wind of the impending retribution, and the brothers made plans to escape before the warriors returned.

"What am I gonna' do with you?" Betsy asked with a frustrated sigh. She had run out of patience with her sister's insecurity. The love between the two siblings still ran deep, but the *like* between the two had started to unravel.

"Nothin'. I didn't know somethin' needed gettin' dun?" Susan replied. While trying not to sound hurt by her sister's accusatory notion, Susan begged Betsy to quickly find and pick some more blackberries so she could make another pie.

Susan had felt the rocks above the fireplace, and they still held enough heat. Whoever built the cabin that the Harpe brothers occupied had built an oven that provided an excellent baking space, just as long as the rocks retained the fireplace's heat.

Frustrated, Betsy yanked the small basket out of her sister's hands. She then marched off to pick blackberries that she did not want to pick.

As she left, she gave a parting verbal jab, "You're so a scared of everything!" Each sister knew the argument had not ended. It just reloaded for the next round.

"Let's go right now. We can get away from here, from them. We can start over." Betsy proposed. She had returned with a basket of berries, and while picking them, she had worked everything out in her head.

"I can't leave him, I'm his woman," Susan explained.

Astonished at Susan's response, Betsy took a moment, gathered herself, and said "You're nothing more than his slave. So am I. Did you forget the knife at your throat when Pa traded you away to save himself? I surely don't," recalled Betsy.

Susan replied, "Pa had to. He had no choice." Betsy waited for Susan to finish her sentence. She then pounced on her sister's remembrance.

"It'd been better we all died then and there. Better than this. Look what Pa brought us to," quipped Betsy.

"Remember how Ma and Pa would talk on and on 'bout things? Then Pa would make a decision. That's how married folks do it. You never talk. He never says but a few words to you and then nothing nice. You just fix his food or lay on your back for him. If that's your idea of what men and women do, I want nothing of it."

Betsy continued, "He beats on me, and then he beats on you. That's not love. He don't care for you at all. You're no one to him. You're just a dumb animal who will do what he wants, when he wants you to do it." Susan listened but didn't budge.

After that, their first real opportunity to escape from the Harpe Brothers passed. Over time, Betsy's expressions of love and affection for her sister slowly diminished. Likewise, her resentment grew because Susan would do nothing to anger Micajah. Betsy took a lot of abuse- physical, verbal, and sexual just to keep Susan from harm. Susan's fear kept her from reciprocating.

"Hurry up and pack. We're leaving." Those six words explained everything they needed to know. Susan and Betsy had heard those same six words twice before, but never with such urgency. Either Micajah, Wiley, or both had run afoul of somebody's rules.

The speed by which they moved indicated the level of illegal activity they had committed. The sisters didn't know exactly what crime until Micajah rode up on a horse they'd never seen before. He led another behind him.

BACK IN THE INDIAN village, that same young boy of ten noticed the militia first. He ran as fast as he could to warn the others. He didn't get far. Major James Ore's militia, a contingent of mostly frontiersmen who had seen the violence the Indian raids had wrought on their neighbors, tore thru the town of Nickajack.

They met little resistance because the warriors were still celebrating down in Turkeytown. Like the little boy, most of the victims included unarmed women and children. Still, with the determination to end the Indian raids, the militia spared no one. To the people living along the frontier, they considered the Nickajack Expedition a welcome success.

A fortunate few escaped that day, including Micajah and Wiley Harpe and their women. As for the spoils of war, the militia men found little of value- with one exception, a freshly baked blackberry pie.

Chapter Six: Wedded Bliss

After living with the Indians and leaving the Nickajack Expedition behind them, they moved further west. Along the way, Wiley befriended a preacher's daughter by the name of Sally Rice. Wiley, immediately smitten, knew the time had come to claim Sally as his wife.

Wiley grew more anxious as the four climbed yet another hill on the path to meet the girl. Both sisters found it hard to see Wiley as a hardened criminal by how he acted. He flitted about like a little boy never staying on task a sufficient amount of time to complete much of anything. Wiley's "don't tread on me" swagger all but disappeared. When he spoke, words poured out of his mouth as fast as an arrow flying through the air. Susan, mildly amused, walked alongside his horse and watched his antics. Even Betsy, who brought up the tail end of the travelers, cracked a smile.

Oh, if he could only be like this all the time, Betsy pondered. Micajah rode ahead by a few paces, and for some reason, never said a word. He knew nothing would ever go on as it had before.

When Wiley slid down off his horse, he made a special point to whisper in Betsy's ear. "I don't want my Sally knowin' 'bout what we been doin'. Do you hear me?" Betsy turned her head away. Wiley didn't appreciate her refusal to listen. He twisted her head by the chin so they saw each other eye to eye.

He repeated, "Do you hear me?"

Betsy angrily pulled away, and just as angrily replied, "I hear you."

"Good, don't you be tellin', now." And with that, Wiley climbed up the hill.

The sun's daily arc came close to dipping below the horizon in the western sky when they reached the small, but well-kept, white church on top of a hill. A person could see its bell tower for quite a distance, and the ringing of the church bell carried almost as far. Directly to right of the building lay the obligatory cemetery with gravestones dating back some fifteen years or so. With numerous stops and starts, a less than stellar rendition of the church hymn "Amazing Grace" floated out an open window and down the hillside.

Wiley reached the church and tiptoed up the squeaky stairs leading to the front door. He knocked and without waiting opened the door and peeked in.

"Yes? May I help you?" asked the well-groomed man who looked up. The older man had been busily straightening out the sanctuary for the next day's Sunday service. A young girl of sixteen squealed with delight when she recognized Wiley. She immediately stopped playing the new pump organ that the church had recently purchased, and ran, literally jumping into Wiley's outstretched arms.

Reverend Rice often considered his daughter as his special bundle of contradictions. At one moment, Sally could easily symbolize piety, pureness of heart, spirit, and solemnity. The next moment she could flirt with the best of women Kentucky had to offer. Flirting came naturally to her. She had a deep passion for life, and lately that passion translated into a deep attraction for boys. Yep, Sally was a bundle of contradictions alright. When her daddy thought about Sally's future, he'd often think to himself, *Woe to the one who weds her, and brings her to his bed.*

"Sally, who might this be?" Reverend Rice asked. Sally's father, obviously confused, felt a bit perturbed but not surprised by his daughter's blatant behavior. However, he still kept his composure. Sally kissed Wiley. She stopped to gulp a breath of air and kissed him again.

"Sally! Mind yourself. You are in the church. Who is this man?" Sally's father had reached the point where he expected answers, and until then niceties would have to wait. Sally broke her embrace with Wiley.

"Sorry, Papa." She straightened out her clothes and said, "Papa, this is Wiley."

Wiley stretched out his arm to shake hands. He interrupted his girl when he said, "Wiley Harpe, sir, and you must be the Reverend Paul Rice. Sally's dun said a lot about you, sir. Nice to meet you, Rev." Wiley's cavalier approach toward a total stranger, as well as someone older than he made Reverend Rice flinch. The Reverend Rice remained calm. It took a lot to do so, but he kept his composure. With Sally as his daughter, he had to. She habitually brought home injured or stray animals, heaping mountains of love on them until they didn't need her anymore. When that day came, and it always did, she would sweep them out of her life, never to show a bit of concern about them again.

Reverend Rice wondered, *Is this another one of Sally's wounded animals?*

"Well, Mr. Harpe, Wha..."

Wiley interrupted him mid-sentence, "Wiley, sir."

"Fine, fine, Wiley, what brings you to our town?"

Without a moment's hesitation he responded, "I come to take Sally here as my woman." Sally had a reputation as a vivacious girl in many ways. Over the time since she first met Wiley, she had taken a great deal of effort to conceal how long the two had known each other, and how intimate they had become. Reverend Rice never figured out how she got away to meet a young man without him knowing about it.

"You what?" asked Reverend Rice. He was unprepared for this conversation.

Wiley repeated himself, "I come to take Sally with me as my woman, er, my wife, whatever you wanna' call it. She's goin' with me." Wiley's tone of voice changed slightly from one of pleasantries and pleading to one that stated a fact. Wiley knew Sally would go with him and arguing about it only wasted time. He just had to wait for Sally's father to reach the same conclusion.

"I'm sorry you came all this way for nothing, sir, but my daughter's not going anywhere, especially not going off as somebody's woman." When Reverend Rice finished the sentence, his disdain punctuated the word woman.

"Good day to you, Mr. Har..."

Sally felt everything falling apart. She interrupted her father when she pleaded, "But Papa." Her dream for her future wasn't supposed to end like this.

With a stern voice, Reverend Rice laid down his ruling. "No, Sally, I forbid it. Good day to you Mr. Harpe."

"Wiley," Little Harpe replied.

"Good day, Mr. Harpe." He turned his back on Wiley and headed toward the pulpit at the front of the church. Reverend Rice had many years of practice verbally sparring with the best of speakers. He did not intend to lose an argument to someone the likes of this Harpe fellow. The church filled with the sound of Sally whimpering. Reverend Rice wished Sally would stop and Wiley would leave. He chose a more patient approach to the situation. Surely it would resolve his problem. He overheard Wiley ask his daughter a question.

"My sweet, is that what you want? Do you want me to leave?" asked Wiley. Between the sniffling, Sally shook her head no. Finally, she uttered, "I love you." Her response to Wiley's question simultaneously drew two extremely different reactions from the opposite ends of the sanctuary.

Reverend Rice bellowed, "No! No! No!" and, with unusual quickness, walked down the church's center aisle toward her daughter.

At the same time, Wiley said, "Well then, let's go. Just leave the old goat." He stretched out his arm waiting for Sally to take it.

Wiley judged that Sally's father would reach his daughter before she could get to him. So, in order to alter things Wiley stepped between the two. He then grabbed Reverend Rice with his two hands and pushed the man backwards.

The Reverend, a robust man himself, ripped Wiley's hands off him while he said, "Take your hands off me, young man."

Now angry, Wiley decided he would do more than push the older man if he had to.

He stopped when Sally pleaded, 'Please don't hurt my pa." Wiley threw his arms up in frustration.

Wiley turned and took a few steps, stopped, turned back, and asked, "Are you leavin' with me or not?'

"Yes!" replied the girl.

Rice bellowed again, "No! I forbid it."

Barely above a whisper, the distraught girl muttered, "Papa, I have to."

While looking at Wiley with anything but a look of Christian fellowship, Reverend Rice asked, "Why?" She hesitated to answer. Her father turned to look at her.

"Because, I'm going to have a baby."

"Huh, I'm gonna' be a daddy?" Wiley exclaimed, surprised about the news.

Stunned, the Reverend Rice sat with a plop. He closed his eyes for an unusually long time. Sally's news profoundly affected him, but she didn't know how. She watched her father for any signs indicating how he felt about her news. She looked at Wiley. He shrugged his shoulders. She looked back at her father.

Finally, in a soft, questioning voice, she asked, "Papa?"

Reverend Rice looked up. His face had that cold as a block of ice look. He said, "You Harlot!"

Sally wailed, "Papa!"

"Don't call me by that name again. You're not my daughter. I no longer have a daughter," proclaimed Rice. The preacher spewed forth in anger, instead of the love and compassion that a caring father should have shown.

Uncharacteristically, Wiley spoke up while trying to console Sally. "Dammit, you're a horse's arse, you know that?"

"How dare you use the Lord's name in vain, and within this church too. This is his Holy Temple. Get out, both of you. Get out, now!" declared the Reverend Rice.

Wiley took Sally in his arms and said, "Let's go."

With his consuming anger still unappeased, the Reverend Rice berated Wiley and Sally all the way down the hill. He quoted every piece of scripture he could think of as a verbal bludgeon. In the end, it didn't soothe the deep hurt he felt.

Standing by the horses, Micajah heard, "For out of the heart proceed evil thoughts, murders, adulteries, fornicators..." While the minister blathered on, Big Harpe pulled out his rifle, and aimed at the head of Reverend Rice.

At the last second before Big Harpe shot, Wiley yelled, "Mickey, No!" knowing that a murdered father-in-law would ruin everything. Big Harpe, one who rarely missed, shot above Rice's head. Sally's father heard the bullet hurtle past him. Reverend Rice stopped and said no more.

Mickey tossed the empty rifle to his brother and said, "That's my wedding present to you."

Wiley, in sincere gratitude said, "Thank you."

As Big Harpe mounted his horse, he heard Wiley promise, "We'll get married as soon as we can. I promise." Sally, between her sobs, hugged her beau.

Micajah yelled back, "Come on you two fornicators. Let's go." He then led his party- bound for the heart of Kentucky.

Wiley, in a rare show that he could keep his word, sought out the next justice of the peace and married Sally. It was an awkward moment since Wiley and Micajah always did what they could to stay away from people representing the law. Both brothers never imagined they would willingly stand before such a man without a gun stuck in their back.

It bothered Micajah that Wiley was the first to get married. He could hardly fathom Wiley leading in anything. Big Harpe would never let that happen again. He took Susan by the hand and pulled her toward the justice of the peace. There, Micajah proclaimed that he too would like to "git hitched." Unprepared for the event unfolding in front of her eyes, Susan never said anything except, "I do".

Chapter Seven: The Perfect Victim

The Pharris Inn's Grand Hall, festooned with Christmas decorations, covered a space of approximately sixteen feet by thirty-six feet. Few would call it grand by Philadelphia or Charleston standards, but for Kentucky, it had little competition.

Dan Pharris always dreamed of building himself a castle, and his Inn came about as close to a castle as he would ever get. Pharris dreamt big. People from all around came to see his pride and joy. Regretfully for Pharris, he didn't understand how the world of business worked and ended up penniless.

He had to sell the Inn to the Johnsons for a fraction of what it cost to build. Unlike Pharris, the Johnsons could stretch a dollar further than anybody else around. Some said, further than they should. However, few complained because people realized that when the inn succeeded, so did the town and neighboring farms.

Most people didn't know about the Johnson's chicanery. Most would have gladly vouched for the owner and his wife if given the chance. They didn't know about that side of the Johnson's clientele, the ones who profited off the misery of others. The Harpe brothers did.

Early on, Wiley took it upon himself to keep a mental list of all the people they met, just as his Scottish father had. He never shied away from a conversation, and by doing so, he got a sense about whether a person was a *Stiff-rump* or a *Sleekit*.

In most cases, Wiley's list of *Stiff-rumps* consisted of people who stayed within the law, were God fearin' folks, or leaders within a community. Those people who made Wiley's *Stiff-rump* list would normally have the respect of most people in a community. Wiley purposefully stayed away from them. *Stiff-rumps* always brought them trouble.

A *sleekit* had the makings of a good fit for the Harpe Brothers. A *sleekit* saw the world in shades of grey versus an absolute black and white, and they acted accordingly. When Wiley first met John Roberts at the local alehouse, he classified John as a *sleekit*, However, after their dispute he didn't know for sure. Wiley had heard things, not so righteous things about the Johnson's, and after talking to them, he knew he'd found a pair of *sleekits*. Together they hatched a plan that would bring them some money. All they needed was a well-to-do victim to make the plan work.

Thomas Langford became their next victim. Langford, anxious to get up Louisville way by New Year's had settled in at the Pharris Inn. He waited to latch on to some fellow travelers heading north. Everybody discouraged traveling that 30-plus mile stretch of land to the north alone due to the common Indian raids and attacks from highwaymen. The Johnsons convinced Mr. Langford to wait for somebody safe to accompany him. To his dismay, encouraging him to wait also meant he kept spending more at their establishment. Langford's patience grew thinner every day.

The time had come to put the plan into play. Mrs. Johnson placed the Harpe's party of five at a table close to where Langford sat for supper. Once they finished eating, both Wiley and Micajah berated Mrs. Johnson over the high cost of the meal. They refused to pay. Thomas Langford came to Mrs. Johnson's defense when he said, "Why are you doing this? Mrs. Johnson's a fine woman who doesn't deserve you yelling at her. If you need money, let me pay for it. I've got enough to spare." The trap door to their plan slammed shut.

They thanked him for his generosity and welcomed him to join them. He gladly did so. A good deal of time had passed since he'd flirted with three young women, and he loved to flirt.

After supper, the men talked about their travels. With mock surprise, Micajah and Wiley's played their parts to perfection as they listened to Thomas' diatribe about being stranded.

"Why, we's headed that way ourselves, first thing tomorrow. You're welcome to come along if'n you'd like," Wiley stated. His well-trained smile sold Langford on the idea.

"Excellent! I'd love to. I thought I would have to stay here until hell froze over. Thanks to you folks, good fortune has finally shined down on me," chimed the Englishman with his proper accent. The post-dinner conversation soon turned into drinks around the fireplace and an evening of music, dancing, and laughter.

With Christmas just days away, Thomas pulled out his violin, his most prized possession, and commenced playing carols. Betsy sang along with the ones she knew. Mickey and Wiley listened while drinking a local brand of whiskey.

Thomas started a new tune. Betsy interrupted him "Start over. I know this one." He played an introduction, and when the time came for Betsy to sing, she began "O, come all ye faithful, joyful and triumphant."

With the music as a background, Sally sat next to Susan.

"You're sure a quiet one. Since we met, I can't remember a time when you've said more than a handful of words. Why?" Sally asked.

"Just like to listen, I reckon," replied Susan. Sally's presence didn't make her nervous like most folks did. She attributed it to the fact that Sally was younger than her, and Sally wouldn't allow Susan to shy away from talking.

"What's with your sister and you?" Sally asked.

"She's just lookin' after me, that's all," replied Susan.

"Why? Do you need looking after? You look fine to me," Susan giggled slightly.

Sally continued, "You remind me of my older sister, you being quiet and all."

Susan asked, "Where's your sister now?"

"She died a few years back while havin' a baby," Sally responded.

"Just like my mama," acknowledged Susan. With something in common to discuss, the two talked on. A friendship blossomed between them,

"Come on you two. Let me teach you a new song," Thomas called out as he waved for Susan and Sally to join them.

"I bet I can play that thing as good as him," Mickey declared to no one in particular. Clearly the whiskey affected Micajah.

Thomas gathered the three women to his side and said, "I've nothing to give you as Christmas gifts, and seeing that all of you are with child, I thought I might teach you a lullaby that my dear mother sang to me when I was a wee one. You could sing it to your babies when they get fussy. It goes like this." He then drew his bow across the strings of the violin and began.

Ye may be the only one,
So be kind to all, not some.
Hope, pray for peace,
Lord, please release your turtle dove.
And, love, always love,
'Till the journey's done.

WILEY, BEING THE JEALOUS type, and having seen Thomas monopolize his wife's attention for far too long, looked to regain her love and affection.

Once the women finished singing the new song they learned, Wiley called out to Thomas, "Hey, you old scooter, do you ever play somethin' fast? You know, somethin' a fella can dance with his wife to?"

Thomas took up the challenge and without hesitating whipped up a cluster of notes making them fly off the tips of his fingers to the sounds of a gigue.

"Sally, come dance, my sweet," Wiley called out. Sally had the will to make the dust kick up and whirl as she glided over their Grand Ballroom floor but will alone wasn't enough. The extra weight of the baby she carried kept her from staying on the floor for long. A nearby empty chair looked more appealing with every one of her husband's twirls. Sally finally fell into the chair, leaving Wiley to dance alone. He did too, that is until Micajah acted up.

Miciajah stumbled while mumbling something about wanting to play "that thing", and claiming he could do a better job than Langford. Wiley threw himself between his brother and the older man just in time. It took all Wiley's might as well as all of Susan's to keep Big Harpe away from Langford. Wiley pulled Susan over to help because she stood closest to the confrontation.

She helped direct Micajah in the direction of the sleeping quarters when she heard Wiley tell his brother, "Don't ruin it now. You can play his violin all you want after everything's done tomorrow." Susan asked herself, *Did I hear that correctly?* She couldn't figure out what "everything's done" meant.

His comment bewildered her and the whole incident felt ominous. She felt she needed to warn somebody, but how could she alert someone about a possible danger when the proof was little more than a feeling? Even if she did, who would she tell?

Should she tell Betsy? Susan and her sister still loved each other, but ever since that day at Nickajack when she ruined their chance to get away, conversations between the two were cumbersome and rare. They didn't know how to get past it. Both sisters missed how they used to share everything with each other. Furthermore, Susan did not want Betsy scolding her again for being afraid of everything.

She wondered, *What about Sally?* Sally wanted Susan as a friend, didn't she? Sally planned to treat her like the older sister she once had and practically said as much. But how could she tell Sally when Sally's husband was the one who said what she had heard. She didn't want to lose a new friend over something that might be a simple misunderstanding.

Maybe I should tell Mr. Langford. Susan thought. He deserved to be warned. He could decide the importance of what she heard and then act accordingly. However, if she heard it wrong, what then? She knew how important reaching Louisville as quickly as possible meant to him. No, it would embarrass her to tell him and then find out that what she heard didn't amount to anything at all. She didn't want to ruin things for a man who had acted so nicely to them.

What about Micajah? What would he do to her if she told anybody at all? Beat her, that's for sure, and she didn't want another beating.

At that moment, Mrs. Johnson came looking for Wiley. Susan quickly decided that she'd tell her. Mrs. Johnson spoke up before Susan could issue her warning.

"I see Wiley's not with us right now. Here, give him this. It's his share. The plan turned out better than we anticipated. Mr. Langford's already paid for your breakfast. Good night."

The owner's wife disappeared just as quickly as she appeared, leaving Susan with no options left.

Anxiety!

She knew it would come.

 Anxiety!

She told nobody.

 Anxiety!

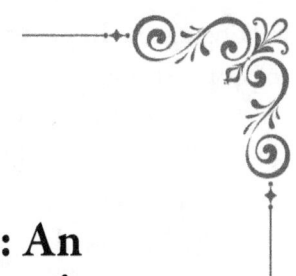

Chapter Eight: An Englishman's Demise

The brothers talked little at first as they journeyed along the west side of the quick flowing river. Wiley attributed their silence to the winter's chill in the air. The slow progress of the cortege took on a dirge-like feel, especially when each fetus pushed down on the bladder of his or her mother. Numerous stops along the way frustrated Micajah. He'd hoped to make far better time.

Wiley took notice of a freshly fallen tree floating by. The hollow maple fell victim to the intense storms that passed through the day before.

In jest, he called out to Langford, "There's the canoe you was askin' 'bout last night."

The Englishman bantered back, "Yes, but I doubt it would hold the six of us. You'd have to walk behind us."

Wiley chuckled. He wanted to let his seething anger boil over but he couldn't, at least not yet. That would come soon enough.

A possessive husband, Wiley disliked how his vivacious wife continually talked with Thomas. The common interest they had in music naturally pulled Sally and Thomas into a friendship, one that would likely last for the whole trek toward Stanford.

Thomas paused, turned back to Micajah and said, "It looks like there's a clearing up ahead. What do you say we stop and rest for a moment?" Satisfied with the brothers' response, Langford gladly shifted his attention back to the stunning Sally, and the two started walking again. Thomas took his violin back up and swept the bow across the strings.

Dissatisfied with its inaccuracy of pitch, he handed the bow to Sally and asked, "Would you, Sally, my dear?" Looking forward to learning another tune, she took it.

Sally then asked, "You amaze me at how you can tune it while you're walking. How do you do it?"

He responded, "It just takes a bit of practice. I'll have to tune it a lot in this cold weather." Thomas held the instrument close to his ear, plucking a string every so often against the sound made from another, as he tightened the violin's pegs. Satisfied at last, Thomas took back the bow, played a brief melody, one with flair, of course. He posed the question, "Now, what would you like to hear?"

"Play something happy," Sally responded, as the two walked toward a bend in the path. Sally and Thomas reached the clearing first. Still a ways back, Wiley stopped and waited for Betsy. She brought up the rear as usual. He took hold of the reins of two of the three horses they had between the six of them.

Micajah had ordered Betsy to tend to the horses that day. She had to tug and pull them all morning. The work exhausted her. Betsy appreciated Wiley's help. She didn't know why he did it, but she appreciated it, nonetheless. Wiley tied the horses off to a tree and pulled something out of one of the side pouches. Betsy couldn't see much, not with the animals blocking her view. Susan could.

Before they started out that morning, Mr. Langford noticed that Susan appeared quite ill. He assumed she had come down with some weather-related illness. Never in his mind could he imagine that she was suffering from a panic attack, an attack that reached epic proportions and had him at the center of her worries. Thomas insisted she ride on his horse and not walk like everyone else.

Sitting atop Langford's mount, Susan watched everything unfold in front of her. She watched Wiley give his brother the half-working dueling pistol that once belonged to her pa. She didn't say a word.

She watched Big Harpe turn, and briskly walked up behind Mr. Langford, placing the gun toward the man's back. She was too terrified to call out a warning. Then she saw him pull the trigger. The horse beneath her bolted from the noise of the gunshot. Wiley had to take hold of the animal to stop him from running, yet Susan didn't flinch, still frozen in fear.

All morning long, Susan felt as though her stomach would soon heave its contents, and her heart would explode over what she heard the night before. She knew danger chased after Langford, but certainly not grave danger. She kept trying to convince herself of that.

She could accept them robbing him without speaking up. She hoped that he could work his way back to the inn. Once she saw the man fall, she knew she could accept murder as well. It sickened her until she did vomit, but she accepted killing without making a peep. Fear had taken complete control of her- mind, body, and soul.

Chapter Nine:
Aftermath

The noise of the gunshot startled Sally. She looked at Thomas and started to ask a question. Then she noticed he'd dropped the bow. Instead of holding the bow, he held his hand over a gaping hole in his chest. Blood splattered everywhere, on her dress, and on the violin. It then dripped off the musical instrument and on to the ground. Mostly, the blood soaked the front of his red brocade vest. Thomas tried to form a word but failed. Sally watched in amazement as his eyes lost their focus in a matter of seconds. He fell forward on top of his violin and lay dead at her feet.

Sally screamed. She could not stop, an ear-piercing sound that irritated Micajah to no end. With the dueling pistol still in his hand, Micajah quickly walked up to her, so their faces were inches apart.

He bellowed at the top of his lungs, "Be quiet." It sounded twice as loud as her screaming. He emphasized the point by raising the pistol up to her face. She got the message. She tried to calm herself and sat on a large rock located in the clearing. She wrapped herself up as tightly as possible and shook in silence.

Big Harpe kicked the body over so he could get to the violin as well as all of Thomas' other belongings. He reached for the blood-stained instrument, only to find that it had collapsed under the weight of Langford's body when he fell dead. Micajah leaned over the corpse and complained.

"Bastard. Ya shoulda' let me play it last night. Micajah then flung the broken instrument into the river. He watched it float away.

Big Harpe pulled Langford's body by one arm toward the river's edge. A trail of blood seeped into the ground behind him. He plopped the body down in the mud. The water curled around the partially covered head and lapped at the eyes that stared up into Heaven.

No innocent bystander, Wiley took the pistol out of his brother's hand, and threw the deadly weapon as far as he could toward the center of the river.

Wiley said to Micajah, "The less evidence the better, don't you think?" Micajah grunted in agreement. Wiley went to Langford's horse and rummaged through the saddlebags to see what they could collect for their efforts. That's when he noticed that Betsy had disappeared.

"Where's your sister? Wiley asked Susan. Susan pivoted on her horse looking in all directions for Betsy. She turned back to Wiley and shrugged her shoulders.

Wiley called out, "Mickey, she's gone."

Big and Little Harpe walked in opposite directions along the edge of the mostly deciduous forest. They called out Betsy's name and threw threats and curses at her for running off. They saw nothing as they peered into the darkness.

Big Harpe said, "I know what to do. She didn't git far, not with her sister still bein' here." Micajah went to Susan and unceremoniously yanked her off the horse. Susan tried to lessen the fall, but she still landed with a thud. Immediately, Susan recalled that a fall caused her mama's death several years ago. She prayed that the same would not happen to her or harm her baby.

Before Susan could recover from his initial blow, Micajah pulled her to her feet, and turned her toward the forest.

Big Harpe yelled, "Do you remember how we first met?... That's right, with a knife at your sister's throat. Well, take a look." Micajah stood behind Susan. He had twisted one of Susan's arms behind her at an unusually high angle causing Susan considerable pain. In Big Harpe's other hand, he held a knife to her neck.

"If you wanna' see your sister alive again, you'd best git here right quick," declared her brother-in-law.

Betsy waited as long as she dared before showing herself. She'd hidden behind an outcropping of boulders. They offered her excellent cover, but they could not offer what she needed most of all, sufficient time to figure out how to free her sister from the clutches of evil.

Betsy stood and walked forward. She knew that Micajah would punish her. Big Harpe didn't disappoint. He hauled off and kicked her in the belly when she came within striking distance. She doubled over in pain and fell to the ground. The pain didn't subside. It grew to an excruciating level. Unlike Susan, Betsy didn't pray for her baby's good fortune. Instead, she almost relished the idea of putting an end to all of her misery.

Micajah quickly threw Susan aside, and just as quickly dragged Betsy by her hair to the dead man's feet. He then threw down his knife. It sliced through the ground leaving only the handle showing.

Betsy wondered, *Could this be my only chance?* She grabbed the knife. Micajah waited.

"Go ahead, do it," he said. "You're more trouble than you're worth anyway."

Betsy wanted to attack. Oh, she really wanted to attack, but a soft plea from Susan convinced her otherwise. Instead, she laid the knife down, flat on the ground.

Micajah leaned over, put the knife back in her hand, and said, "Cut 'im open from stem to stern, and pull out his innards."

Astonished at big Harpe's command, Betsy yelped, "What?"

Micajah, once again, pulled Betsy's hair so she would move to the place he commanded.

"You heard me. Cut 'im open from stem to stern." He pointed with his finger to a spot just below Langford's neck, and slid his finger all the way down to the man's groin,

Micajah continued, "Then, pull everything out."

"I will not," Betsy declared with a disdainful voice.

"Oh, yes you will. Now, do it!" Big Harpe, yelled with all his might just inches away from her ear, sending a shockwave surging throughout Betsy's body.

Betsy ripped back what remained of the brocade vest and plunged the knife deep into Thomas' bloody chest. She knew he laid dead in front of her, but it still felt like she had just murdered him again.

Betsy had eviscerated chickens before, but never a man. She didn't know if she could do it. She started by sawing upward with the knife toward the neck. Many of the ribs in the ribcage cracked when the bullet pierced his heart, but not all. Pushing the blade in and out, as well as applying constant pressure up toward the head, she made slow progress. When she heard a rib crack, she paused. She had to take control of her emotions. Her stomach churned when the second, and then another rib cracked.

Cutting through the layers of skin, from where the sternum used to be down to below the man's belly button, didn't require as much physical exertion, but it still, by far, passed as the most challenging task she'd ever been forced to do. Ripping through the diaphragm muscle required Betsy to reach into the chest cavity, grab hold of the muscle with one hand, and whittle away at it with the knife in her other hand. She shook violently as she heard the muscle tear apart. Betsy wiped her tears away. Her hands were covered with Thomas' blood. The combination of her tears and his blood created oddly shaped designs on her face, designs a warring Indian might have worn.

She could think of nothing worse than the blood. The heart no longer pumped which meant the blood pooled wherever it could find the lowest point. It puddled in the cavity of the chest, found its way out and seeped to the mud below. Betsy tried to avoid getting near it, but it still soaked into her dress leaving a large red stain. A distinct sweet-sour smell permeated the air directly above the body. Betsy held her breath as long as possible, but she had to breathe at some point. Thankfully, a brisk winter breeze blew the odor off in the other direction.

MICAJAH, WATCHING BETSY work over the body, turned to Susan and said, "Go find some rocks, and give 'em to your sister." He then turned toward Sally who, still wrapped into a ball, rocked back and forth.

Micajah said, "You too, Sunshine." At first, Sally didn't realize Big Harpe had called her. Ever since the actual shooting, she tried to erase the entire disgusting incident by recalling the happier parts of her life as a young girl. Then, when he used a nickname she had never heard before, it confused her.

"Me?" asked Sally who was still in a daze. Sally found it difficult to comprehend much of anything, let alone carry on a conversation.

"Yeah," Big Harpe responded with a twinge of "How stupid can you be" sarcasm. Micajah looked at the immobile girl and said, "Are yuh goin' to move, or what?"

Still confused, Sally asked, "What?'

"Are you daft? Wiley, of all the women, why'd you pick Sunshine? You git her to look for rocks before I lose my temper," Micajah muttered to his brother as he walked away.

Sally, a consummate flibbertigibbet, could talk, and talk. She could go on forever about the weather and matters of no particular consequence, but when faced with a crisis, or a subject of some weight, she emotionally closed down. Micajah had aptly identified her usual personality with a single word, "Sunshine".

Sally possessed an effervescence that enabled her to pull the most morose person out of their darkest emotional cave. She made friends quickly and easily. One could see why Wiley picked her. What young man wouldn't fall for Sally? Her beauty, friendliness and willingness to explore her own sexuality would cause any young man to claim he had found his own personal goddess.

Wiley felt an emotional tug of war between two extreme opposites. Sally - with her vitality and loyalty, contrasted with Mickey's cynical, sadistic view toward people and the world in general. Sally and Mickey forced him to walk a tightrope in a way he had never experienced before, and he found it hard to maintain.

Up to the point Micajah's bullet blasted open Thomas Langford's chest, Sally's perception of Wiley, her husband, leaned toward warmth, pleasure, and mirth. During the time of their very short courtship, Wiley spoke little of Mickey, and when he did, he spoke in general terms. Both Sally and Wiley enjoyed the comfort of a physical closeness instead of learning about each other as complete people. She barely knew Micajah existed, nor that an enormous dark cloud floated over him. When she met Big Harpe and saw his evil nature, Sally worried about Micajah's almost mythical influence on Wiley, the father of her baby. Now, Sally had to adjust her way of thinking about her husband with the reality of a body at her feet.

Wiley came to his bride and asked, "Whatcha doin'? Why aren't you lookin' for rocks like Mickey said?" Sally said nothing but glared at Wiley instead. Her glare sent a clear message he could hardly miss.

Still, he missed it. Wiley asked, "What? Are you sick or somethin?"

Sally responded, "You could say that." Anger poured out as she continued, "Wiley, he killed a man. Why didn't you stop him?" she asked.

Wiley sat down next to her and said, "Oh, that."

Sally quipped, "Yes, that. He killed Thomas. What's going on here? Did you have anything to do with it?" Wiley felt relieved to find out that Sally didn't see him participate in the murder. It gave him the opportunity to tell a story about what happened that portrayed him as an innocent bystander, just like her. Sally desperately wanted to hear that story. She couldn't, she wouldn't acknowledge that her husband murdered people.

When Wiley finished telling his story, a story full of inaccuracies and lies, Sally embraced him. She believed him because she dearly wanted to believe him. She needed to believe him.

Whispering in Wiley's ear, Sally proposed something he didn't expect.

"Let's leave right now, just the two of us. We could go back and tell the authorities what went on. They'd believe us. Then we could settle down and raise a family, our family - you, me, and the baby." Sally's solution gave him pause.

After a nervous delay, Wiley said, "I can't do that."

"And, why not?" Sally asked, peeved over his response.

"'Cause he's my brother. You don't think I would turn in my brother, do you? Besides, even if I did, he's bigger and stronger 'n me. I'd hafta' fight him, and I'd lose. No! I won't turn on my brother. I won't do it," Wiley declared.

"Fine, then I'll do it." Sally's' response, like a geyser building up steam and ready to blast, grew in intensity, just waiting to erupt in disgust toward Wiley and Micajah. As the two continued arguing, Micajah took back his knife from the defeated Betsy. He dipped it in the river to wash off the blood. Later, he walked over to where Wiley and his bride still carried on a heated discussion.

When Micajah overheard Sally's last comments, he asked, "You'll do what?"

Micajah purposefully used his knife to dig out crud from underneath his nails as a way to intimidate Sally. It worked. Sally glared at Big Harpe and he glared right back until she looked away.

Wiley tried to shield his wife from his brother, "Uh, Sally was just sayin' that she'd best get some rocks. Weren't you, honey?" His explanation didn't fool anybody.

Micajah said, "Then git to it, Sunshine."

Sally refused to look at either man, and in a fit of rage, marched off to fetch some rocks.

Wiley asked his brother, "What's with the... Sunshine?"

"It's my new name for your Mrs. It fits her don't you think?" Big Harpe never dreamed he would have to test the loyalty of his younger brother, but that's exactly what he felt he needed to do. It unnerved him.

Wiley responded, "I do, I really do."

Micajah put his test into play, "You should call her that."

Wiley quickly replied, "Uh, no!" Mickey harrumphed. Micajah didn't blame his brother for differing with him. He blamed Sally instead. He knew a wife's henpecking would begin sometime, but he did not think it would start so soon. Big Harpe's harrumph turned into a scowl.

Sally dropped off some rocks, mostly small stones, with a couple of larger ones interspersed in the pile. Without looking up, Betsy said, "Thanks." At that time, Betsy had already pulled out most of Thomas' insides.

It amazed Sally that throughout the disgusting ordeal where they forced Betsy to desecrate another human being, the woman, not much older than herself, still had the wherewithal to say thank you. She had talked with Betsy some, but not about anything of importance. Sally watched Betsy take the brunt of Big Harpe's ire, protecting her sister to the best of her ability. Betsy seemed to have such a resolute spirit, an inner strength that kept her fighting. So many others would have given up in the same situation. Why did she stay and fight?

Sally thought, *I need to learn more about Betsy.*

Having done what Big Harpe demanded of her, and with her clothes soaked in blood, Betsy rose and waded into the river to wash away the physical and emotional grime.

She needed a good cleansing. She didn't care about the chilling numbness the river caused. Nor did she care about what Micajah would say. Her mind had taken on what she thought would classify as the worst of all possible things she would ever have to endure, and she survived. Because of it, her determination grew stronger. At the same time, and for the first time, a bit of her spirit disappeared.

Unlike Thomas who died from an external force, Betsy questioned if a person could slowly die from the inside out? Each day, could a person feel less and care less about anything and everything? And, if so, could nothing be done to stop it? She dreaded the thought of becoming a walking corpse without the capacity to feel, to show any emotion, or even to cry.

As Betsy waded back out of the water, Micajah commanded Betsy to "Dump 'im in the river."

Betsy replied, "I can't do it alone. He's too heavy."

"Give her a hand," Big Harpe demanded as he looked at Susan.

He then turned to Sally and said, "You too, Sunshine." Sally quickly despised her new moniker.

The three women struggled with the body, especially with the current in the river flowing faster than usual.

The water was up to their waists. With her teeth chattering, Sally said, "Someone ought to say something over the body."

"I know what," replied Betsy. In the icy cold water, with Thomas Langford's body sinking to the muddy deep, the three women paid homage to the man they barely knew by holding hands and singing the end of the song he taught them.

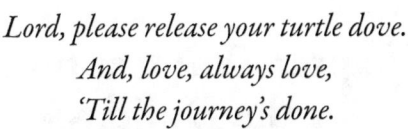

Lord, please release your turtle dove.
And, love, always love,
'Till the journey's done.

PEEVED BY THE WOMEN'S action, which Micajah took as a protest, Big and Little Harpe stood on the shore watching. Big Harpe called out, "You done?" He turned and walked off.

As always, Wiley followed.

Chapter Ten: Captured for the Holidays

Several years passed since Joseph Ballinger came to Kentucky by way of Tennessee. Most of his neighbors thought of him as a congenial type of fella, just as long as they stayed on his good side. Those who didn't, met the side of him that earned Ballinger the nickname, Devil Joe.

Rumor had it that in his earlier days, he fought like the devil, hence his nickname. It didn't matter whether he fought alone or led men into battle. Those he faced would never forget how he fought with such ferocity. At Cowpens, a revolutionary conflict between the British forces under the leadership of the ruthless Colonel Tarleton and patriot forces led by General Daniel Morgan, Joseph fought with a great deal of courage and valor as he led his fellow patriots in the conflict. Because of it, he all but guaranteed that the "Devil Joe" moniker would stick with him for the rest of his life, whether he liked it or not.

When things needed handling, the people of Stanford often turned to Devil Joe as the man who could get things done. People trusted him, and willingly put up with his peculiarities.

As he grew older, he learned that using his brain instead of his brawn made life much easier and safer too, especially when someone asked him to do those dangerous but necessary tasks. Still, Devil Joe knew what it took when things got tough, and he didn't shy away from it. No, Devil Joe could still fight as ferociously as ever.

Joseph Ballinger prepared for all the likely scenarios once he heard the news about a couple of murderers heading up to Stanford. He knew that dealing with the murderers would eventually fall to him, so he quickly took action.

The day started peacefully enough. Everything changed when a bloated body floated past the Pharris Inn and on into town. It didn't take long before somebody noticed the body. Someone else identified the body as that of Thomas Langford. A blood-stained, elaborate red vest that hung loosely over his shoulders helped identify the corpse; and by the looks of it, someone had intentionally murdered the man. It took less than an hour's worth of talking to folks about town before the authorities learned that Mr. Langford stayed for a while at the Pharris Inn. The Johnsons, proprietors of the inn, shared with the authorities that Langford left earlier that morning with Micajah and Wiley Harpe, along with three women. They'd headed out for Stanford.

Soon thereafter, a dispatched courier raced northward along the opposite side of the river to where the Harpe's traveled. Staying on the opposite side reduced the likelihood that he, too, might end up murdered. The horseman risked his life when he forded the river near Stanford.

Devil Joe Ballinger had sufficient information and time to figure out how he would capture the culprits. He had a good idea where he would find them. He had successfully led many raids on a place called "Liberty Inn" before, and suspected Liberty Inn would, once again, house his prey.

Many people often wondered why Devil Joe always felt so confident. He answered, "Yuh gotta' be prepared." Since the weather had turned colder, he knew the party would need to seek shelter. The inn had a reputation of serving the wants and needs of those living outside the law. The path the Harpe brothers took didn't have many places for a man to hide. Ballinger assumed correctly. Three horses bedded down in the Inn's barn, one of which matched the description of Langford's horse.

"Men, hot buttered rum fer y'all when this is over," Joseph declared.

The raid began just as he expected. Members of the posse surrounded the inn and waited for the innkeeper to head toward the barn, or the privy, whichever happened first. Ballinger knew the owner would eventually appear. The two had run-ins on numerous occasions, and the innkeeper rarely deviated from his habitual patterns. Once detained, the innkeeper provided all the information Joseph sought. He then politely excused himself, for he did not want, or need any hassles with the law, any kind of law.

Ballinger and his band totaled six. Devil Joe assumed that six men would be more than enough to deal with two murderers. Based on experience, he felt confident that the women who traveled with the murderers would not cause a ruckus. Still, one of the six had to watch them, just in case. That left five. It took all five men, and a little bit of luck, to bring down Big and Little Harpe.

According to Joseph, a successful raid depended on no one on your side getting hurt or killed, and your prey being brought back trussed up like a chicken waiting to lose its head.

This raid succeeded... barely.

After kicking away the long rifles that leaned against the nearby wall, Billy, the youngest of the posse, tripped. He fell, landing face down right in front of Big Harpe. Quick to respond, Big Harpe yanked his tomahawk free. Thanks to the loud cracking sound at the windowpane, Big Harpe stopped and looked up. If he hadn't looked, Billy's brains would have smeared the floor. When Micajah turned back, Pete, the most experienced of all the members of Devil Joe's posse, was pointing a rifle at Micajah's head. Big Harpe dropped his weapon the moment he saw the odds of success piling up against him.

"Merry Christmas! Y'all dun' murdered that feller Thomas, uh..." the man in charge paused.

A member of the posse leaned in and stated, "Langford."

"Langford," repeated Devil Joe. He continued, "We're takin' y'all in."

Once they had disarmed, gagged, and tied the two brothers, Ballinger went through Wiley's pockets, looking for anything that someone could use against the brothers in a court of law. He found nothing. Before moving on to Big Harpe, Devil Joe took a bite of a piece of sweet-cake that had been intended for Micajah. Devil Joe felt duty bound to finish off the delicious morsel.

"Umm, this is good," declared Joseph, while looking at the three pregnant women.

With one of Ballinger's men resting a rifle in his arm, yet still directed toward the women, Devil Joe began talking.

"I know the owner didn't make this, lifting up the cake for all to see. Hell, he can't cook worth a damn. Sorry ladies, worth a darn. One of y'all cooked this?" In a timid fashion, Susan raised her hand. When she lowered it again. She slid a small bag off the table and hid it in a pocket of her skirt. Nobody noticed, except for Micajah, who for the first time ever, winked at her.

The time had come to check to see if Micajah hid anything in his pockets.

Ballinger walked up to Micajah and said, "Feller, stand up." Big Harpe stood and growled through the gag while doing so. Taken aback, Ballinger looked at Micajah for a moment, and scratched the whiskers on his chin.

He turned to Pete and said, "Pete, you check 'im out."

Pete roughly did as instructed. Joseph then walked back up to Big Harpe and said, "You made a mistake. You shoulda' used more rocks." Ballinger watched Big Harpe's eyes closely. He hoped Micajah would give away whom he should talk to first. Angered over how quickly they traced the murder back to him, the older brother tossed a red-hot glare at Betsy.

"Aha," Ballinger exclaimed. Joseph followed Micajah's eyes directly to Betsy.

"I want to talk to her alone," he pointed. "Y'all need to go in that other room." After a great deal of moving about by everyone, Betsy sat alone in the room, waiting anxiously. Ballinger reentered the room, took the chair once used by Micajah, pulled it towards her, sat on it backwards and began.

Right off, Devil Joe asked, "Didja' stuff 'im with rocks?' Betsy, never looking up, nodded her head in shame.

"Was you the one who dun the cuttin' im open, too?" Once again, Betsy nodded without looking up.

"Nasty stuff, that. How come you dun' it?" asked Joseph. "Oh, before I ferget." Ballinger abruptly stood up and left the room. Betsy, with her nerves already taut as a whalebone corset, began to quiver at the thought of having to wait any longer. However, no matter what she desired, she had no option but to wait.

Joseph crossed over to the room where everyone else waited, and said, "I promised you fellers a hot, buttered rum. I fergot. Which one of you ladies done the cookin' of that sweet cake?" Devil Joe asked. Sally, barely noticeable, pointed toward Susan.

Ballinger looked at Susan and said, "Come here, Missy." Susan stepped forward.

"Do you think you can rustle up some more of it for the boys here, bein' Christmas and all?" Anxious to please, Susan smiled and nodded.

Devil Joe smiled at her when he said, "Use whatja' need. The owner won't mind." He then turned to Billy, the youngest of his men, and said, "Billy, come here." Billy set his rifle safely down and stepped forward. "Son, go with her and get her anything she needs, but don't let her get away neither." Still rattled over almost dying, Billy thankfully accepted the less demanding assignment.

Still, he stood grim-faced and determined to show that he still belonged as part of the posse. He refused to allow any signs of weakness to appear as he led Susan toward the stockroom.

Ballinger, making sure Susan heard him, shouted out, "And, don't ferget the rum."

Ballinger returned to Betsy and asked, "Let's see, where was we?" He kept snapping his fingers until he recalled his question. She couldn't make out if Ballinger's flighty behavior came to him naturally or if he pretended. Devil Joe never let on, one way or the other.

"Oh!... How come you dun' it?"

At first, Betsy shied away from answering any of Ballinger's questions. Her reticence didn't bother Joseph one bit. He excelled at slowly drawing out a person's story. Once he heard everybody's version, he'd have a pretty good idea of what happened. Slowly, and with a little patience and coaxing, Betsy finally came around.

"When everything was goin' on, where was you?" Ballinger asked. Believing her answer might absolve her of any connection to the crime.

Betsy jumped at the opportunity to answer, "In back, behind the horses." Ballinger made a mental note of how vehemently she responded.

Half as a question, and half an assumption, Joseph continued, "So, you didn't see much of anythin' did yuh?"

Betsy replied, "Not much."

Ballinger continued, "What did ya do when you heard the gunshot?"

"I ran into the woods and hid behind a rock," Betsy's replied. The interplay between Betsy and Devil Joe picked up its pace.

"Why?"

"I wanted to get away."

"From who, them? That big feller, he's your husband ain't he?" Betsy shook her head.

Devil Joe raised his hand high as if he measured Micajah's height.

He then lowered it to identify Wiley, "Him?" Again, she shook her head. Ballinger looked directly at Betsy. He then glanced down toward her ripe stomach. Ballinger's moral compass spun around. It took a couple of seconds for Joseph to refocus on the task at hand.

Ballinger asked, "So, you wanted to git away. What stopped you?"

"Mickey said he'd kill Susie if I didn't come out. He woulda' done it too... I made a promise."

"What promise?" Ballinger asked. Betsy then went on to explain her promise to her mother to take care of her sister. She then described, in gory detail, what role she played in the murder.

After hearing Betsy's testimony, Ballinger offered some consolation, "It's alright what you done. You saved yer sister's life."

Startled, Betsy curtly responded, "I ain't proud of what I done. It mighta been for the right reason, but I desecrated that man's body. It felt like I killed him all over again. He was so nice to us, too."

She paused for a time, then Betsy then cried out, "Oh Pa, why did you lead us to this?" Afterwards, Betsy sat in silence for a long time while she stared off into a place beyond anyone's reach. Joseph knew he would gather nothing more from her. He decided he would talk to her again, later. When he rose from his chair, he lightly patted her knee, hoping it might offer her some comfort.

Ballinger turned away from Betsy and called out, "How's the cookin' goin? I'm famished."

A women's voice replied, "Not yet."

After sending Betsy to the waiting area, he had Sally brought in. Ballinger patted the chair in front of him and said, "Come here, Missy." Looking into her nervous eyes, he began, "I'm guessin' we've got time to talk fer a spell, Mrs. Harpe. Do you mind if I call you Sally?" He began with the usual questions. Sometimes, he would purposefully make an incorrect assumption, just to see if Sally would correct him and thereby prove her honesty. Sally provided straightforward answers, or at least she thought so. Without realizing it, all of Sally's answers showed a bias against Micajah, and for Wiley. Ballinger repeatedly challenged the accuracy of her answers, and when pushed, what she said fell apart. What she claimed as truth laid buried somewhere beneath phrases like, "I think so, I suppose," or "I don't remember."

Devil Joe didn't admonish her. He pitied her. She'd told the story that put Wiley in the best light. She didn't want her husband to die. When choosing a loved one, she had done a poor job of it. Of the two people in the room, only one believed that Wiley was innocent. Devil Joe looked skeptical.

Ballinger abruptly stopped asking Sally questions when Susan announced she had finished the sweet cake. Sally's answers added very little. He had grown tired of her biased account and appreciated the break.

The time had come to have a little chat with Susan. Devil Joe walked back to where Susan busily cleaned up after making the cake. He motioned for Billy to leave, which the young man did. Susan failed to notice any of the changes that took place behind her and jumped when she heard Ballinger speak.

"Thank you, Mrs. Harpe fer doin' that. I'm sorry, did I give you a start?"

Susan replied, "That's alright."

He continued, "I think wherever there's food a cookin', that's my favorite part of the house, what with them smells and all. Wouldn't you agree?" Susan hummed in agreement.

"I hope you don't mind me askin' you some questions while yer workin.'"

Susan remained silent, which Joseph took as tacit approval.

He continued, "Mind if I call you by yer given name?" Again, Susan remained silent, and again, Ballinger believed he had permission to proceed.

"Your sister told me that you was the only one on top of a horse when the shootin' took place. Is that right, Susan?"

Susan spoke softly when she replied, "Yes." She wished Ballinger would leave and she felt another panic attack blooming. Susan innocuously searched her pocket, without drawing any undue attention to her action. She did so just to make sure the coin pouch, Langford's money pouch, remained safely tucked away. Feeling the pouch gave her a perverse sense of comfort.

"Think you can tell me who shot the man?" asked Devil Joe.

"I can't," Susan said.

"Can't or won't?" asked Ballinger. "You clearly saw who done it." Determined to keep what she knew to herself, Susan bit her lip so hard, she drew blood, but she didn't tell.

"Let's leave that for a moment and back up some. I hear that some sort of scuffle took place between that big feller and Thomas Langford the night before he got shot. Is that right?" Susan nodded her head.

"And you and Wiley helped break it up, right?" Again, Susan nodded.

"Didja hear anything that went on?" Susan shook her head. She paused for a moment like she wanted to say something, but finally decided against it. Ballinger picked up on Susan's body language and pressed forward.

He said, "I'm sorry, you want to say something?" Susan felt queasy as the battle within her raged. The guilt she felt, when she didn't tell anyone about what she overheard Wiley say, roiled at a fever pitch. She couldn't tell which emotion came across as more debilitating- guilt or fear. She crossed her arms over her stomach and doubled over in the chair. In a normal situation, someone would excuse a person so they could find relief, however they may. Devil Joe knew his questioning far exceeded anything normal.

He pressed forward, "Clearly, you need to say somethin'. What's botherin' you?" Susan whispered, "Wiley." That's all she could say.

Ballinger leaned closer so he could hear, and asked, "What about Wiley?' The emotional wall of fear crumbled as Ballinger picked and prodded for more and more details.

"One final question. You knew that feller was in a heap of trouble. Why didn't you do something? As hard as she tried to look at Devil Joe, she couldn't. She found it impossible to settle down at all. When she spoke, her words came parsed out like stuttering as she continually gasped for air.

"I was scared."

"Of who, them?" Ballinger pointed in the direction of Big and Little Harpe.

"Yer more ascared of a man with a rope 'round his neck than of what the good Lord will think of you when you meet yer maker?" Susan hung her head down low.

Joseph paused for a moment. He then said, "Bein' scared ain't no reason fer a man to die."

Susan felt she'd barely hung on to the bottom rung of a crumbling ladder. Her self-esteem had all but disappeared.

She thought, *How could other people care about me when I don't deserve to be loved?* Looking for some way to redeem herself, she wrapped her hand around the coin pouch in the pocket of her skirt.

Susan thought, *I should give this to that man.* Her fear clawed its way back in control.

What will Micajah do to me if I do? Susan thought.

She pulled the pouch up, ready to give it to Joseph, but stopped when Devil Joe rose and said, "Excuse me." He then turned and left.

She did not stop him. Instead, fear won out as she let the pouch drop. And, at that moment, Susan fell off the lowest rung.

Ballinger called out, "Alright boys, we're almost done here. If any of y'all wants more of that cake, now's the time. A couple of you boys hitch up that buckboard we saw back in the barn. Oh, and saddle up Langf... that dead feller's roan. I want her." He pointed to Betsy, "Ridin' up front with me."

During the quiet journey on the last leg north to Stanford, Devil Joe asked Betsy more questions. Devil Joe agreed to keep Betsy's hands free if she promised not to run away. She agreed.

Ballinger rode for a spell. He then asked, "Why are you here?" Flummoxed, Betsy didn't know how to respond.

She answered, "You're bringing us to jail?"

"Oh, no, no. That's not what I meant at all. I guess what I'm tryin' to say is, why are you mixed up in all this?"

Betsy fell back on the only answer she knew, "I made a promise..."

Ballinger interrupted her, "I know about that. You told me about that already. But why are you STILL here. Why do you stay?"

Frustrated, Betsy answered, "I don't know what you mean?"

Joseph began, "Look, your maw didn't want you to give up everything and fail, jest so yer sister can succeed. No parent wants that."

Betsy interjected, "I'm watchin' over Susan, tryin' to keep her alive."

"And, if I'd be a guessin' man, I'd guess you've done that more than once already. But she's a married woman now. You can't be watchin' over her forever. It ain't right... What do you get by stayin' other than a heap of hurt from all the beatings?" Ballinger questioned.

After thinking about it, Betsy explained, "She's my sister. I love her." Her comment, tepid at best, had a difficult time convincing her, let alone convincing Joseph.

Ballinger, noting the weakness of her proclamation, responded, "I'm sure you do. Your sister loves you too. I'm sure of that, also. But something's not right. What is it?" Again, the conversation lulled as Betsy mulled over what Devil Joe had said.

Betsy broke the silence, "I'm afraid,"

Joe questioned, "Afraid, of what?"

"I'm afraid of not being needed, of bein' all alone." That sentence came out laboriously slow.

It took some time for Devil Joe to come up with a worthy response. She dearly needed one. He finally said as they entered into Stanford, "Sooner or later, everybody's got to step out on their own. It's the nature of things. Even the tiny bird has to fly at some point. You can't keep usin' the excuse that 'you're protectin' her' as a way to hide yourself. It ain't good for her. It ain't good for you, neither."

Feeling the need to validate why he showed such concern for Betsy's well-being, he continued, "I've got a daughter- gettin' close to yer age. If'n she got messed up in somethin' like this, I'd hope somebody'd come along and talk some sense into her."

Ballinger's demeanor changed when they arrived at the jail, "Well, here we are."

As Devil Joe helped Betsy off the horse, Betsy asked, "What's gonna' happen to us?"

Ballinger replied, "Pretty soon, I reckon, they'll take y'all on over to Danville. They got a better set up than we do here. When the circuit judge comes back around there'll be a trial for them two boys. A hangin' will take place not too long after that, I reckon."

"Will they hang us too?" asked a concerned Betsy.

The question startled Devil Joe, "You women?"

He continued, "Naw! No woman been hung around here fer as long as I can remember. There may be a trial fer y'all, but most likely, they'll find y'all innocent. They'll probably jest run you out of town."

AS DEVIL JOE AND BETSY conversed while riding ahead of the wagon, Big Harpe concluded they didn't have a chance of escaping at that moment. But he felt he could set something up when he got the chance. At first, he didn't know what to do. Then he remembered the pouch.

Micajah, the first of the four prisoners loaded onto the wagon, landed with a loud thud. The next thud belonged to Wiley, who they threw aboard the wagon like a sack of potatoes. Both were hog tied. Devil Joe's men treated Susan and Sally with much greater care when they assisted the women up into the wagon, especially after Devil Joe admonished them earlier for not treating the women as true ladies. Still, both Susan and Sally had their hands tied, albeit in front of them. As luck would have it, Susan wound up next to Micajah, and Sally next to Wiley on the cramped back end of the wagon. Before they left Ballinger warned them to avoid any funny business, and not to talk to each other.

Both brothers ignored his command the moment the wagon pulled out. Big and Little Harpe twisted, tugged, and pulled at the ropes that bound them. Even with the help of Susan and Sally, untying the ropes was impossible. Pete had done his job well and smiled at the brothers' curses.

As they traveled toward Danville, Micajah noticed that, when the trail narrowed, the guards pulled their horses back behind the buckboard and out of earshot. They returned to their original positions- one on each side of the wagon and one following behind, when the trail widened again. He also noticed that Pete had a heck of a time with the team of horses that pulled the wagon. With Betsy riding up front with Devil Joe, she'd unconsciously diverted Ballinger's attention away from his primary duty.

Micajah needed to talk to Susan, but he wanted no one to notice, He needed a diversion.

He whispered to his brother, "Every time the guards pull back, kick up a storm." Without knowing why, Wiley did as instructed. After a couple of trial runs, Micajah felt satisfied that Pete was too busy with the horses, and he couldn't eavesdrop. At the same time, the others rode too far behind to hear anything,

When the horses pulled back a third time, Big Harpe turned to his wife, and in a soft voice said, "Do you still have the pouch?" Susan tried to pull it out of her skirt pocket.

"No, keep it," Micajah said.

Susan asked, "What if they search me?"

"No man's gonna put his hands on you, especially when you're about to have a baby. Anyways, if somebody asks about it, just tell 'im we was savin' it up to buy a farm. They'll believe you," Micajah finished as the guards returned.

For a fleeting second, Susan dreamed, *Oh, if his lie were really true.* Once again, Ballinger's men pulled back.

Big Harpe began again, "Hide it so only you know where it is. Don't tell nobody, not Betsy, not..." He pointed with his head toward Sally, "Nobody, you hear me? Sometime somebody will show up fer it. When they do..." He paused as Ballinger's men returned. On and on, the pattern continued until Susan understood what was expected of her. The Harpe brothers kept up their disruptive act even when they no longer needed to. They did it out of pure spite, and because of it, Wiley got the butt of a rifle jammed against his kidneys. Big Harpe's intuition proved right. The Harpe brothers now had a plan for staying alive.

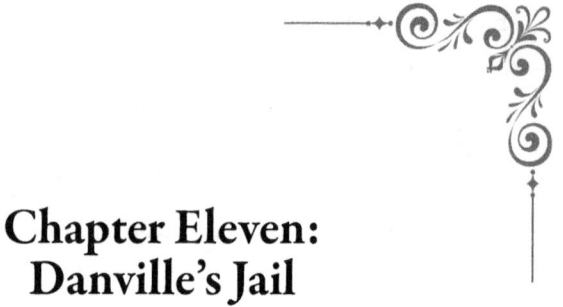

Chapter Eleven:
Danville's Jail

Short of jumping up and down like a child having a tantrum, Thomas Biegler, the Danville, Kentucky's jailer did all he could to present himself as the one who would guard the prisoners.

However, for reasons unknown to Biegler, Henry Palmer, the sheriff of Mercer County, would hear none of his complaining. Biegler left the meeting angry and confused. He had built a reputation as being a fair, just, and cautious guard. He'd never had anyone escape nor had anyone ever been seriously injured before. Biegler looked forward to the challenge before him and had already taken extra precautionary measures to make sure everything went as smoothly as possible.

Instead, Biegler found that he would protect his friends and neighbors from three supposedly dangerous women, all of whom were pregnant. Furthermore, Jonas Edwards, his part-time assistant and full-time roustabout, who some in the town considered untrustworthy, would watch over Big and Little Harpe.

To Biegler's surprise, the sheriff would not budge from his decision. Sheriff Palmer didn't share that his wife had a few choice words to say over-throwing pregnant women into jail. She may not have had the legal right to express her views on the subject, but she had a voice, and boy, did she use it.

Furthermore, if an earful from his wife didn't get the sheriff's attention, word got out that the three women who accompanied the murdering scoundrels were expecting, and their anticipated delivery dates were fast approaching. A cadre of well-intentioned do-gooders from the community's largest church determined that Susan, Betsy, and Sally would have the best of care. Anything less than the best, they considered unacceptable. "Not in Danville" became their common motto. The sheriff didn't need a boisterous group of women berating him every day, not with the next election just a few months away.

Thomas Biegler stewed. He understood how and why men thought and acted the way they did. That knowledge served him well as a jailor. He didn't know women. He didn't want to. Biegler, an avowed bachelor, also didn't know anything about babies. Oh sure, he knew about making babies. Once he sprouted a beard, two widows, one young and the other not so, volunteered to tutor him on the finer points of making babies. Nobody volunteered, nor did he ask, for tutoring on how to bring a baby into the world or how to care for one.

The day Susan, Betsy, and Sally arrived in Danville, Biegler went through a list of procedures with the women. He informed them of what to expect from him, and what he expected of them- just as he did with any prisoner. However, when the time came to search the women for contraband, he didn't. Instead, he depended on their honesty, and asked each of them if they had anything they should turn over to him. He did not dare search the women or physically put a hand on them at all, that's if he wanted to keep his job. Micajah had guessed correctly.

Captivity started just as Tom Biegler expected it would.

He purposefully insisted on the three women calling him "Mr. Biegler", just as he had done with every other prisoner in the past. He would use their last names as well. The formality of using a proper salutation and a family name, as opposed to using a prisoner's given name, kept an emotional wall in place between the guard and the prisoner. Biegler desired this kind of separation. He never wanted to connect with those he guarded. Through experience, he'd seen how becoming too close to a prisoner led to opportunities for a prisoner to put a guard in a compromising position.

With the women, Mr. Biegler had to adjust the way he normally addressed prisoners since two of them had the same last name. After a brief discussion, the women agreed to address Tom Biegler as Mr. Biegler, and he in turn would address the women as Mrs. Susan and Mrs. Sally, because they had married, and Miss Betsy, because she had not yet married.

"How quaint," Sally expressed. But since he insisted, they had little choice but to go along with what Mr. Biegler wished. Soon thereafter, the women started mimicking the Mrs. or Miss usage to make the days pass faster.

Conversations like, "Oh, Mrs. Susan, would you pass me that bowl?"

Susan would respond, "Why of course, Mrs. Sally. Miss Betsy, please pass this bowl on over to Mrs. Sally, would you please, dear?"

Betsy responded, "Why I'd be delighted to. Here you are, Mrs. Sally."

"Thank you, Miss Betsy. Thank you, Mrs. Susan," Sally finished. It became common banter, and they would have a good laugh over the silliness of it all.

Mr. Biegler also learned something he had never known about expectant mothers before. The weight of a baby on a woman's bladder necessitated the women's use of the facilities more often than usual. Three pregnant women who needed to repeatedly "go", quickly became a bother. Readily accessible facilities would alleviate the problem, but people had limited options back then. The women had the choice of using the chamber pot or having Mr. Biegler escort them back and forth to the outhouse. The outhouse stood a distance away from the jail so the pungent smell from the privy would not seep back into the building.

Mr. Biegler grew weary of the syrupy sweet pleas, or the more urgent ones, depending on the immediate need of each woman. He felt as though the lyrical, "Oh, Mr. Biegler," or the more desperate, "Mr. Biegler!" calls for assistance, one right after the other, had the designs of a plot to irritate him. If so, they succeeded.

A little over two weeks passed when, in the early evening, he heard a "Mr. Biegler." He ignored it, and continued to read his book, Thomas Paine's, *The Age of Reason*. Again, he heard "Mr. Biegler." This time it sounded twice as loud for two voices called out in unison. He set his book aside, rose, and answered what he expected to be one of their usual requests.

"Yes?" he asked, bothered over being interrupted.

Betsy, energized by what would soon take place stated excitedly, "Mrs. Susan's water broke."

"So?" Mr. Biegler casually responded.

Betsy did not say another word. Instead, she gave him a look, a *You just don't get it yet, do you?* face and waited. It took a while before he realized why they called him.

Biegler nearly hit his head on the doorframe when he jumped as he said, "Oh!" Biegler, a rather tall man, left an imposing impression on those who met him. However, at that moment, when her statement finally sunk in, Mr. Biegler no longer looked like an imposing man. Instead, he reminded Betsy of her younger brother who quite often got into things beyond his ability and floundered about until someone came to his rescue.

"What do I do?" Mr. Biegler asked.

"Fetch a midwife." Betsy responded. That's exactly what he did.

HE BROUGHT BACK THE slave Hany Brown. She was a middle-aged woman who learned midwifery at the feet of her mother - Venus Brown, who in turn learned the art from her mother. Hany had a solid reputation as a midwife. She was sought out by white folks as well as slaves. Her owner quickly recognized how valuable a skill Hany possessed.

That's why he agreed with Hany to keep a record of all the times she successfully delivered a baby. A stillborn didn't count. Furthermore, the slave owner agreed to set aside a portion of what he charged for her service to pay for her freedom. The agreement benefitted both owner and slave.

As far as Hany could tell, she would earn her freedom when she turned sixty, just as long as people kept making babies. Everybody thought of reaching sixty as a daunting goal since the life expectancy of a slave fell far short of that. Still, it motivated her to work hard and excel at what she did. To Hany, the notion of freedom stood out as the most worthy of dreams.

When called on to deliver a youngin, Hany wasted no time taking charge of each situation. She learned that when dealing with the birth of a child, everyone else felt overwhelmed. Therefore, they appreciated her expertise and leadership. She'd also learned, with several lashes across her back as a reminder, that taking charge in other areas outside her field of expertise didn't reap the same benefit.

Hany climbed off the wagon that Mr. Biegler used to fetch her. She received no help climbing down, nor did she expect any. Biegler used that time to tie off the team of horses instead. He didn't want to chase after an empty wagon, especially not then. Thomas Biegler looked confused, and a bit perturbed, as he watched the slave woman bury seeds at the entrance to the jail.

How odd, he thought. She hadn't gone in to see about Mrs. Susan like someone would expect. She planted seeds? He concluded that it had to be some type of voodoo, witchcraft, or superstition. Hany's first act disturbed Biegler a bit. However, he knew he'd have to accept it since, when it came to finding a midwife, he had no other options. Hany's second act disturbed him so much more.

The diminutive slave hustled Mr. Biegler out the entrance. The door slammed behind him on his way out. Biegler considered the jail as his domain - his responsibility and home away from home. Nobody ever dared take control of it before. Yet, here came this tiny five foot nothing of a slave woman who did so with no difficulty at all.

How could I lose control so quickly? How could this happen? Biegler wondered as he opened the door to reclaim what he believed was rightfully his.

Not to be trifled with, Hany saw Thomas Biegler enter. Without a moment's hesitation she yelled, "Get out!" He stood his ground. Just then, Susan screamed out as another contraction occurred. This time it lasted longer than previous ones and was far more painful. When he heard her scream, Mr. Biegler hurried toward the door.

Biegler paced outside the jail for the next twenty or so hours. He never dared enter again.

Thomas, a man who planned for every contingency, found it very frustrating to wait for the birth of a baby. Like a multitude of others, Biegler craved order and consistency in his life. Being out of control bothered him. Once he heard a tiny cry, his anxiety finally waned.

A few minutes later, Hany, disheveled and exhausted, opened the door, and said, "Massah Biegler, that woman, Missah Susan, she be wantin' you to come in right quick."

Biegler took a step toward the door and then stopped.

"Oh no, I don't think so. I'll wait awhile," Biegler nervously replied.

"But you gots to. She's done got somethin' 'portant to say to you," Hany insisted as she stepped out of the way.

The fire in the fireplace crackled as Mr. Biegler entered the jail. Sally and Betsy busily moved about- cleaning up, gathering things, and throwing things in the fire. Sally approached Biegler with a bucket of water that needed to be thrown out. She looked for his approval, which he gave with a nod. She exited.

Susan, lying on a rope bed, every so often reached over with her free hand and touched her child. The nearby fire cast a flickering shadow over both mother and infant. The newborn snuggled into the crock of the mother's arm.

Thomas Biegler had never seen such a tender moment before. In fact, he had never seen a newborn baby before. He'd grown up as the youngest of five, all boys. His mother died while giving birth to him. His father, a *do it my way or else* man, banker by trade, hired an elderly spinster to keep the house clean. She also prepared meals for the family, but nothing else. Thomas had only one vague memory of the woman. It had something to do with a bowl of frosting for a cake and her giving him a spatula to use to lick the bowl clean. Biegler attributed his appreciation for fine food to that old woman. Other than that, female influences on him as a child didn't exist. Even his tutoring, supplied by a male teacher, came with a one-sided perspective. Hearing his personal history finally made sense to his prisoners as to why he had never seen nor stood near a newborn baby before.

"Mrs. Susan how are you?" asked Biegler. As one would expect, Susan felt weak and tired. Still, she put her hand out for Thomas Biegler to take. He quickly grabbed a chair and sat down beside her. In an uncharacteristic move, he put her hand in his. He knew he had just bent his rule about keeping up an emotional wall between prisoner and guard, but at the moment, it didn't seem to matter.

Susan had put some serious thought into what she planned to say. With the delivery taking so long, she had plenty of time to think about it.

She began, "I haven't seen too many men in my life that I'd call good, just two really. One I let down, and I have to bear that guilt to my grave. You'd be the other one. You didn't have to, but you've been fair and kind to us. You and Thomas Langford had the same first name. That's why I'm going to call my baby Thomas. I hope he grows up to be a good man just like the two of you."

Flabbergasted, Thomas Biegler instinctively pulled his hand away from Susan. He didn't know what to say. Nobody had ever gotten that close to him before. Without question, he knew he'd not only bent, but compromised beyond repair his own rule, and it didn't bother him a bit.

Susan asked, "Do you want to hold the baby?"

"Oh, no, I better not." Thomas beamed when he took a moment to say the baby's name. "Thomas is the first baby I ever seen up close. I don't want to break him," replied Biegler.

"You won't," said Susan. With the help of Miss Betsy, Thomas Biegler took hold of his namesake, an infant no more than an hour old. The child fussed a bit at first, but eventually he fell asleep in the arms of a "man's man." Biegler thought, *Maybe being a bachelor isn't so good after all.*

A few things changed once little Thomas was born. After seeing Hany do wonders with her potions and such, both Betsy and Sally requested that, when their time came, Hany would deliver their babies, too. The sheriff happily agreed to their request since Hany charged less than any other midwife in the region. He could also show the growing number of women who hounded him daily that he had done something pro-active for the women in his jail.

Mr. Biegler kept calling Sally, Mrs. Sally, and Betsy, Miss Betsy. But for Susan, he'd dropped the "Mrs." The first time they heard Mr. Biegler call Susan by only her given name, Betsy dashed off a surprised look to Sally, just as Sally did to her. The two then looked to Susan for an answer. Susan could only shrug her shoulders in surprise. Unlike how he communicated with the women earlier, Thomas Biegler started chatting about almost anything with Sally, Betsy, and especially Susan. During one such conversation, he learned from Betsy that Susan excelled at cooking. Thus began a new cooking arrangement. Susan happily agreed to have Mr. Biegler provide all the ingredients and supplies that she needed for cooking sumptuous meals. It made Susan happy to be cooking again. It made the others happy, too.

One evening, Susan tested the waters about the name change. Thomas had just finished hanging another rope from one end of the thick-walled cabin used as a jail, to the other end. He knew the demand for diapers would certainly increase, so he prepared for the inevitable. They had finished eating, and he sat in the rocking chair, which he purchased. While rocking little Thomas, both he and the baby nodded off next to the warm fireplace. It painted a serene picture the women never dreamt possible.

Susan tapped on Mr. Biegler's shoulder, and said, "Tom. I made some pudding. Would you like some?" Susan intentionally called him Tom, and nothing else.

"Thank you. That will be a fine finish to a fine meal," Thomas replied. Susan didn't know what surprised her more- how he accepted being called Tom, or how he spoke to her in such an informal and complimentary way.

When Sally tried calling Mr. Biegler by his first name, he roundly reprimanded her, and reminded her to continue calling him Mr. Biegler.

Sally said, "What about Susan? She called you Tom."

"That's different," he replied, and he left it at that.

In less than a month after little Thomas entered the world, Hany Brown returned to the jail once again to ply her trade. This time it was for Miss. Betsy. In the dead of the winter of 1799, Betsy gave birth to a redheaded, brown eyed, healthy baby boy by the name of

Johnny Roberts. She named him after her brother whom she had always called Johnny. Not John, but Johnny.

FORTUITOUS MOMENTS happen to everybody, whether they deserve them or not. Micajah and Wiley had worked out an escape plan. Wiley quickly recognized the Sleekit tendency in their jailer, Jonas Edwards; and it didn't take much encouraging for their jailer to join in the plan. The brothers' escape plan depended on Susan placing Langford's money pouch in Jonas' hands and doing it without raising anyone's suspicion. That meant Susan needed to know beforehand when to expect a visitor. Micajah and Wiley hoped for a fortuitous moment. They got it when Johnny, Susan's and Betsy's younger brother, knocked on the wrong cabin door.

"Susan, Miss Betsy, you have a visitor," Mr. Biegler called out as he opened the door. Johnny, fourteen going on twenty, peeked around from behind the jailer and grinned at his sisters. Both Susan and Betsy squealed with delight when they saw him. He stood taller and his voice had changed, but to his sisters he remained their impish little brother.

For the rest of the afternoon, the three siblings laughed over good times, bemoaned the bad, and sidestepped those memories that were too painful to discuss- especially those about their pa. During the entire visit, neither sister asked, nor did Johnny offer any news about him. Johnny told of how Samson, the family dog, finally passed away. After that, nothing remained at the homestead that kept him there. He decided the time had come to go out on his own. He would go and make a life for himself. As with all visits, this one finally drew to a close.

Just before leaving, Johnny turned to Susan and said, "Oh, before I forget. The big one, Micajah? He wanted me to tell you that someone will stop by in a day or two to see about his baby." After another round of hugs and kisses, Johnny bid them farewell. They would never see him again as he disappeared into the fabric of the new country.

A couple of days later, the visitor who Johnny spoke of appeared at the door. Jonas, the Harpe Brothers' jailer, surprised the women when he unlocked the door and walked right in. They had mistakenly assumed that Mr. Biegler possessed the only key. Furthermore, Betsy found it strange that the timing of the visit happened just as Mr. Biegler stepped away. He didn't stay long, nor did he speak with Betsy or Sally, only Susan. Jonas pulled Susan aside so no one else could see them. Susan made sure nobody saw her place the money pouch in the jailer's hands. He then left. The other two tried prying information from Susan about the visit, but she stayed tight-lipped no matter how they persisted.

Just days after Jonas dropped by to look in on Micajah's baby, a loud pounding on the door to cabin woke everybody up. Normally, anyone wishing to enter would ask if everyone was decently dressed before entering. They wouldn't want to embarrass the women.

That day was different. Two men rushed through the door with their rifles at the ready. A grim-faced Sheriff Palmer followed close behind. Thomas Biegler stepped in behind him. He looked uncomfortable. The women didn't know that the Sheriff had verbally thrashed Biegler over Micajah and Wiley's escape. On almost every other day, Biegler stood a hand taller than Sheriff Palmer when the two stood side by side. Not so, this time. The women had never seen this side of their jailer before. Biegler, with his shoulders stooped over and his eyes cast downward, looked more like an old hound dog who had been kicked after getting into trouble.

Sheriff Palmer spoke, "Morning ladies. Sorry for the interruption. Your menfolk escaped sometime last night, and Mr. Edwards..."

Sally unintentionally stopped Palmer when she asked, "Who's Mr. Edwards?'

The sheriff responded, "Jonas, the jailer watchun' them two boys. As I said, we can't find hide nor hair of him neither. Do any of you women know anything about the escape? Know anything that might help us catch them two boys?"

Sally and Betsy gave convincing blank stares. They both added an innocent shrug of their shoulders for emphasis. At the same time, Susan, doubting she could convince the sheriff of her innocence, pinched her baby's rump. It caused him to cry, right on cue. She turned away and drew the infant close to her breast so he could feed. By doing so, Susan had successfully placed her back to the sheriff without drawing any attention to herself.

The sheriff turned toward Susan and quickly noticed she nursed her child. He shied away from looking directly at her and asked, "How about you, Ma'am? Do you know anything?"

Susan raised her head, just a little, and vigorously shook her head no, a little too vigorously for two people in the room who observed her response. Susan went on to say, "No, sheriff. I haven't seen nor heard anything about my husband since we got here." She should have just said no.

Betsy immediately flinched when she heard Susan lie. Betsy bit her tongue to keep quiet about it. She knew Jonas had visited Susan only a couple days before.

Biegler didn't know about Jonas' visit, but he sensed she'd hidden something from the sheriff. *Did she just lie? Does she know how much harm this is causing me? Why would she lie?* For Susan's sake, he kept his doubts to himself.

"Well, thank you ladies." The sheriff turned and exited, as did his two deputies. Thomas Biegler waited for them to pass. He intended to stay and make sure Susan had told the truth, but when he heard

Palmer's peeved voice call out his name, he had no choice but to leave. The door slammed shut and Biegler locked it on his way out.

Betsy could hardly wait for the cabin to clear out before she challenged her sister.

"Did you lie to him? Did you lie to that man?" Betsy asked, as she looked at her sister with a stern face.

"Well, are you goin' to say somethin'?" Betsy asked.

Susan finally let loose her pent-up anger, saying, "Yes, I lied. There! You satisfied?"

"No, I'm not satisfied," Betsy bellowed. "How could you?"

The babies started crying again. After a bit, once the babies had settled down, Susan responded in measured tones, saying, "Micajah told me what he wanted me to do before we ever came here."

"But why?" Betsy asked.

"Cause for better or worse, he's my husband. I don't want nobody dyin' with a rope round their neck," Susan responded.

News of the Harpe Brother's escape spread quickly, as quickly as an army of ants does when a child's stomping foot disturbs their home. Sheriff Palmer readied himself for a heap of hurt, political hurt, as the swarm of public opinion rose up against him. He had to do something quickly to mitigate the damage. Therefore, he fired Thomas, his loyal and trustworthy jailer. Sheriff Palmer would have much preferred firing that reprobate Jonas, but since Jonas disappeared too, the only option the Sheriff had, if he wanted to win his re-election, was firing Thomas.

The women heard a loud rap on the door. One of them responded, "Yes?"

Thomas partially opened the door and asked, "May I come in?"

As he entered, Thomas uncharacteristically kept his distance away from the women when he asked, "Mrs. Susan, may I have a word?" Susan whipped around to face Thomas when she heard "Mrs. Susan". She knew something had gone wrong.

She slowly rose and looked at Betsy who said, "Don't worry, I'll watch the baby."

Once she left, Sally mouthed to Betsy *"Mrs. Susan?"* Also confused, Betsy shrugged her shoulders.

Susan looked scared when she went to talk to Thomas.

She wondered, *Did somebody find out about the money?* She looked crestfallen when she returned. When the other two saw her puffy eyes and the strained muscles in her face, they knew something was wrong.

Susan relayed how sheriff Palmer, as well as most of the community, blamed Biegler for the Harpe Brother's escape, even though Jonas had also vanished. Thomas Biegler had broken his own rules, and because of it, he besmirched his reputation beyond repair. Effective immediately, the sheriff decided to remove Biegler from his responsibility as the jailer.

Thomas apologized to Susan for taking liberties. His pretending to live a life as part of a family should never have happened. He also relayed how he'd decided to head down south and start over.

Susan listened in bewilderment and shame at what she heard. He had never touched her. How could he have taken liberties? She appreciated the gentle, male companionship he had shown her, as well as the genuine affection he had given little Tommy. Did he consider that taking liberties? If so, Susan craved more, not less. She knew marriage to Micajah came with expectations, but playing house the past weeks, albeit innocently, restored her belief that a bright future might still be possible. Susan didn't want it to end.

Susan now realized how every action or inaction has a consequence. Thomas Langford died because she didn't act. Now, Thomas Biegler had to leave because she did act. Oh, how she hated that fear controlled her life.

Confused, Thomas Biegler didn't know what to think about the entire mess, but he'd already decided he would keep everything he knew to himself.

Because Susan named her baby after him, it opened a new world to him. Thomas already missed the talks he had with the three women, mostly talking with Susan while sitting by the fireside and holding little Tommy in his arms. It intrigued him how women thought and looked at things, not right or wrong, just differently. In a man's world, going alone, succeeding or failing by one's own efforts dominates a man's thought. Biegler learned how women differ.

A woman always has someone, usually children, consistently calling on her assistance. Until he got to know Susan, Biegler never thought long, nor too deeply, on the importance of building relationships, including affection, and quite possibly love. He would miss holding Tommy most of all. To hold something so tiny, so fragile, stirred an emotion in him. It finally dawned on him that not making babies but caring for them made living more meaningful.

Was it a ruse? he wondered. *Did Susan know all along about the escape? Did she help make it happen?* What little evidence he knew implied she participated somehow. Jonas had visited her the day before, and when he first told the women of the escape Miss Betsy and Mrs. Sally looked as surprised as everyone else. Susan? She turned away and refused to look at Thomas. He'd grown fond of her, very fond. He found it hard to believe she would betray the trust he had shown her, especially when she named her child after him. Still, he lost his job because he trusted her. He just did not know.

No matter how he felt, Thomas had to move on. He took account of his resources and found he had sufficient funds to head south. He doubted his old gray mare would survive such an ordeal, so he chose to buy another horse. Hopefully, he could trade the mare for something of value. Soon afterwards, Thomas bid the women a final goodbye, full of remorse and regret.

THE DAY AFTER, SALLY gave birth to a sweet baby girl whom she named Abigail, the court in Danville met and ruled to release the women. The day after that, Sheriff Henry Palmer asked some of the leaders who campaigned so hard on the women's behalf, to accompany him to the jail. There, he made a great political show by speaking about the people of Danville's generous spirits. He gave Susan, Betsy, and Sally a collection of parting gifts. The sheriff knew the speech would bode well for his re-election. Not included in the speech but later, Sheriff Palmer issued a stern warning to the women to never return to Danville again.

The women, all very grateful, found among the gifts different sizes of clothes for the babies, some diapers, and some things to wear for themselves. That last Sunday, Danville's leading church passed an offering plate for the three women. As custom had it in churches at that time, men handled the giving and collecting of an offering. Some men gave willingly, some did not, and some gave grudgingly after receiving a jab in the ribs from their wives. The sheriff handed Betsy a tidy sum of money sufficient to travel for quite a while, especially since someone anonymously donated an old gray mare.

Despite the compassion shown by the folks of Danville, their leaders made a dispassionate decision to force the women to move on. They were a pitiful sight. The three mothers and their charges, one less than a week old, had no choice but to travel onward.

The struggle they'd face took less than twenty-four hours to show itself. On the first day, they got off to a late start and traveled no more than a handful of miles. The next day they woke to a bone-chilling spring storm that drove each drop of moisture sideways.

With little more than a single tree nearby for protection against nature's onslaught, they used anything they could to create a canopy. The tree anchored one side- their old, gray mare the other. Unfortunately, the canopy collapsed every time the mare moved closer to the tree. The mare, also uncomfortable, looked for relief like everyone else. Each mother kept a watchful eye on the mare's hooves for fear a child might end up under the heel of the beast.

Chapter Twelve: Revolt in the Ranks

Things looked promising on the third day as the sun's rays broke through the clouds. That's when an argument broke open. They traveled a distance when Sally looked at the sun. She noticed that things weren't as she expected.

"We're heading south," Sally proclaimed. Her statement was more of a realization than anything else. This bothered Sally for she'd assumed the Harpe Brothers went west to avoid the law.

With her anger rising, Sally asked Betsy, "Why aren't we heading west?"

Betsy replied, "Goin' south's how we get to Knoxville. The Sheriff told us to go back there."

"You did what that old geezer told you, and you didn't ask us?" Sally quipped. She then plopped down on a nearby tree trunk. Sally decided, "I'm not going any further."

Betsy, not concerned about Sally's threat, said, "Suit yourself. Come on Susie." Betsy trudged forward. She turned when she saw that she trudged alone. Susan had plopped down next to Sally. Betsy faced a revolt. "What are you doing?" she asked. Sally knew of the sisters' conflict, so she put her arm around Susan's waist to encourage her.

"I'm not goin' neither," Susan said timidly. Ever so slightly, her confidence grew.

"Micajah told us to meet him at a place called Cave-in-Rock," Susan told her sister. "What? How do you know this?" Betsy asked. Astonished, she listened with her jaw dropped. Susan told how they should take the Green River west and stop by the Stegall homestead when they got close. From there, they were to go to the Ohio River, then on down to Cave-in-Rock.

When Susan stopped, Sally jumped in, "Our husbands want us. I know Wiley's not the best of people- but good or bad, he's my man and he's out there." She pointed west. "He wants me. So does Susie's. We belong with them. I'm heading..." Sally adjusted her statement. "WE'RE heading west, and nobody's gonna stop us."

Betsy knew if Sally traveled alone, or even if the two traveled together, they wouldn't make it. They'd face too many dangers. All three traveling together was the only chance of survival. Betsy doubted they were prepared for what they'd find when they reached their men.

"You're doomed if you go west," Betsy said.

"We're doomed if we don't. Can't you see, they'll come looking for us. Besides, if we go back, we'll have to go past where Langford died, Right?" Sally asked.

Betsy responded, "Yes."

"I'm not doing that." Sally exclaimed.

"Me neither." Susan added.

Betsy stood silently for several seconds. She then said, "Me neither...come on." She picked up her belongings and marched off to the west. Susan and Sally hurried to catch up.

BETSY, A RELUCTANT yet steadfast leader, brought them to the headwaters of the Green River. During that time they promised to keep as invisible as possible. The rumors they heard about the Harpe's ghastly attacks appalled them and they knew that if anyone connected them to the brothers the result could end horribly. They kept their promise, too, what with Micajah and Wiley spreading fear across the region, all the way from Illinois to Tennessee.

Thus, their westward journey began. After trading the old gray mare for a canoe, they floated on the still waters of the Green River toward a place some called Wilderness' Edge. Each remained deep in thought as they pulled away from the shore. Sally worried about her future with Wiley. Susan wondered if God ever wanted her to be happy. For Betsy, a question kept recurring. How many challenges must she face before her time in Hell was over?

Chapter Thirteen: The Stegall Place

People would call Moses Stegall a situational man. He had no moral compass to guide him. Both Micajah and Wiley had a compass. Evil guided it and they stayed true to it all the way to the bitter end. Moses, he'd make decisions for himself, and his family based on what prevailing conditions arose.

He continually straddled the proverbial fence between good and evil. If coming down off the fence on the side of good benefited him, then he would do so. If evil prevailed, then Moses had no qualms about climbing down on the side of evil.

Moses Stegall had made the Harpe Brothers' acquaintance at Hughes Inn, a notorious hangout on the western side of the Cumberland Gap. Wiley immediately recognized Moses as a fellow sleekit. Moses told the Harpe Brothers about Mason and his gang of river pirates located at Cave-in-Rock. He showed Micajah and Wiley how to reach his place as well as how to reach the cave.

Later, Moses joined a posse hell-bent on capturing, more likely killing the two brothers. The Harpe Brothers terrorized the state of Kentucky with their ungodly and ghastly acts of violence. Cashing in on part of the hefty reward was too much of a temptation. He had to join the posse. The Harpe Brothers, more than a little upset that Moses turned on them, vowed vengeance against Moses.

THE THREE WOMEN MADE good time on the river that day. They had just passed a peculiar outcropping of rocks on the north side of the river that resembled a buffalo, just as the jailer in Danville said it would. Once they spotted the small stream feeding into the Green River, they wound up fairly close to the Stegall homestead. All three looked forward to stepping foot on solid ground, talking to somebody other than each other, and enjoying a good night's sleep under a roof again. They could hardly wait.

"Smell it?" Susan asked.

Betsy replied, "Uh-huh."

Sally chimed up, "What is it, a fire?"

"Yeah, a big one too." Betsy answered back.

Sally asked, "Is it still burning?" Like the other two, it concerned her.

"No! I don't think so, but it hasn't been too long since it was," Betsy responded with an air of authority.

"How can you tell?" Sally asked.

Betsy said, "The smell's still strong."

With the canoe safely stored out of sight and each baby nestled in a papoose, the women walked toward where they believed they would find the cabin. It disturbed them that the smell of the fire grew as they walked closer to their destination. When they rounded a bend in the path, they abruptly stopped. Directly in front of them stood a partially burnt cabin and a pile of ashes that someone once called a barn. Apparently, a spring shower passed over at the right time, otherwise the cabin would have met the same fate as the barn.

With great trepidation, Betsy, Susan, and Sally took refuge in the nearby forest. They hid behind some large boulders and built a temporary shelter out of nearby branches for the babies. The infants remained relatively safe for a short time. The women watched for any signs of life. They discussed all the possible options available to them. Mostly they waited. For what they did not know.

At long last, Betsy stood and said, "I'll go look and see what I can find." Neither Susan nor Sally stepped up to stop her.

Betsy knew that to cross the open space in front of the cabin could be dangerous, so she chose a circuitous route. As she passed behind the burnt-down barn, she noticed a powerful, pungent smell. She assumed the burnt carcasses of animals trapped in the barn during the fire caused the odor. She had it partially right. She moved on quickly. Susan and Sally watched as Betsy paused at the partially open cabin door. They wondered why it took her so long to enter. They would have hesitated too had they seen what she'd seen.

Betsy stalled and wondered, *Can I do this?*

Clearly, the Harpe Brothers had caused this. Instead of hiding any evidence that could connect them, they carved a crude picture of a harp on the wooden door. The etching of the harp gave the destroyed cabin even more of a macabre look, especially when dried bits of coagulated blood-filled parts of the primitive etching. The Harpe Brothers were sending Moses a message. Betsy knew she shouldn't enter, but her morbid curiosity led her through the door.

She pushed the door open wider and peered in. Darkness dominated the room even though daylight shone through the part of the cabin that had burned away. The cabin stank, oppressively so. Betsy identified the smell of charred wood as the main odor, but she smelled something else, too. When she stepped in, she stepped into the remnants of hell.

A swarm of flies lifted up to avoid Betsy's shoe when she stepped in a slowly drying puddle of brownish goo that once flowed red. When the danger passed, the flies settled on the sticky mixture once again to lay their larvae, some of which had already grown into squirmy little maggots. Betsy's footprint joined the footprints of two others on the floor of the charred cabin. It didn't take much to assume those prints belonged to Micajah and Wiley. It disturbed her to see dog prints too, most likely coyote, she assumed. From the look of things, those prints showed that an animal pulled something heavy through the open door and out into the yard. A long, dried streak of brown followed the prints of a dog. Ripped shreds of blue calico cloth stuck to the blood-soaked wooden planks of the front porch.

A buzz startled Betsy. At first, she thought something might be cooking in the fireplace, but the fireplace no longer burned. She heard it again. It sounded like it came from inside a cave, but a cave inside a cabin seemed illogical. The sound came from the direction of a baby's cradle. Overcoming her desire to flee, Betsy edged her way toward the cradle. She noticed that someone or something moved inside it.

She wondered. *Is there a baby snoring beneath that polka dot blanket?*

Betsy crept closer, and for a second, closed her eyes so she could gather control of herself. She leaned over the cradle then opened her eyes again. The polka-dots moved. As one would expect, she wildly waved her arms, and the swarm of tiny critters, both the walking and the flying kind moved away. A white blanket was now covered with a legion of little black things racing to create a different design. A buzzing sound still came from under the blanket- louder this time. Should she run? Should she look? Giving in to curiosity, Betsy pulled the blanket back. A buzzing swarm of bees came towards her.

Betsy tried to move, but she couldn't. Her muscles wouldn't obey her. She could feel a buzzing creature on her cheek. She dared not move, not a twitch. It didn't move at first. It occasionally buzzed. The distinct stench of death, finally free from the blanket that muffled it, rose up and spread throughout the cabin. The smell slithered into her nostrils. When combined with the already acrid odors of all things burnt, all the fresh air in the room disappeared. The heavy mixture made her want to gasp, but she couldn't.

She dared not move. A bee walked over her ear. She wanted to scream. She could feel another- the tiny feet pressing against her cheek, leaving minuscule indentations behind when it walked toward her eye. She wanted to blink, but she dared not move, not a...PAIN! excruciating PAIN! throbbing PAIN! She faded quickly.

When Betsy woke, she could only see out of one eye, her left eye, the one that intrigued the bee. Everything she saw had an opaque yellowish glow about it. Strangely enough, her other eye registered nothing. It went black. She could feel her left eye swelling by the second and feared her ability to see would soon be gone. She could hear too, but only on her left side. That seemed odd.

Betsy wondered. *Is this forever?*

She looked around. The buzz no longer punctuated the room. The multitude of other insects disappeared as well. Everything had an eerie yellow look to it. The cabin looked well-kept and welcoming. There'd been no fire. A woman wearing a light blue, calico dress busily prepared a breakfast of eggs and sausages. Betsy expected to smell the food cooking. She smelled burnt wood and death instead.

Betsy said, "Hello," or at least she thought she did. The woman acted as though she had not heard a word. She repeated the salutation again. The woman ignored her. Off to the side lay a baby in a cradle. The child fussed, for he had kicked down the pure white blanket, and because of it, decided to cry- a good, strong, healthy cry.

Betsy called out, "Your baby's crying." The woman didn't hear her.

Betsy tried to move toward the cradle, but she couldn't. Then came a knock at the door. Two men entered, Micajah and Wiley. Betsy immediately knew she had to warn the woman.

She yelled as loudly as she could, "Get away! . . . Get Away!" Betsy could somehow see and hear them, but for some reason, nobody could see or hear her. She tried to step in Wiley's way as he approached the cradle, but she couldn't move. Watch and listen, that's all Betsy could do as the events unfolded.

In anguish, Betsy repeatedly yelled out, "No! No! No!"

She could do nothing to stop the brutality. She could only watch in horror. She couldn't move in a time that had already gone by.

Susan and Sally didn't hear Betsy's initial screams with the wind blowing toward the house, but they did hear her screams of, "No."

Sally stood up and said, "Come on. That's Betsy. She needs us." Sally started toward the cabin. She stopped when Susan wouldn't budge.

"What's wrong?" Sally asked.

Susan sat with her back against the boulder, her arms wrapped around her knees and tears dropping onto her lap. Without looking up, Susan said, "I can't."

Sally knelt down in front of Susan and with a firmness in her voice, said, "This may be the only time, but for once in your life you get a chance to hold up that promise of yours. Your sister needs you." It took a couple of seconds for Susan to build up her courage, but she did, and off they ran toward the cabin.

"Wait," Susan said. She hurried to the burnt-out barn and found a sturdy stick she could use to wallop somebody with if she had to. When she returned, Sally smiled slightly and nodded. Susan's emotional wall of fear collapsed. She decided that if she were to meet her maker that day, she'd go out swinging.

Of the two, Susan ran faster. She kicked the door open wide. It made a thud as it hit the cabin wall. Then, with her eyes squeezed shut, Susan swung away, over and over again, left and right, right and left. Luckily, she didn't hit her sister.

"Susie, stop," Sally yelled. Susan did and dropped the stick.

Sally urged Susan, "Help me pull her out."

The two pulled Betsy out to in front of the cabin. Betsy could not stop shaking. She felt clammy. Her skin lost all color except for her puffy eye - all purple, blue and lined in red.

"We need to make a poultice," Sally declared. She headed toward the cabin door. Susan held her sister in her arms, trying to soothe Betsy who seemed unaware of her surroundings. While comforting her sister, Susan knew she'd overcome her own fear for once, and that felt good.

Sally stood at the door and took a deep breath. She let it out. She took another. She figured she would have about forty seconds to go in and find the things she needed and get out again. Sally prayed that what happened to Betsy wouldn't happen to her. She took a deep breath, held it, and ran in. Sally didn't find everything she needed, but she found enough.

When Sally went to fetch water to form the poultice, she had to fetch it from the well by the side of the cabin. While drawing the water, she noticed something moving off about fifty feet away. Sally couldn't recognize the animal she saw, but she'd never forget seeing the partially eaten remains of a woman dressed in a blue calico dress.

Although the brothers played sadistic games on victims in anticipation of death, or gruesome ones with the remains on those they had already dispatched, they usually killed their victims relatively quickly. Then there came the others, the ones who knew them best. Those, they killed slowly by tearing them apart from the inside out. For Sally, she had to face the fact that Wiley might have another history other than that of a loving and caring husband. For Betsy, they'd just torn away a chunk of her compassion, her ability to care for what happened to the innocent ones. When the brothers rode off that day, they left a lot of people forsaken.

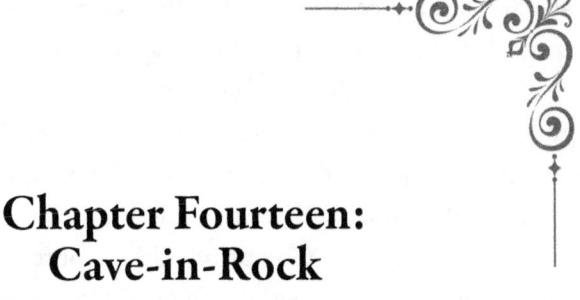

Chapter Fourteen:
Cave-in-Rock

"There it is!" Sally exclaimed as she pointed to a massive dark hole. It was in the western bluffs along the Ohio River that jutted skyward. "That jailer was right. You can see it for miles." Betsy and Susan looked. Susan saw it. Betsy couldn't. Her eyes remain blurry. They'd also grown sensitive to bright light. With the sun blazing down from above, as well as the glints of light bouncing off the tiny, white-capped waves, a glare from both directions made it hard for Betsy to see much of anything.

Betsy told Sally, "We need to cross to the other side." She knew it would take some time, so she closed her eyes and waited. Her recurring vision of the young boy who kissed her at the fair many years ago popped into her head. The boy grew smaller and disappeared. She then saw a hand, hers she thought, scurrying through the family Bible. Betsy felt confident her vision had some purpose to it, mainly because it kept playing over and over in her mind. However, she couldn't make much sense of it. Then the Bible vision jumped forward. It startled her. An unrecognizable image sat and read the "Whither Thou Goest" Bible passage and flashed out of sight. Betsy wondered, *Was she supposed to protect anyone in need so they might find happiness? Was that her role in life?*

Sally called out, "We're almost across."

Betsy put her thoughts behind her and felt around for a stick with a white cloth attached to it. She held it firmly and waved it over her head once she found it. "We made it this far. We don't need anybody shootin' at us now," Betsy said to whomever would listen.

"Welcome to Cave-in-Rock," A heavily armed man said as he pulled the canoe up to shore. Betsy sat confused. She looked around in every direction searching for a large ship with sails and a couple of cannons. She anticipated seeing something impressive moored in the river outside the cave. Completely disappointed, she thought, *Even Pa's bedtime stories were nothing but lies. How typical!"*

Betsy didn't see what she expected to see in the pirates either. She expected them to look like buccaneers- men with peg legs, hooks for hands, a few missing teeth, and an eye-patch or two. Surely, somebody around the place wore an eye-patch. She would find no valor here, no heroes- hardly anyone she could call a worthy opponent. She didn't even hear an "Ahoy, Matey" when she stepped ashore. She wanted to hear, "Ahoy, Matey."

A gray-haired man stood at the fifty-five-foot-wide entrance to the massive

cave. He worked his way over the layers of rocks down to the water.

The pirate who pulled the canoe ashore said in whispered tones, "That there's Colonel Mason, Samuel Mason."

The man then said to the Colonel as he helped Sally out of the canoe, "Colonel, we got visitors."

"I can see that, Luke. Be sure to help the other ladies too." Mason replied.

Sally walked up to Colonel Mason. He put out his hand for her to take. While using his hand for balance she said, "Thank you, Colonel Mason."

"Ma'am, you have me at a disadvantage. And you might be?" Mason asked.

"Where are my manners? I'm Sally Harpe and this is..." Sally then went on to complete the introductions.

After she finished, Colonel Mason said, "So, y'all's Wiley's and Micajah's womenfolk. Well, come on up." Before he led them up to the cave, he instructed Luke, "You be sure to bring all their belongings."

Sally could wait no longer. "Colonel is Wiley around?" she asked.

Mason responded, "No. They're out gallivanting around. Those two don't stay put for long. I expect them back in a day or two." Sally pouted. Her troubled questions about Wiley would have to wait.

Equally curious, Betsy asked, "Colonel, where's your ship?"

"There's no ship," Colonel Mason replied. Her question had him at a loss.

"Then how do your pirates swing out over the water to board the boats?" Betsy asked in all seriousness. It took a second or two for Betsy's question to sink in. When it did, Colonel Mason guffawed at the image she'd conjured up of him standing at the helm of the three-masted schooner chasing down much smaller boats as they floated by on the Ohio.

"Missy," Mason sputtered, "We don't go out on a boat to capture anybody. We bring them to us." He continued while chuckling, "A boat."

Betsy muttered, "Well, that doesn't seem fair." The winds finally blew in a storm that forced everybody to hunker down. Betsy, unable to sleep, jumped when Mason came over and started talking. As a reason for doing so, he used the pretext that Betsy reminded him of one of his daughters. That, and she made him laugh.

Mason asked, "What made you think we had a boat?" Betsy relayed how her Pa used to tell bedtime stories, mostly about Pirates, and pirates always had a ship. At that point forward, they had a pleasant conversation that lasted well into the early morning.

Mason acted like a perfect gentleman, just as she hoped. From their conversation, and from what she had seen earlier, he had the leadership's cut of the jib about him.

Both Betsy and the Colonel found it odd that they so easily opened up and shared personal secrets and feelings with each other-Feelings they seldom shared with anybody else. Betsy told the Colonel about her fear of dying by half. She told of how she still felt everything just as she always had, but the ability to show expressions of emotion was slowly disappearing.

"I feel like I'm drying up from the inside out," She stated. Betsy blamed Micajah and Wiley for tearing away how she showed others that she cared. She blamed her pa even more for bringing the two evil men into her life.

At the same time, Mason shared how he, born into a prominent and wealthy family from Virginia, had the best of things and never felt deprived. He admitted that his unquenchable thirst for the fast life eventually led him to a life of crime, when he began stealing horses at the age of sixteen. He regretted doing so and wished he hadn't.

Mason said, "Oh, how I wish I could go back and start all over again. I dream of a second chance." Little Johnny fussed. The Colonel got up to leave. Before he did, Mason asked, "Did I hear you say earlier that you women sang?" Betsy hesitantly nodded,

"Good! I expect you to sing at the hootenanny tonight. It's my birthday."

Chapter Fifteen:
Capturing the Floating
Fortress

T he night storm, full of flashes that crisscrossed the dark sky and
crackling thunder that refused to quit, paled when compared
to the sounds that woke Betsy that next morning.

A roar of musket fire jarred the women awake. If it hadn't, the
crying of three infants surely would have. When the women turned
in the night before, Mason warned them to remain inside the cave
if they heard any shooting. That morning they heard bullets hailing
down from the bluffs above on an unsuspecting boat. The boat's
captain died instantly. The last thing he heard was somebody giving
a command to fire.

The three remaining crew members, responsible for delivering
four hogshead casks of tobacco to the port of New Orleans, dove for
safety inside the building atop the 15 by 50 ft. flat bed of timbers,
called a Floating Fortress. The boat's designer claimed it to be
impenetrable, especially with loopholes available on all four sides of
the cabin. Supposedly, a crew of four could fend off an attack since
the loopholes let them shoot at those attacking without being shot
themselves. That is, if all four made it safely inside and deadbolted
the door. Unfortunately, when the captain died, he fell in front of the
door, which made it impossible to close it.

Betsy's curious nature wouldn't let her stay put. She edged her
way toward the entrance of the cave. Mason felt someone tiptoeing

behind him. When Betsy cleared her throat, he recognized who foolishly interrupted him.

"You shouldn't be here. Get back in the cave," Mason said with a stern voice. Betsy did so, but peaked out when he wasn't looking.

She watched in fascination at how Mason led the attack. The forecasts on the boat, two four and two aft, gave a Colosseum look to it. The Colonel had to work quickly as the boat floated down the river and out of control. The boat's design required the captain to act as a rudder. He directed the boat's path with the use of a long pole that had an oar at one end. The job required that he stand in plain view on top of the cabin. Once he died, the boat floated freely.

It surprised Betsy to see grappling hooks flying through the air. Mason then unleashed the Harpe brothers. He didn't know whether to thank or curse Stegall for delivering them to him. Moses, once a pirate himself, introduced the brothers to Mason. What the Harpes lacked in loyalty, they made up for it in their eagerness to fight. The brothers exceeded all of Mason expectations; but just in case, Mason always slept with one eye-open and his hand on a loaded double-barrel pistol.

The final attack didn't take long. Mickey and Wiley jumped on the boat and moved quickly behind a cask. Wiley yelled as he popped out from behind the cask and popped back in again. The scared man who guarded the door chose not to close it for fear of being shot himself.

Moving the captain's body out of the way was just too great a danger. Besides, he felt comfortable with his shooting skills. The man shot at Wiley and the lead ball lodged into the side of the cask. Suddenly unarmed, the man tried to reload, but Big Harpe's tomahawk, flying through the air with deadly precision, stopped him. He died soon afterward.

The man in the middle, the one whose leg was shot when he dove toward the cabin, put up more of a fight, but he too succumbed to

Big Harpe's superior strength. The fight inside the cabin allowed a 16-year-old boy time to escape their chamber of death. Alone and scared, the boy took refuge behind the cask. The lad thought of jumping but chose against it. He couldn't leave his older brother behind. Even if he did jump, the prospect of pirates shooting down from above didn't seem very promising.

"Where is yuh, boy?" Wiley called out as he worked his way up along the side of the boat toward the bow. Micajah came out of the cabin while Wiley played a cat and mouse game with the teen. With the cask as his only protection, it would only take a matter of seconds before the boy also perished.

Betsy had seen far too much of the insanity as she stood behind the colonel. She said, "Colonel, they're gonna kill that boy." Betsy saw a resemblance between the boy and her younger brother. It disturbed her.

Mason replied, "Probably."

Betsy pleaded, "You've got to stop them." This didn't match her childhood recollection of how pirates acted at all.

The Colonel asked, "Why?"

"Because he just a boy. That's why. He doesn't need to die. He's just a boy, like you was." Betsy continued to plead, "Colonel, give him a chance. He's just a boy. Let him live." Betsy rushed around to face Mason and looked into his eyes. She then said, "Samuel, give him the second chance you never got." Mason mulled over her plea. Her request struck a nerve.

"Wiley," Colonel Mason yelled, "Leave him be."

Wiley didn't like what he heard, not when he was about to stick the knife in and take away the boy's final breath. "What?" he countered.

Mason repeated his command, "I said, leave him be."

Wiley couldn't leave him be. It scraped against his way of thinking. Therefore, instead of thrusting forward, he swept his blade across the boy's chest that left a large, gaping wound. The boy fell.

Mason shot his rifle into the air and Wiley turned. "Enough," Mason said. Wiley stopped but Micajah didn't. Everybody knew taking on Big Harpe in a close quarter struggle led to an early grave. That's why all the other buccaneers stayed away from them. Big Harpe moved toward Mason. It didn't surprise him that the other pirates aimed their rifles at him. He didn't care. Wiley wisely tugged at his brother and whispered something into his ear. After hearing what Wiley whispered, Big Harpe stopped and smiled. Micajah called out, "As you wish Colonel." He turned back to the boat and threw the bodies into the Ohio. All three floated downstream with their eyes gazing into heaven.

The Colonel turned to Betsy and said, "Well, it's clear they haven't killed you by half yet. I doubt they ever will. You got your wish. Go get him."

Micajah blocked Betsy's path when she stepped aboard. In a soft voice nobody else heard, Micajah said to Betsy, "You can't save 'im no matter what you do." He walked away.

Chapter Sixteen:
Wiley's Dilemma

When he saw Mickey whisper something to Betsy, he rushed over and asked, "Where's Sally?"

Betsy responded, "In the cave."

"And the baby?" He wanted to know.

Betsy replied, "Your daughter is in the cave, too."

Wiley turned to Micajah and said, "Did you know that? I have a baby girl." Micajah grunted.

Wiley took a couple of steps toward the cave. He stopped and asked, "What's her name?"

Betsy deferred saying, "I'll let Sally tell you."

Before Wiley could get much further, Micajah asked, "What about the...you know, the..." He didn't appreciate being rebuffed like this.

Anxious to share his news with anyone who would listen, Wiley turned to his brother and proclaimed, "Did you know that? I have a baby..." The rest of his sentence dissipated into thin air as he rushed into the cave. Big Harpe didn't ask about his own family. He didn't care.

Even though Micajah would never admit it, he needed his brother's company. If he ate alone, traveled alone, or just stood around waiting alone, sooner or later he would end up cursing the world. This time was no different. Once Wiley rushed into the cave, Micajah looked and acted uncomfortable. Then he muttered to himself like some demented old man and walked away. Betsy was happy to see him go.

Wiley and Sally hugged and kissed to the hoots and hollers of some of the pirates in the cave. He then asked, "Can I hold her?" Sally placed the infant in his arms. It felt awkward at first, but he quickly got the hang of it.

Sally said, "Her name is Abigail. It was my mother's name."

"She'll make you weak," Micajah interrupted. His statement, given from the entrance of the cave, silenced everyone else's comments. Sally bristled when she heard it. Still euphoric at the opportunity to hold his baby, Wiley had no intention of feuding with his brother. He chose a more innocuous path to deflect Micajah's anger. Wiley responded, "No, lack of food will make all of us weak. I'm hungry."

Micajah spoke up, "That's not what I meant."

In fast order, Wiley replied, "I know what you meant." His curt response stung Micajah. It took all of Micajah's willpower not to lash out at someone.

Wiley turned to Sally and said, "Come on." He picked up the baby and gathered some things. He also grabbed a hunk of cheese and a loaf of bread when they departed. Soon thereafter, Micajah also left.

Wiley led his family off to look for a quiet place to spend the day. They found a pond near a stand of evergreens. Sally hoped it would offer the privacy she desired. With her permission, Wiley swept tiny Abigail up in his arms to introduce himself to his daughter as he went walking around the pond. Imagine Sally's surprise when she heard Wiley squeal, "She squeezed my finger." Sally thought, *This is how being married is supposed to be.*

While Wiley gave his infant daughter his undivided attention, Sally busied herself by preparing a meal. She jumped when she heard someone behind her whisper, "Someday, Sunshine. Just you wait.

Someday." She immediately knew who it was, but chose to keep the incident to herself. She would not let Micajah ruin things this time. No! This time Wiley belonged to her, all to her. Sally turned to make sure that Micajah had disappeared before turning back to Wiley and calling him to come eat.

Later, with Abigail asleep by their side, they cuddled on a cushiony, soft bed of pine needles. Neither Wiley nor Sally knew that Big Harpe had watched from the shadows of the forest.

Afterwords, a whistle pierced the air. Wiley knew what it meant. He hoped that his wife hadn't heard it. She had, and quickly recognized that her husband was being summoned. Wiley tried to postpone the inevitable. So, too, did Sally with kisses and intimate embraces. Once again, the battle for Wiley's loyalty stirred.

Another whistle – this time louder and longer.

Wiley finally said, "I have to go." Sally pleaded. She did all she could to keep him by her side.

Knowing his brother's temperament, Wiley told Sally, "I really have to go."

"Why? Why can't he wait? You're with me now. Doesn't that matter?" She beckoned him to stay.

Wiley offered a reason. He knew the reason was weak, but that's all he had. "Cause we done made plans already."

Sally asked, "Plans? What plans?"

Wiley reluctantly responded, "Me and Mickey, We's cookin' up a hummer of a surprise for the Colonel's party."

Sally mimicked, "Me and Mickey, always Mickey. What about me, about us?

We are married, you know."

Wiley shot back, "I know."

"Do you?" Sally questioned. Her question gave Wiley pause. He didn't know how to respond, so he reached out to touch her. Sally pushed his hand away and said, "Go! Go do what you have to do. But when you return, we need to talk. I've got some questions that have been..."

Wiley interrupted her, "I know. We'll talk. I promise."

Sally pressed him for an answer, "You promise, but when?"

Wiley spat back, "I don't know when yet. But if'n I say we will, then we will!" The heated argument made Abigail start to cry.

The whistle interrupted their lives yet again. This one sent Wiley over the top.

"Damn it! I hate this! Him pushin' me one way. You pushin' the other. Why can't you just let me be me?" He took a deep breath and slowly let it out again to calm himself. Wiley then continued, "All right! We'll talk. I promise. Right after the hootenanny." Wiley walked in the direction of the whistle.

Chapter Seventeen: The Boy in Need

In a single day, Susan, Sally and Betsy experienced all there was to know about a buccaneer's life. Boredom, stretching on for hours, swallowed up much of the day. Then, with little or no advance warning, a few minutes of great intensity would overcome all else-followed by boredom again. Susan pushed it away by traipsing through the woods in search of herbs and spices. Sally spent her time planning how to preserve her marriage. Betsy tried with all her might to keep a young boy alive.

"Oh, you're awake. How are you feeling?" Betsy asked as she wedged the torch she held into a crack in the wall. Menacing shadows danced about when the torch flickered. Still, the boy appreciated the light, for he'd been alone in the dark cave for too long.

He took a gasp of air, "It hurts somethin' awful. I can hardly breathe."

Betsy leaned over and felt his head, "Your fever's gone up." She leaned over to pull the boy up so he could breathe. She noticed a large bump on the back of his head that she hadn't seen before.

"What happened to me," The boy asked.

Surprised, Betsy asked, "You don't remember?" He winced when he shook his head.

"Where am I?" the boy asked while Betsy cleaned his wound. She danced around the whirlwind of questions coming from the lad.

"You're in a cave. They call it Cave-in-Rock. Do you remember floating down the Ohio?"

The boy replied, "I do."

"Well, pirates attacked you when you reached here. That's when you got hurt," she said.

"Does my brother know about me? Where I am?" The boy asked.

Betsy asked, "Who's your brother?"

"He's Tom. He was on the boat with me," the boy explained. Betsy's eyes opened wide. She turned away so he couldn't see her lips quiver. He waited for an answer.

He finally asked, "He's dead ain't he?" Betsy could only nod her head. She looked anywhere but at the boy. She felt guilty; she wasn't sure why. Her heart ached for him.

All of the sudden, questions entered her mind that were buried long ago. *I pleaded to save the boy. Should I have tried to save them all? Should I have taken Micajah's life while he slept? Would mankind have forgiven me? Would God? Does it really matter? Why don't I have the courage to give up my life so I can stop the murdering?*

The silence between Betsy and the boy continued for way too long. She looked at him. He closed his eyes. She saw his tears following a smudged trail off of his face and down to his side. He could do little to wipe away the tears because of his wound. Betsy lightly touched his cheek with her sleeve to wipe away his tears. He opened his eyes, looked at her and smiled. She smiled back.

The boy closed his eyes once again and prayed to God about the loss of his brother. Betsy tended to his needs.

"Do you know who did this?" The boy asked. Betsy hesitated, but eventually nodded.

He continued, "Who?"

Betsy resisted. "I can't tell you. I'm tryin' to save your life, not get you killed. You'll go after them for sure if I tell you. You're no match for them. They'll kill you like that." She snapped her fingers. "Just to get back at me. I can't. They'll ki..."

The boy interrupted her, "I need to pray for them not kill them."

"What?" Betsy thought, *Surely, I must've heard him wrong.* "Whatdja say?" Betsy asked.

"I need to pray for them, not kill them. I pray that I never kill anybody," the boy responded.

Confused, Betsy sat back and stared at the boy. She looked at him intently. Had the bump on the back of his head affected his thinking? Was he crazy? Nobody prayed for the Harpe Brothers. Oh sure, Betsy had no doubt that the Harpe brothers name crossed the lips of many AS they prayed. They prayed they would never meet the Harpes. They prayed for their victims, or that somebody would catch and kill them. Betsy always heard prayers against the Harpes, but never had someone prayed for them. That was, until now.

The boy confused Betsy. She wondered, *How does someone pray for men like Micajah and Wiley? They're not like normal folks. No, Satan scraped off the walls of the dungeons of hell for men like them. The devil places them at the threshold of an innocent and unsuspecting family. There, they wait to inflict vile acts of hatred on anyone inside. That's how it happened to us. Just how does one pray to God FOR men like them- the Devil's devoted ones?*

"Betsy," Susan called out as she walked further into the cave. "That Mason fellow, he's lookin' for you."

Betsy responded, "Tell him I'm comin'." She turned to the boy, "Now, don't forget. You get some rest. I'll check on you after the hoopla's over." She placed her hand lightly on his shoulder to reassure him that he was safe. She turned to leave when the boy asked again.

This time Betsy responded, "Micajah and Wiley Harpe. Now, get some sleep. Betsy caught up with Susan and exclaimed, "I don't even know the boy's name."

Susan responded, "You can ask him later when you see him again."

Chapter Eighteen: The Hootenanny

Mason considered his hootenanny a roaring success, that was until the sky fell. Plenty of rum and food always made for a successful evening. His favorite moment occurred when Betsy, Sally, and Susan sang. The second most surprising part of the evening happened when some buccaneers took a shining to the women's babies. Liquored up, they would jump about. Some called it dancing. The man would whirl a baby around in his arms until the child vomited. Each man laughed it off, wiped themselves clean, and jumped into the Ohio. Without fail, they would do it again and again. The women worried about their babies, even complained some, but they could do nothing to stop it.

The Colonel worried a bit about not seeing either of the Harpes, but he figured if they didn't want to join the festivities, so be it.

Little did the Colonel know that the Harpes had planned something special for his hootenanny. While everyone else was celebrating, Wiley snuck back into the cave and pushed the injured boy through a small, chimney-like hole in the back of the cave. He left the boy with Micajah so he could fetch the horse they had stolen earlier that day. It took some work to get the boy through the hole, but when Micajah yanked on the boy's hair. The rest followed, soon thereafter. He trudged on with the Harpes.

On top of the bluffs, the boy hurt, he was exhausted, and his bleeding started up again, but he made it up.

Micajah warned, "Don't be thinkin' of runnin." The boy didn't think he would get far even if he tried. He was instructed to sit against a tree and he complied. Darkness gradually set in. The storm that blew through earlier left a clear sky, not a cloud anywhere. A full-blown moon had just eclipsed the day before, and tiny stars twinkled with each passing minute.

Micajah also sat. They sat facing different directions with the tree trunk between them. The boy could tell they waited for something, but he didn't know what. With a lot of stumbling along the way, the boy recited, "The Lord is my shepherd; I shall not want, he maketh me to lie down... beside still waters, He restoreth my soul. Yea, though I... Yea, though ..."

Micajah asked, "You a churchgoer, boy?"

"When I get a chance," The boy replied.

Micajah commented, "Never saw much need for it myself." The boy didn't know what to say so he kept quiet. After a bit, the boy returned to quietly reciting the Scripture passage while sniffing to hold back the tears and trying to appear brave. He kept stumbling over the same passages.

Micajah interrupted the lad when he heard the boy recite something about walking, "You ain't walkin'. You're gonna ride through the valley of the shadow of death. Only the best for you, boy."

Neither spoke for a while, then Micajah finally said, "Well, it's time you shimmy out of those clothes, boy."

"What for?" asked the frightened lad.

Micajah responded, "Cause, I dun told you to... Now git to it, boy." The boy reluctantly did as he was told. He then sat back down in a tight ball. Big Harpe heard the boy sniffling again. Uncharacteristically sympathetic, Big Harpe felt the boy deserved an explanation.

"You're the center of the show were puttin' on, and we want everybody to see how pure and innocent you is."

Wiley reappeared pulling a reluctant mare by a rope.

"Boy, this is your special day," Wiley said. The boy refused to look up.

Wiley continued, "You oughta' be more grateful. We dun went out and stole you a horse. Took most of the day it did. Ain't she a beaut?"

Micajah and Wiley hoisted the naked and struggling boy up on the horse. They tied his hands around the horse's neck, and his feet beneath the mare's midsection. They then took the boy's pants and wrapped them over the horse's eyes.

Wiley continued, "There, fit as a fiddle. And listen.... Do yuh hear it? ... Hear them singin? A choir of angels is callin; you. Now, say thank you."

The boy's lips were moving, but Wiley didn't hear the boy saying anything.

Wiley leaned in to hear the boy whispering, "Hallowed be thy name. Thy kingdom come. Thy will..."

Wiley yelled, "Say thank you. Damn it!" He then punched the boy in the jaw and broke it.

Wiley continued, this time in a more peaceful tone of voice, "Say thank you."

With a great deal of labor, the boy mumbled something vaguely recognizable as a "thank you".

"That's a good boy," Wiley said. The boy then said something else. He missed what the boy said the first time.

Wiley leaned into the boy and asked, "Whatdja say?"

The boy gathered what little strength he had left. He looked at Wiley and said, "I forgive you." Startled, Wiley took a step back.

Macajah asked, "Whad he say?"

Not sure how to react to the boy's forgiveness, Wiley said, "I forgive yuh."

"What?' The boy's comment angered Micajah a great deal. He pulled Wiley aside, and asked the boy, "What? Whad yuh say?

The boy could do little more than mouth the words, but the message reached its target. "I forgive you. May God forgive you, too."

Micajah's anger rose to a height rarely seen before, "What? How dare you. Nobody said nothin' 'bout bein'' fergiven." Micajah slapped the rump of the horse. The mare lurched, and then blindly galloped forward off the ground above the cave and into space.

Micajah yelled, "I'll see you in Hell, boy!"

A shrill, discordant, multi-pitched scream, two in fact, acted like a hellish clarion call the moment the horse's hooves had nothing to run on but air. Everybody below looked up. The screams grew louder and demanded their attention. No one had an inkling of what they watched.

At first, they saw an ever-changing angular shadow that increased in size with every passing second. It blocked out more and more stars behind it. The shadow mesmerized them. When they heard the ghastly screaming a millisecond later, everybody realized something big was falling down on top of them. That's when the scrambling began.

The concussive thud, when the boy and horse smashed against the limestone boulders, jarred everything. It made a large, drum-like sound that echoed out over the river. The pressure of the air suddenly created an invisible wave that bowled everyone over. The once-blazing fire, the main source of illumination, extinguished itself for a couple of seconds while all the oxygen in the area disappeared. A hot cloud of dust and silt rose up from the crevices between the boulders, only to slowly settle back down like a blanket over the area. Miraculously, no one died, or received any serious injuries; no one, that is, except for the boy . . . and the horse.

Just as miraculously, no one shot the Harpe Brothers as they came down off the ground above the bluff.

Giggling like schoolboys who had pleased themselves with the gruesome prank they pulled off, Big and Little Harpe worked their way down the steep slope by the entrance of the cave. Neither one could stop yapping away as they relived what they considered the highlight of the entire evening.

"Which one do yuh think screamed the loudest when they was in the air?" Wiley asked.

Micajah answered, "Oh, the boy, without a doubt. Did you feel the thud when they hit?"

Wiley continued, "Sure did. Wish we coulda' been down there when they come down. That had to be somethin' worth seein'." Wiley continued, "What was with that little runt goin' on and on with him sayin' 'I fergive you, I fergive you' over and over again.?"

"Dunno," Micajah stated. "S'pose the boy was scared."

Wiley unwittingly cut off Micajah when he mimicked the boys' last words, "I forgive you. I forgive you."

Micajah thought on it a moment and then said, "Huh, like he thought we was needin' forgivin.'"

Wiley reached the ground in front of the cave. He asked as he turned around, "Whadja' think?" His enthusiasm over the violent stunt quickly faded when he saw several rifles aimed at him.

Wiley gazed past the guns, looking for his Sally, He spotted her standing beyond the carnage. Their eyes met. With his shoulders shrugged and the palms of his hands facing up, he gestured, *This, this is who I am.* Sally wept and turned away. Her troubled questions faded, for she finally saw the gory truth.

Micajah, hearing no one talking, asked, "What's happenin'?"as he reached the bottom. Once he turned, he knew.

Colonel Mason, a few steps away from the carnage, lashed out at the two brothers, "You two are damn fools." He continued, "I want the whole lot of you outta here first thing tomorrow morning."

Colonel Mason walked down to where the boy and horse landed and surveyed the deadly sight. Somehow, the boy ended up beneath the horse while the two dropped through the air. Both the animal and the young man died instantly. The weight of the horse crushed the young man on impact.

Mason turned to Wiley and Micajah and said, "You're gonna clean this up." He pointed to the deadly sight. "I don't care if it takes all night. You're gonna clean it up." Mason, working to maintain his composure, finally lost it.

"Hell, what were you thinking? I told you to leave him be. It was your woman who asked me to." Wiley started to talk but the Colonel wouldn't allow it.

"Shut your yap!" He continued, "Luke, if either of them starts talkin' back, shoot 'em. I don't want to hear their voices ever again." Mason vented his anger by pacing back and forth across the cave's entrance.

"I told you to leave him be, and what did you do? Run him off a cliff. Just for the fun of it. You two are sick bastards. Both of you!" Mason continued to pace. He took a deep breath. "It's one thing to kill a man when you have to, but to kill someone for fun? Animals don't even do that. You're sick!"

Mason bellowed, "Get this," He lost all the words for how to describe it, "cleaned up." He pointed to a group of five river pirates "You five make sure they do a good job. And don't let 'em get close to you. You can shoot 'em if you have to. They're nothin' more than rabid dogs, anyway." Mason entered the cave, only to come right back out again. "And, if I ever see you two around here again, I'll shoot you down myself. It'll be fun!" Mason reentered the cave while muttering, "Damn fools!"

Almost everyone else, not assigned a task, followed him into the cave. As one of the last ones outside, and feeling sad about the boy, Betsy looked at the mutilated body and sighed. When she turned toward the cave, out of the corner of her eye she noticed Big Harpe staring at her. She turned to him. Big Harpe slowly swept his hand in a grand gesture over the dead boy and horse. She recalled the threat he made earlier in the day, and then understood. *No matter what she did, she couldn't save anybody*. Micajah smiled menacingly at her.

BETSY OPENED HER EYES. Blood dripped off her fingertips, and her arms looked as though she'd dipped them in the same deep red juice up to her elbows. Morning had broken. The sun, a scorching red-hot orb, rose up behind an unimposing hill. A single tree, having several twisting and turning branches, stood atop the hill. Betsy walked toward it. With every step she took, she walked on the bleached bones of those who died at the hands of Big and Little Harpe. Their bones did not crack or creak as one would expect, instead, when stepped on, each bone recalled that person's final anguished cry, and plea for mercy.

Beneath the tree were two beasts- part man and part wild dog. One was big, the other little. They fought bitterly for the right to tear the latest of the Harpe's victims to shreds. This time it was a naked, broken boy of sixteen. In the tree, a head hung from a branch- a human head. Betsy looked up at it but could not tell whose head hung there. Its eyes popped open and watched Betsy come closer. No matter how hard she tried not to, she could not help looking at it. She felt mysteriously pulled to it until she stood directly in front of and below the pockmarked, maggot-holed head of Micajah Harpe.

Then it spoke saying, "No matter what you do, you cannot save them."

Big Harpe's head laughed, mockingly. It would not stop laughing.

Shivering, Betsy sat up with a start. A cold sweat chilled her spine. She would not sleep anymore that night.

Chapter Nineteen:
Micajah's Anger

Betsy's lungs ached. She didn't know how much longer she could hold her breath, three seconds maybe, five at the most. Micajah's hand, wrapped tightly around her hair, held her head in place under the water by the river's shore. *Just how long does it take to die by drowning?* Betsy wondered. At that point, Betsy's worry about dying by half seemed frivolous, when faced with the reality of actually dying.

Being held upside down for so long, she didn't know if she could right herself even if she had the chance. Up, down, left or right, all sense of direction disappeared.

Big Harpe's large paw yanked her head up into the air. She gasped for as much of it as she could. "Damn you! Don't you ever do that to me again. Do you hear me?" Micajah threatened. Betsy's long black tresses, covered with mud, hung like a dirty rag over her face. Big Harpe tightened his grip and plunged her head under again. He pushed her so far down her face scraped along the rocks at the bottom. When he yanked her up again, he did so with such force she felt as though her neck had twisted completely around. He then threw her to the ground.

"Never again. Do you hear me? Never!" Big Harpe sputtered. Betsy tried to respond, but everything she said came out as nonsense.

Several hours passed since Mason's men trussed up the Harpe brothers. Mason warned the women to keep them tied up until they reached the Cumberland River. All three women knew that Betsy would be the one who would pay the price for Micajah and Wiley's embarrassment. She steeled herself for the anticipated onslaught once they were untied.

Both Susan and Sally pleaded for Betsy's release but it was useless. They even took the blame for big Harpe's predicament, but he knew better. Micajah figured that if she had let them kill the boy at the beginning, all of this would have never happened. But no, Betsy had to butt in. It was all her fault, so it was only right that she would pay the price. She would have, too, if Wiley hadn't interrupted at that precise moment.

When Micajah first set eyes on Betsy, her "I will stand my ground no matter what" behavior intrigued him. He'd never met a woman like her before. The women he met wilted whenever he exerted his will upon them. Betsy fought back. Each time, she would suffer the consequences for her obstinance, but still, she resisted. Big Harpe enjoyed the challenge she provided at first. However, as of late, he grew weary of his feud with her. He determined the time had come to end it, and in order to end it, he had to kill Betsy. Micajah considered the present as good a time as any.

When Wiley said, "They're coming," That's when Big Harpe pulled her up and tossed her aside. Wiley walked away following his brother. Sally thought it strange that Wiley stepped in at that particular moment. *He could have just as easily waited for a few seconds more, and let Betsy drown.* Sally wondered, *did he do it on purpose?* Afterwards, Betsy never spoke of the incident again.

On one of the brother's excursions away from Cave-in-Rock, before Colonel Mason expelled them, they made contact with a small band of renegade Indians. Surprisingly enough, the spot where Colonel Mason told Betsy to release the brothers was the same place where the Harpe Brothers planned to rendezvous with the Indians.

The next couple of days passed uneventfully, but then came the third day.

Early that morning, Wiley told Sally, Susan, and Betsy where they should wait until the brothers returned. They heard commands like that before, and it always ended with someone dying. The women overheard bits of the men's conversation, and from what they gleaned, they knew about the plans for an Indian style raid on three families traveling in Indian territory, just west of the Mississippi River. Wiley told the women to wait by an outcropping of large flat rocks just around a bend in the river.

Once the men left, Susan volunteered to watch over Betsy's little Johnny. Both Susan and Sally noticed how quiet and withdrawn Betsy had become since the day she almost drowned. They talked it over and agreed that giving Betsy time might help her snap back to her old self again. She appreciated and accepted their offer.

Betsy looked for a quiet spot to hide away from the noises she anticipated hearing. During that time, she spotted a finely detailed cloth doll someone had made with loving care. However, one of the buttons used for eyes fell off. By the look of the doll's current condition, Betsy assumed a little girl lost it in the past week. The water-logged doll had snagged on a bush where the branches dipped into the river. Betsy gripped the doll as she closed her eyes and laid back on a large rock to absorb the sun. Then, before the screams came, she tried her best to dream of something special so nobody could steal her precious few moments of peace.

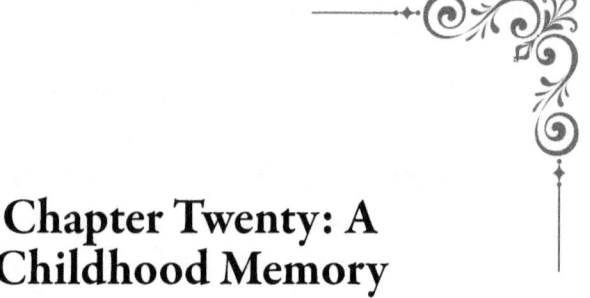

Chapter Twenty: A Childhood Memory

Anne Roberts sat on the porch in her favorite rocking chair. She'd found some free time, and completing various sewing projects seemed like a good use of that time. Betsy was no more than six years old at the time. She ran up to her mother with tears rolling down her puffy, red cheeks.

"Mama, Mary lost an eye. Look!" Betsy said while sniffling. She held out her cloth doll for her mother to take.

Anne responded, "Oh my, she sure did. What happened?" Betsy shrugged her tiny shoulders.

Anne continued, "I don't have any buttons that match this one. Let's see what we can do." Anne reached down into a jar of buttons that she had placed at her feet when she started sewing. "Here's a couple of blue ones we can use. She'll have eyes just like you. Will that do?" Anne replied. Betsy vigorously nodded her head while wiping away her tears. In no time at all. Anne repaired Mary so she looked better than before. Anne said, "Here you go, Punkin." She gave Mary back to Betsy.

"Thank you, Mama, but I'm not a pumpkin," declared the little girl.

Anne reassured her, "No, you're not. You're a Punkin. You're OUR Punkin. Isn't that right dear?" Anne asked her husband just as he happened to walk by. John Roberts seemed to know that some reassuring platitude needed saying. So, he added, "Yes you are, and such a fine young punkin a..."

Something or someone tugged the child's doll out of Betsy's hands. The yank of the doll jarred her back to her present world. She looked up to see Micajah standing over her.

Micajah said, "Oh good." As he used the one-eyed doll to wipe off the blood, skin, and brains from his tomahawk. He then threw the doll into the river. Betsy showed no emotion at all as she watched the doll meander slowly downstream and out of sight. Half-death drew closer.

Chapter Twenty-One:
Alone

The brothers decided the time had come to search for a new place to hide, especially since they knew of one posse already trailing them. They assumed others did, too, since the governor of Kentucky had placed a hefty bounty on their heads. The brothers set out to find a secluded place that offered more cover than their present hideout – yet another cave, a shallow one on the side of a shallow hill. Heeding Wiley's advice, Big Harpe sent Betsy to check out a place called Campground. He considered her the best choice since she was the most expendable of the three women. Wiley told Susan to watch little Johnny for Betsy while Micajah ordered Betsy to go alone, look over the place, and report back what she saw. Once again, Sally observed how Wiley acted in a way that protected Betsy from Micajah's wrath. She didn't know what to make of it.

Betsy's journey left her standing in the middle of nowhere in search of yet another nowhere. She knew her time alone offered her the best chance of escaping. Freedom could be hers if she would only forsake her child, her sister, and her friend. She wondered, *If I do run, can I live with myself afterwards?* Lately, her devotion to the safety of the others was fading. Just turn and take a step in another direction. That's all she needed to do.

Betsy felt sorely tempted. She questioned whether or not she would make a better mother than her sister, especially after feeling herself slowly dying from the inside out. *What child would want a mother like me?* she wondered. Besides, it seemed as though Susan had matured in spite of all they had lived through. Why shouldn't she give up Johnny? Turn and take that first step in another direction, that's all she had to do.

She didn't. What stopped her? The vow.

Chapter Twenty-Two:
A New Hideout

Betsy suspected the place called Campground would differ from anything else she had ever seen before. She didn't know why it was called Campground, but she finally found it in the middle of a dense forest. The forest stretched north and south for miles along a winding creek. Betsy figured a person could get lost in there if needed. A loud noise coming from within the forest piqued her interest. She thought she heard geese squawking.

As she worked her way toward the noises, Betsy was surprised that what she thought were geese were people. She knew the importance of staying out of sight, but the distant sound of violin playing pulled her closer. The familiar sound brought back memories of Thomas Langford.

People singing hymns, some of which she remembered as a little girl, hypnotically pulled her through the forest until she came upon a man-made clearing in the middle. Campground was an outdoor tabernacle. She never expected to see so many people sitting and standing around.

She stumbled upon a church meeting. Sunday passed a few days ago, at least she thought so, but this was a revival meeting. Revivals, in those days, consisted of a series of daily church services totaling up to two weeks. Some lasted longer. The purposes of revivals, even now, include restoring religious fervor, confessing sinful nature, and saving lost souls. A preacher, not a local one, usually a circuit rider, preached at the services.

From Betsy's vantage point in the back she had a clear view of everything. A stand of mature oak trees bordered the tabernacle on the East side. This part differed from the rest of the forest. Dead leaves, broken limbs, and the lack of sunlight squelched the weeds and grasses from taking over. A person could see someone coming from a long distance.

Folks, probably local parishioners, took the time to improve the East side. It had privies, and a fenced-in area for keeping horses. Several rough-hewn tables, used for potluck meals and smaller meetings took up considerable space close to the altar. There was a firepit between the tables at the altar which made it possible to roast a pig or help illuminate an evening service. The firepit stood at the edge of the altar on one side, and a garden of wildflowers bordered the other.

Betsy watched from the shadows as a man of some importance introduced the preacher. People sat on tree stumps or fallen trees that laborers lined up- one behind the other. They anticipated hearing a powerful sermon and leaned in as the man of the cloth took his place. Reverend Joshua Talent didn't disappoint them.

Chapter Twenty-Three:
The Sermon

He looked over the crowd and said, "Yes folks, we are smack dab in the middle of Bible thumpin' country, and let me tell you, I'm mighty proud to be here, mighty proud. Amen?"

His "Amen", phrased as a question, drew a rousing response from the crowd. However, it failed to meet his expectation, so he said, "Amen?" again. This time the response reverberated. It satisfied Reverend Talent as he said for the third time, and with great fervor, "Amen!"

"You know, folks, I've preached me a mess of sermons in my day. Quite a few of them have been outdoors like this one here; but, never, NEVER have I preached me a sermon in front of a Jesus tree before. And oh, what a magnificent tree it is that y'all have chosen to glorify His name with. Oh, you mighty oak. Amen?" Once again, a full-bodied "Amen" returned from the crowd. "Amen," he repeated. This time the word ended with a peaceful hum that drifted back through the crowd.

The giant oak tree received its name because an enterprising young man carved the name of Jesus on a plaque. He then nailed the plaque to the side of the tree. The plaque hung about eight feet above the ground.

The "Jesus Tree" and the podium were about ten feet apart leaving plenty of space for a preacher to move around it when he got the itch to move when he spoke. A local artisan carved out a tree stump to create a unique podium. Those who cleared the land around the altar purposely left twelve trees standing. They gave each tree the name of one of the twelve disciples.

"I've titled this sermon "Forgiveness: An Amazing Gift from God." Reverend Talent then knelt on one knee and remained perfectly still for a long time. Most people thought he prayed. Others believed he used that time to build up his strength. No matter what, his action startled the crowd. Throughout the sermon, all eyes focused on him- wondering what he would do next. And so it began.

The preacher started slowly. He didn't stay slow for long. He staked out a patch of land on the left and on the right of the ornate pulpit. Back and forth he crossed, left and right, right and left. Every time he turned to the retrace his steps, his extra girth swung around and hurried to catch up. Those who watched him felt exhausted. Surprisingly, the preacher seemed to gather more energy with every word he spoke.

He didn't speak in measured tones either- no march-like precision for him. When he spoke some phrases received close attention. He cradled them with care, like a mama cradles her newborn child. These precious words were the ones he wanted his listeners to mull over. He rattled off other parts of his sermon so quickly that a nearby woodpecker couldn't peck fast enough to keep up. However, nothing compared to his voice, a voice that left the crowd spellbound.

His deep, bass utterances rumbled high among the leaves when he articulated a point with gusto, which he did quite often. When he whispered, he did so with such clarity that his soft, low, basso-profundo made the frogs, crickets and other living creatures from the nearby pond fall silent and listen. The sermon lasted well over an hour. Afterwards, one man approached the preacher and said, "Brother Talent, that was a stem-winder of a sermon. Indeed, it was."

BETSY JUST HEARD SNIPPETS of the sermon since she stood in the shadows at the back of the crowd. Snippets such as, "When someone is angry, they are sinning" and "The ability to forgive is a gift from God." Still, what she heard began to make sense. Betsy moved closer. She wanted to hear more.

She found herself nodding in agreement when she heard, "It is harder to live a life where anger consumes you than it is to let it go and forgive." Once again, she crept closer. She let out a soft, "Huh," when she heard the preacher say, "Forgiveness is as much for the one doing the forgiving as it is for the one receiving forgiveness."

Engrossed in the sermon, Betsy failed to hear the noise behind her.

"Hello." She heard the soft greeting from a woman who stood behind her. It startled Betsy.

Without realizing it, the mature woman had positioned herself in such a way that Betsy's only escape required she interrupt the sermon. She didn't want to do that or draw any attention to herself, so she stayed put and waited for the worship service to end. She thought she might escape during the closing prayer but the woman grabbed Betsy's hand and squeezed it before she could move.

"Please don't leave," The woman whispered. She squeezed Betsy's hand again. With the service finished, the woman came up beside her.

She said, "Child, you must be famished. We have plenty of food. Please stay." The woman wrapped Betsy's arm in hers as though they had grown up as dear friends who hadn't seen each other in ages. "Ooh, you're chilled to the bone. Here, put this on you." The woman pulled her own shawl off her back and wrapped it around Betsy's shoulders. She would not take no for an answer. "Now, let's get you something to eat, shall we?"

WHITHER THOU GOEST

Betsy, overwhelmed by this woman's generosity, obediently followed. Nobody had shown Betsy so much kindness since her Mama died. Nobody could, since everyone around her lived under the same dark cloud she did.

Chapter Twenty-Four:
Questions

After being introduced to so many people in the crowd, Betsy felt like she was royalty. At long last, the woman introduced Betsy to Reverend Talent.

The preacher said, "Thank you, sister. Welcome, child."

She tried to give the shawl back, but the woman said, "Keep it. I'm sure you will need it later." She then walked away.

The preacher patted a space next to him on a large tree trunk. He said, "Betsy, please sit." With a heaping plate of food in her hands, she sat. The gregarious preacher instantly made her feel at ease. A joke here and a kind comment there left her hoping to learn more. She'd only heard tiny parts of his sermon, and hoped he might offer her a brief synopsis of what he said. However, with so many people stopping by to say farewell, he spent much of his time saying goodbye, or promising to pray for someone.

During one conversation, Betsy overheard the preacher say, "I won't be out this way for quite a while. I'm bound for the Carolinas, a place called Swannanoa Valley."

Betsy made a special note of it and intended to talk to him about it later. The crowd slowly filtered away.

Betsy asked, "Do you have time for some questions?"

"Why of course I do. I love questions," the preacher replied.

He interrupted her before she asked her first question, "Just a minute." He waved for a man he called Brother Paul. Their quiet conversation lasted for only a brief moment. Brother Paul nodded his head and set off to do what the preacher asked of him.

The preacher turned back to Betsy and asked, "So, Miss Betsy, what questions do you have?"

While Betsy and the preacher talked, Brother Paul stoked the fire in the pit until it once again glowed. He also made sure Miss Betsy and her family would have everything they needed to turn a meal into a feast.

Betsy asked, "What about revenge?" At the same time, she nervously glanced around the edge of the forest. The preacher picked up on her anxiety and intended to ask about it if given the chance.

He replied, "Getting even or looking for revenge doesn't work. Vengeance is like an uncontrollable beast. When a person calls upon the beast and frees it from the chains that bind it, just so they can get some temporary satisfaction, they are asking for trouble. The beast destroys everything and everyone in its path, including the one who freed it. You can't control vengeance, it controls you. That's why the Almighty God declared 'Vengeance is mine.' No, forgiveness is the key that takes away your anger- Seeking God's forgiveness for all your sins, seeking the forgiveness of those who you hurt, and forgiving the people who hurt you. That's the key. Let the judges deliver vengeance. That way, justice is served. You? You stick with forgiveness. It will give you peace."

"Sorry for steppin' in, but my family's waitin' for me. Preacher, everything's done as you requested." He then turned to Betsy, "Miss Betsy, I hope your family shows up soon. I hate to leave you all alone, what with them Harpe Brothers lurkin' about." Brother Paul and the Reverend then said their goodbyes. Brother Paul offered Betsy a, "Good day, ma'am." He climbed aboard his buckboard and rode out of sight.

That left Betsy and the preacher all alone. As the two walked toward the buggy awaiting him, the preacher said, "Now, I have a question for you. Have you asked the good Lord to forgive you of your sins?"

Betsy replied, "Oh... No... What's the use. When my time comes, I'm sure he won't want me in his heavenly choir."

The preacher questioned, "Why not? Can't you sing?"

"No, that's not it. I'm not worthy. I'm no Moses or King David. My sins are bad! God don't want me," exclaimed Betsy.

The preacher responded to her doubt, "God doesn't look at sin like man does. There's no list of really bad sins and not so bad sins. Sin is sin. It's going against God's will. Moses was a murderer. David, an adulterer and a murderer. Even if the people they led thought they spoke for God, them two had to get right with God first. They had to ask for forgiveness. It's the reason why God sent his son Jesus to die on the cross as a perfect sacrifice and rise from the dead three days later."

"So?" Betsy questioned.

"So, anybody who asks to be forgiven is forgiven," The preacher replied.

She asked, "What does he want from me?"

The preacher offered, "Miss Betsy, I don't know what he wants from you, but I know this. God wants everybody spendin' eternal life in heaven a singin' in his choir."

With an earnest interest in what the preacher said, Betsy asked, "Can you..." She paused for a moment when she heard Micajah's muffled curse. She hoped that only she heard it.

Her mind raced, searching for some way to stop another killing. That's when she said, "You know the one who needs savin'? It's my Pa. He's one who needs savin'. He done his family wrong. If you can change him, then I'll listen. You oughta look him up when you go back to Swannanoa Valley. He lives near Morristown."

Surprised by Betsy's sudden turnabout, the preacher promised to visit him. It didn't matter to her whether he did or did not since she only used her pa as a pretext for sending the preacher safely on his way.

He wanted to stay and talk some more but sensed the time for talking about heavenly matters had passed. Therefore, he bid her farewell, and climbed aboard the buggy that awaited him. He alone claimed all the available space possible in a rig designed for two. The buggy's wheels went full circle all but three times before he stopped. He twisted around to look at Betsy and said, "And oh, about them Harpe boys. I wouldn't fret none. I got it on the best of authority that them two are nowhere around here. Besides, God's watching over you child."

She watched him ride away, singing, "Amazing Grace how sweet the sound that saved a wretch like me. I once was lost, but now I'm found, was blind, but now I see," as he traveled out of sight and sound.

Betsy knew it to not be true, any of it. How could it be? But oh, how she wanted to believe the gregarious preacher who spoke with such assurance.

"Sweet Jesus, I thought he'd never leave," Wiley's acidic voice pierced the quiet of the forest, as he bit into an apple, part of a table of food the worshipers left as a gift to them. Betsy shuddered when she heard him. Her muscles ached in anticipation of his brother. Wiley reached the table first. The others followed close behind.

Micajah walked toward her with that typical snarl of his, and said, "You was supposed to come back and tell us."

"I couldn't..." Before she could finish her sentence, Micajah walked away. He showed no interest in hearing her excuse. He yelled out, "Wiley, go get us something to drink."

Betsy worried about what that night would bring.

Chapter Twenty-Five:
The Missing Virtue

A quandary - that's the situation in which Wiley found himself - in a quandary. *How could he convince Sally and Mickey to stop fighting over him? Why did they feel it was their right to exert their will upon him? Why didn't they feel the same way as he did?* After stealing some liquor, as his brother demanded, Wiley had time to think about his dilemma.

The horse he rode, a gentle mare he named Lady was his loyal companion. Wiley knew the horse would never beat anybody in a race. Nonetheless, he had a sense that the mare would give all that she had to give if called upon, and he appreciated such loyalty. Of all the things to value, loyalty was the virtue he valued most of all. Unfortunately for him, loyalty was rare these days.

It wasn't clear whether the uncanny timing of Lady's whinnies, something Wiley construed as the horse actually listening to him, or the nearly empty jug of corn liquor led Wiley to chatter on so, but something did. He recalled sad, childhood memories of his Pa beating his ma into submission. His older brother adopted the practice and gradually did the same to him. Over the years, Micajah's constant pressure on Wiley wore the boy down until Big Harpe's wishes and desires became Little Harpe's commands.

Except for the time when Wiley asked Micajah not to shoot his future father-in-law, he couldn't remember an instance when Mickey showed any loyalty to him in return. Everything was always what Mickey wanted. "Well, not this time," he declared.

With only Lady to hear, Wiley yelled out, "Damn you, Mickey! I won't do to Sally what Pa done to Ma." A few paces later, he yelled again, "No matter what YOU want!"

Wiley found Sally's silent treatment even more disturbing. Sally had opened his eyes to a new way of living, and it had some appeal. However, just when he needed her the most, to counter the enormous amount of pressure exerted by Mickey, she shunned him. He knew what she wanted, but in no way would he turn on his brother. That would be disloyal.

Wiley felt the feud spiraling out of control. Because of it, he spent more time talking to animals and babies. They made no demands upon him.

"You know, Lady. Me and you is loyal to a fault. They's expectin' us to do what THEY want, WHEN they want, with nary a question, even when it ain't right. They want you to act like some dumb animal." He chuckled, "Sorry, gal." Wiley rode on awhile, eventually stopped, took a swig from his jug, and muttered, "Why not just chuck it all." That's when he thought of Abigail, his little girl who cooed and kicked her feet in delight whenever she saw him. He would go back because of her.

Chapter Twenty-Six:
No Crying Babies
Allowed

It frustrated Micajah that he had to wait for Wiley to return with something to drink. He never understood how Wiley did things, nor did he especially care just as long as Wiley did as he was told. Still, he put up with the frustration because Wiley was kin, in fact, his only kin, and that deserved allowances.

Big Harpe had a strange way of defining kinfolk. In his brain, he recognized that all three babies, Thomas, Johnny, and Abigail were all related to him by blood, but in his heart, until those little ones could somehow meet his needs, they did nothing more than irritate him. Micajah found it ridiculous how Wiley acted like a buffoon when he fawned over little Abigail. It aggravated him that he had to compete at all for his brother's devotion, but to compete for Wiley's attention against a tiny baby frustrated him even more. What he feared would happen when Wiley married Sally had finally come home to roost, just as he'd predicted.

Micajah didn't want to hear the babies crying, nor listen to some inane conversation, let alone contribute to it. He started a second fire, some fifty feet away.

As Micajah's parting comment for the night, he said, "No babies cryin'. You hear? Keep 'em quiet, or I will." Everybody knew what that warning meant. He settled in by his fire and waited for Wiley to return.

All three mothers worked diligently to keep their babies out of danger by keeping them quiet. However, no matter what a parent does, sometimes babies cry. It's what they do. Unfortunately for Abigail, she would not stop. Big Harpe warned Sally, not once but twice, to stop Abigail from making all that noise. In spite of her mother's efforts, little Abigail refused to stop crying. Sally had run out of ideas as well as run out of patience.

Micajah warned Sally a third time.

Without thinking, Sally sharply spat back, "If you think you can do better, why don't you ...."

She stopped suddenly when she realized the horrible mistake she'd made. Micajah stood up and walked briskly toward Sally.

"Oh God. No. Please don't," Sally pleaded as she saw him coming toward her. For every step he took she took a step backwards. She kept Abigail in her arms, as far away from Micajah as possible. Both Betsy and Susan, unwilling to let a tragedy happen without putting up a fight, repeatedly called for Micajah to stop. They tried every argument and plea that came to their minds, but Micajah wouldn't listen. It seemed as though an evil force had taken over Big Harpe's mind and body.

Betsy rose in a hurry to block Micajah's forward progress. Susan scooped up the two infant boys who once again began crying. She ran a good distance away from Micajah as a precaution. Micajah threw Betsy off to the side with very little effort. Again, Betsy rose to intercede, and once again, Micajah threw her aside as if she weighed nothing more than a leaf falling from one of the nearby trees. Betsy fell, and when doing so, she wrenched her back, making it difficult to move quickly.

Sally stood as Abigail's last wall of defense. She chose to use the fire as a barrier against Micajah's onslaught. She could have run, but knew that Big Harpe would catch up with them. No, Sally considered the fire as her best option. If he moved right, she would do the same. If he moved left, so would she. At the same time, she pleaded for her baby's life, and prayed that Wiley would soon return.

"I'll keep her quiet. I promise. Please don't hurt my baby," Sally begged.

Sally's plan worked for a few seconds. Impervious to the pain, and in two steps, Micajah walked through the fire. He brushed out any flames with his bare hands. It didn't bother him whether he caught fire or not. Micajah always thought of pain as a distraction he could temporarily overcome when faced with a formidable challenge, even one as formidable as Abigail. Micajah had drilled down in his mind to one single purpose. He meant to keep Abigail quiet at all cost. His ability to reason had shut down, as did all the emotional ties he had with those around him. He'd become a machine fueled totally by adrenalin.

Sally turned to run, but before she could, Micajah tripped her. Abigail flew from her arms when she fell. Micajah reached the infant first.

Sally screamed, then begged, "Oh God, please don't hurt my baby. Oh God, don't do this. Please no!" Sally sobbed and sobbed, so much so that she went into an emotional shock as she watched in horror.

Micajah spun around while holding her tiny baby by her tiny feet. He looked somewhat like a Grecian shot-putter ready to launch a heavy stone. Abigail no longer cried. Instead, she gasped for air. On the third spin, and with all the strength he could muster, Micajah slammed little Abigail into the side of the Jesus tree, Campground's Altar.

Seeing her child's blood splattered on that special tree left an indelible memory Sally would never forget. And, there, for no reason at all, the infant Abigail, like an innocent lamb, lay sacrificed.

Like a javelin flying through the air, Micajah hurled the baby's lifeless body into the underbrush somewhere among the trees of the disciples.

Micajah looked down at Sally and said, "There. No more noise, I warned you." He had risen to Sally's taunt and nothing more needed saying. He then walked back to his personal fire and sat.

Chapter Twenty-Seven:
Battle Royale

Before Wiley returned, Sally traveled through a series of emotional upheavals over the sudden loss of her baby. First, she wailed. On and on she wailed. Then she sobbed uncontrollably. Next, while in the arms of Betsy, Sally grew lethargic, sliding in and out of a stupor, only to ask what had become of Abigail. Betsy sat by Sally. She was at a loss for how to respond. A pall set in over the area.

Wiley arrived. He could sense something had happened, something bad, the moment his feet touched the ground. He walked over to Sally, knelt down beside her, and looked into her hollow eyes.

"What's wrong with her?" Wiley asked Betsy, as he waved his hand in front of Sally's unresponsive eyes. Betsy couldn't think of an easy way to break the news to Wiley, so, without hesitation, she laid the whole gory details out for Wiley to hear.

At first, Wiley denied that Abigail had died.

"Mickey would never kill one of his own." He swore up and down, but the one he needed to convince the most, he couldn't convince. He couldn't convince himself that Mickey hadn't killed his daughter. Wiley got up and walked toward his brother. He still had a bottle in his hand.

"Did you do what Betsy said? Did you kill my baby?" Wiley asked. Big Harpe looked up at his brother but never said a word. Wiley knew it. He knew his brother had murdered his child. "You son of a bitch!" Wiley screamed.

He threw the bottle at Micajah. It cracked open on a tree behind him. Normally, Wiley shied away from confronting his brother, but nobody would call this normal. The liquid courage he'd already consumed left him all "likkered up" and ready to charge.

Once again, Wiley yelled, "You son of a bitch!"

Wiley pulled his knife from its sheath. Micajah rose and yanked free his tomahawk. Micajah swung at his brother with all his might. Big and Little Harpe, the two most vicious killers in all of Kentucky, maybe America, faced off in a life and death struggle that could leave one of them dead by his brother's hand.

Little Harpe, familiar with his brother's fighting style, knew Micajah would swing low across the body with his tomahawk as his initial move. To counter it, Wiley quickly stepped back out of Big Harpe's reach. He barely escaped the deadly blow and felt the breeze of the tomahawk as it swept by.

Micajah, out of position for just a moment, grunted when Wiley successfully slashed at him, drawing blood from his right arm. The wound, not fatal but substantive nonetheless, forced Micajah to favor his wound, and fight more with his other hand. Each time Big Harpe swung his tomahawk, Wiley lost ground- until he couldn't retreat any further. A tree, one of those named after a disciple, stopped Wiley's backward movement.

When Wiley fell backwards over some broken branches, Micajah lunged forward. He raised his weapon to kill his brother.

As the voice of reason, Betsy, devoid of emotion, uttered, "Mickey, don't kill your brother." Betsy never knew for sure why she saved Wiley's life that night. As far as she could tell, it had something to do with her mama's teachings. If she could save a life, she should. Besides, Wiley had protected her a couple of times lately.

Micajah, realizing he came close to doing just that, tossed aside his weapon. Wiley took one last swipe with his knife. That move incensed Micajah since he once again drew blood. Micajah threw aside Wiley's knife and choked his brother until Wiley lost consciousness. He then pulled him by the back of his shirt near the fire where he lay unconscious. Micajah sat, recouping his energy, and pondered the situation deteriorating all around him.

Chapter Twenty-Eight: The Sunshine Dims

To dominate, that's what drove Micajah to act the way he did. Big Harpe always believed that other people should do what he told them to do. Those who couldn't or wouldn't deserved to die, usually in some gruesome fashion. In Micajah's mind, only Micajah mattered.

Micajah regretted killing little Abigail. Not because he valued the baby's life, he didn't. He didn't value anybody's life. He regretted it because it built a wall between Wiley and him. Although he would never admit it, he depended on Wiley, and didn't dare lose him. Faced with his need to dominate falling apart around him, he knew he had to do something, and do it quickly.

Micajah yelled, "Susan." Susan gave the babies to Betsy to watch over.

"What does he want?" Susan asked her sister. Betsy could only shake her head. Betsy watched intently while Big Harpe told Susan what he wanted. Susan balked. However, she ultimately knew she had no choice but to obey. With a look of resignation on her face, Susan rose, walked over to where the still unconscious Wiley lay. Susan then settled in beside Wiley and waited. Micajah had told her to do whatever it took to keep his brother occupied throughout the night.

A minute or so later, Big Harpe got to his feet and slowly walked toward Betsy. She knew that he had developed some plan and wearily waited to hear what he had to say.

"How is she?" Micajah asked in a calm, quiet voice. His question, as well as how he asked it, sounded so uncharacteristic of him. He never cared about any of his victims before, why now? It left Betsy confused as well as worried. Thankfully, Sally had finally fallen asleep with her head in Betsy's lap. Betsy feared what would happen if Sally opened her eyes while Big Harpe stood well above them.

"She's finally asleep," Betsy replied. She continued. "How do you think she feels when..."

Micajah, still in a quiet voice, interrupted her, "Be quiet." He then knelt down beside them, and stroked Sally's golden hair. Betsy wanted to scream, but she dared not.

"Take your hands..." Betsy complained.

"Shhh!" Micajah whispered. "Listen up, and I don't want her hearin' it." He then slowly swept his hand over Sally's arm and further down her leg.

While he did, he uttered, "Such pretty skin, too." Betsy tried to pull Sally away.

Micajah then softly whispered in Betsy's ear. "I'm gonna' f..." Betsy squirmed, trying to escape. "What? Did I hurt your tender ears, your not-so-innocent tender ears? Fair enough. Let me start over. I'm gonna use her, and I want you to help."

Horrified, Betsy pulled back. Micajah grabbed her arm and firmly stopped her from leaving.

Betsy's eyes widened as he whispered more. "I thought you might refuse. If you don't help, I'll strip you nekkid and tie you to that, that tree, that... *Jesus Tree* yonder. You can wait for the wild dogs to feast on you. Oh, and they will too, but not before you git your own personal show.

First, I'll throw your sister's baby, Thomas is it? I'll throw him in that fire so the two of you can smell him as he roasts to a nice toasty brown. You'll git to watch me use your sister, too, 'til she's tiny little strips, just like we done that other girl.

So much for that promise of yours, eh? Didn't think I knew did you? I'm gonna take Sally. No matter what, I'm gonna' use her. You can watch too. Then I'll gut her. Her innards will fall out on your feet.

Your baby Johnny? I got somethin' special planned for him. He'll live. That's right. He'll live. You'll die knowin' that I'll bring him up. He'll grow up to be just like me. I'll change his name, too. The last time you'll ever see "Little Mickey" will be with me ridin' away with him in my arms. Is that what you want?"

Micajah leaned in and slowly licked Betsy on the cheek to intimidate her even more. It was a foul-smelling, slimy, gut-wrenching lick. Micajah stood up and walked back to his place by the fire. He smiled as he sat. She had seen the devil, and the devil had smiled at her.

Betsy sat still, perfectly still. She hoped that if she did nothing at all maybe everything would disappear, just as a rabbit freezes in place hoping its predator will not see him. If Betsy decided to disappear by staying still, then her plan failed miserably. Betsy didn't realize it, but her hands shook wildly, so much so that a drunkard with the shakes would watch in awe. While she shook, her mind raced for answers.

Betsy posed the question to herself. Maybe he's bluffing? She rejected that idea right away. He and Wiley had killed well over twenty people already. Micajah did not bluff.

Betsy considered offering up herself instead of Sally. She thought that if she willingly participated in any sexual activity he desired, he would choose her over someone unable to do much of anything in her present state. Then it dawned on her that sexual gratification didn't matter. The domination mattered. She rejected that idea.

Betsy then thought of running. However, that idea had little merit. She had seen how tenaciously Micajah came after Abigail. Besides, the likelihood of everyone escaping safely didn't seem promising.

Betsy contemplated killing Micajah, but how? She had no weapons. He did. If she got a hold of a rifle, she didn't know how to shoot it. She would need brute strength and surprise to kill Micajah with a rock or a burning stick. Furthermore, she didn't know if she had it in her to kill a person.

Betsy prayed for a miracle, but the assurance Reverend Talent gave her earlier in the day held no power for her. No, Betsy had no options to choose from other than to bring Sally to the slaughter, or to die watching the utter destruction of everyone she loved.

Betsy woke the emotionally and physically spent Sally, and stammered, "Sal...Sally, I need you to come... come with me."

Betsy could not blot out Sally's pleas as she crawled back to the sleeping babies. Her legs collapsed when she tried to walk.

"No, no... d... don't do that... Stop it... Betsy... Betsy, help me... please?"

Betsy wallowed in shame when she saw Sally's face pressed to the soil. The soft lullaby she sang to the two boys may have helped them sleep, but it did nothing to alleviate Betsy's guilt as she heard the young mother scream, "Kill me, kill me, too!" Micajah's hot thrusts of unfathomable hate seared deep into the crevices of Sally's body, mind, and into her soul.

His anger burnt away at her vitality, her thoughts, her emotions, her memories, even her ability to speak - until all that remained was the hollow shell of that once-vivacious sixteen-year-old girl. And, with that, beneath the Jesus tree, the demons of Hell danced over the ruination of one of God's children, and her mother.

Betsy could only question *How can God ever forgive me? How can SHE ever forgive me? How can I ever forgive myself?*

Chapter Twenty-Nine: Fulfillment

U nder a cloudy sky, Betsy embarked on a task nobody else could, or would do. She went to bury tiny Abigail. She waited until the sounds about her switched from ones of lust and abuse to that of snoring. One sound, Sally's repeated whimpering, confused her. Betsy didn't know if Sally actually slept or not, but she couldn't wait any longer. She would have to chance someone finding out, as she crawled in the direction where Big Harpe threw the child's body.

Betsy stretched out her hand, patting the ground in front of her in a large circular motion. It took some time, but, at last, she found a baby's foot dangling off the underbrush near a tree. With it so dark, she felt the foot to make sure it belonged to Abigail instead of some animal. She felt the soft baby's sole and her tiny toes along with the rest of her lifeless, little body. Yes, it was Abigail. Strangely enough, touching the infant's remains didn't faze her as much as she thought it would.

Having no tools to aid her in her quest, Betsy used her bare hands to claw out a small shallow grave. Dirt and blood, she assumed hers, and bits of skin, or other parts of the body, she assumed as not hers, all squished together beneath her fingernails.

Betsy never imagined a lovely shawl, her gift from a stranger, would become the young child's shroud. She took it and wrapped it around what remained of the infant's head. Betsy then placed Sally's child in the ground. It reminded her of the time when she covered her mama's body with dirt.

Betsy knew the grave would not keep the coyotes away for long. The scent of death smelled too strong. Nor could she imagine the horrific sight Sally would take to her grave if she caught sight of wild dogs ripping away and gnawing on the bones of her precious Abigail. Betsy decided to pile as many rocks as she could find on the grave.

She thought *At least that will keep them away until we leave this God forsaken place.*

Betsy knew she should take a moment to pray or say something, but nothing came to mind. All the violence, all the evil, had depleted her ability to show love, compassion, and caring. The Harpe brothers had stolen her ability to show any emotion at all. *Have I turned into an empty shell?* she wondered. Betsy prayed, "Oh God, help me to mourn over Sally's baby. Help me to feel. Help me to cry again." She waited and waited. Betsy felt nothing. Slowly she turned from the grave and crawled back toward the others.

Then it happened. She heard a soft plop, then another, and another. Finally, a rhythmic pattern of plops, all created when tiny drops of rain landed on the leaves of that majestic oak tree. Heaven cried, for Betsy couldn't.

Chapter Thirty: What Price Revenge

The last vestiges of Betsy's dream, more of a nightmare actually, ended abruptly when she felt a presence close to her. Her eyes pried open to look about. She saw nobody close. She didn't see anyone moving around at all. She rolled over and tried to recall a more pleasurable dream from her memory bank of dreams worth remembering.

As of late, the only time Betsy felt fully alive happened in her dreams. Again, she felt a presence, and again, she opened her eyes. Sally startled her. The young women, disheveled, half-naked and worse for wear, sat unusually close to her. Sally looked at Betsy with a blank stare and never said a word.

Betsy quickly rolled back to her first position and squeezed her eyes shut. She didn't want to face Sally. She didn't know if she could ever face Sally again. Even as a little girl, Betsy trained her mind to build cubicles for tucking away anything bad she experienced during that day. She would lock up the cubicle and then start her next day fresh.

This mental manipulation allowed Betsy to face the challenges a young girl should never have to face. When she saw Sally that morning, last night's cubicle, already filled to the brim, collapsed. Betsy's feelings of guilt roared back. She heard some rustling behind her and wondered if Sally had left.

Betsy dared not open her eyes for fear of what she might see. However, her curiosity won the battle. Just as she feared, there sat Sally, still disheveled, still gazing at her with a blank stare, never saying a word.

What would Sally do to her? Betsy wondered, after what she had done to Sally. Betsy felt grimy. Not a physical griminess, but an emotional one. She knew what she would do to anyone who did that to her. She would kill them. Logically, Betsy knew she had to give in to Micajah's demand in order to keep everybody alive, but she knew she had participated in a great evil and deserved to be punished. Betsy sat up and faced Sally. She chose to accept whatever Sally meted out. She would not fight or run. Betsy believed that her guilt would wash away only after she accepted the punishment she deserved. Even killing her came across as fair and just, if Sally chose it.

Betsy lifted Sally's hands and placed them around her neck. She closed her eyes and waited, and waited, and waited. Betsy opened one eye to peek at Sally to see if she would soon do the deed. It appeared as though Sally's punishment would take longer than she anticipated.

Betsy felt movement in front of her. *This is it.* She thought, and she squeezed her eyes even tighter. When Betsy felt Sally's nose touching her nose, her eyes popped open. Betsy watched as Sally slowly pulled her hands away and sat back, never saying a word.

Betsy decided that if Sally would not punish her, then she must punish herself on Sally's behalf. Such a vile act deserved retribution. No longer could she consider herself worthy of other people's affection, loyalty, or even attention. They looked to her for leadership and protection and she had left them wanting. For that, she deserved the ultimate punishment. She deserved to die. Death by her own hands provided the escape she craved. She could not live with it. She would not live with the anguished guilt.

Over the past few hours, Betsy's mind raced from a state of dull nothingness to considering suicide. She kept looking for a way to make sense out of all that had happened. Her constant emotional shifting in search of an answer weighed heavily on her.

While Betsy contemplated methods of dying, Sally had another plan. Moving at a pace similar to where sap drips from a maple tree, Sally reached out and turned Betsy's face to the side. Betsy watched in amazement as Sally moved so laboriously. Sally leaned over and kissed Betsy on the cheek. She then sat back just as she had done before- never saying a word.

Sally's kiss changed everything for Betsy. It stopped her downward spiral. Also, instead of thinking of suicide as the only way to take away the guilt-ridden pain, the kiss of forgiveness offered Betsy an alternative. Sally's kiss rebuilt the compartment in Betsy's mind for storing her guilt so it would not overwhelm her again.

Furthermore, when it came to how Betsy would act, the kiss changed how she thought of herself and how she would get along with Sally and Susan. The kiss was an act of forgiveness. It meant that in spite of what she had done, Betsy could still have a place in Sally's life. She knew it wouldn't be the same. She had tainted her role as leader and protector when she offered Sally up to Micajah's viciousness. Because of that, Betsy became Sally's caregiver.

As the morning passed, the summer sun's rays lifted high enough to filter through the clusters of leaves from the giant Jesus Tree. Susan appreciated the extra hour of sleep. A sinister, evil power forced Susan to participate as an unwilling player and an unwilling observer the previous night. She stirred that morning, once a beam of light finally reached her eyes. *Would their little corner of hell ever end?* she wondered, as she got up and walked over to her sister, and her friend.

"I saw," Susan whispered in her sister's ear after leaning over. "How cou..." For some reason, Susan's eyes shifted over to see Sally sitting there staring off into nothingness.

"What happened?" Susan asked.

Betsy responded, "I don't know. She never talks and barely moves at all." Susan fully intended to give Betsy a verbal lashing for the horrendous deed she had done, but after seeing Sally it no longer mattered.

Susan waved her hand in front of Sally who continued to stare ahead. Susan noticed that Sally cringed when Betsy's child woke up crying. Susan took her sister's place next to Sally when Betsy went to tend to her baby's needs. Sally grew anxious watching Betsy leave, so Susan scooted closer and gave Sally a hug. It seemed to help. She had no idea of what to do when her baby would wake up.

Never one in the morning for saying a friendly, "Howdy-do", Micajah stood up, stretched and grumbled, "Those damn runts. Will they ever stop crying?" Thomas had just woken up a few seconds before, and his cries stole Micajah's last moments of slumber.

Micajah looked around and noticed that Wiley had disappeared. Big Harpe called out, "Anybody know where Wiley got off to?" Susan shrugged her shoulders and so did Betsy. Sally, hearing Micajah's voice, slowly curled up into a ball and began to rock.

As Micajah came closer, he asked, "I'm hungry, any food?"

"Go look on the table." Susan replied.

Standing near to the two, Big Harpe looked down at Sally. "What's wrong with her?" he asked. Nobody answered his question or even looked up. He waited a few seconds for an answer, but when nothing came, he muttered, "Women!"

Micajah walked toward the table by the altar, scratching his backside and searching for food. What the churchgoers hadn't devoured the first time, Micajah, Wiley, Susan, Betsy, and Sally did on the second go around.

By the time Micajah grazed over the table a third time, not much remained, especially since the local critters, large and small, feasted on the crumbs all night long. He found one last piece of shoo-fly pie. However, flies and little crawling things covered it. Hunger will make a fella do things he wouldn't normally do. Micajah dug out as many of the little white crawling things with his pinky finger as he could find. He scattered the flies with the sweep of his hand and stuffed the pie, as well as some critters in his mouth. As one would imagine, this piece of pie did not taste like the pie his ma used to bake. It took more than one try to pass what remained of the pie down his gullet. While doing so he wondered *What happened to Wiley? He don't normally go off by his lonesome first thing in the morning.*

Just as the pie left an unsatisfactory taste in his mouth - Wiley taking off, to God knows where, left Big Harpe dissatisfied too. He looked for something to wash away the taste.

He found a small tin cup half-full of some kind of fluid, most likely a weak tea by the looks of it. Micajah poured most of it out before a fly floating upside down in the middle dropped to the ground. Nonetheless, enough of the fluid remained to quench his thirst.

Micajah pushed aside some debris that covered the table. He sat on the table while placing his boots on the nearby bench. He surveyed the area, and on one of the few times felt calm. In his time of solitude. He felt at peace at the campground.

A horse behind him whinnied. He turned to look at it. Micajah muttered to himself, "Wrong horse." The relaxed feeling he experienced faded once he saw the smaller of the two horses, the ones they took as their prize for participating in the earlier massacre. He always assumed when it came to divvying up who would ride which horse, Wiley would ride the smaller one and he would take the bigger one. They'd agreed on it. From Wiley's perspective, the agreement sounded more like a mandate than an agreement. A smaller horse just plumb tuckered out under Micajah's weight. He knew Wiley knew that. Micajah determined that he'd give Wiley a piece of his mind when he returned.

A mosquito lighted on the back of his hand. Micajah watched it bite him. He thought what sweet revenge as he held his breath, believing that would disable the tiny insect from flying away. It took in his blood, much more than usual.

Micajah slowly pressed down on the bug with a finger from his other hand. The mosquito popped, spewing blood in all directions. Big Harpe took his blood back by licking it off the back of his hand. Nothing would ever get the better of him. He would not allow it. Yep, Micajah liked it there. It had almost everything he imagined he would ever need, just as soon as all the folks stopped coming around.

Susan yelled, "There's a horse comin' in."

Chapter Thirty-One:
Lost in Transformation

If someone thought of Wiley as a manipulated pawn, or an innocent bystander, they'd be wrong. Sally did, in the beginning. Wiley had perfected the use of a charming demeaner to gain access into people's lives and restricted places with ease. Once he passed those barriers, people found a self-centered, amoral, cold-blooded killer who considered killing as a means to an end.

If Wiley desired something, and killing made it possible to attain it, then so be it. Unlike Micajah, Wiley knew right from wrong. He just didn't care. Few ever got to know the real Wiley. Sally did when it was too late.

Micajah thought of murder, and the accompanying gruesome acts, as a right of his. He terrorized and intimidated others into submission. He considered himself to be part of the chosen few to be given the honor to kill. One brother was insane, the other amoral, and their being together fueled a spree of murders.

So how did Sally affect Wiley? People do what they know. All of Wiley's life, violence and brutality engulfed him. Following a deadly path made sense because that's what he knew. In the brief time Sally and Wiley were together, Sally introduced love, kindness and civility into his life. She also helped him better understand right from wrong. It piqued his curiosity. Too bad time ran out before she could teach him more.

Chapter Thirty-Two:
The Sudden Departure

Big Harpe ducked behind a tree, mad at himself for forgetting to bring a weapon. When the horse neared, Susan identified the rider, "It's Wiley." Wiley was riding at break-neck speed. His mount skidded to a stop when he pulled up on the reins. Micajah came out from behind the tree to face his brother. Both men spoke at the same time, certain that what he had to say outweighed the other.

Micajah asked, "Where'd you get off to? Who said you could ride my horse? We agreed, I ride the bigger one."

Wiley issued a warning, "There's a posse comin', and it's a comin' quick." Micajah heard just a part of Wiley's warning.

"What?" he asked.

"There's a posse headed this way." Wiley repeated. He stayed mounted.

"Why didn't ya say that in the first place?" Mickey complained. He grabbed some things, mostly weapons. Not much else mattered.

Micajah hurried back, reached out and said, "Here, gimmie my horse." Wiley wheeled the horse away from his brother. Micajah reached out again. Wiley pulled back further.

"Whatja doin'? We don't have time for this." Micajah argued. When Micajah reached out a third time, Wiley pulled out a pistol he'd squirreled away. The pistol grabbed Big Harpe's attention. He stepped back. He didn't expect this from his brother.

"I'd already done left you. That posse's the reason I come back- to warn ya. Owed ya that much, you bein' kin and all," Wiley said.

Micajah took an aggressive step forward, "Ungrateful bastard."

Having had enough, Wiley aimed the pistol at Micajah. Once again, Micajah stepped back.

"You killed my baby." Wiley glanced over to his wife. He saw her rocking back and forth. "You do that too?" He asked, nodding his head toward Sally.

Micajah protested, "Let it be. What's done is..."

Wiley cut off his brother, "Course you did. You don't care nothin' 'bout me. It's ALWAYS been you." Wiley gave Sally one last look and said, "Damn shame."

Wiley wheeled the horse about and left. He yelled as he galloped off, "Rot in hell, brother." Micajah whipped his knife at his brother. It fell far short of its mark.

Susan heard Micajah muttering as he rushed by, "Ungrateful bastard."

She called out, "What about us?" Micajah stopped once he heard the question. He'd erased the women out of his mind.

He said, "Oh," Big Harpe took a couple of seconds and thought. "Go back... Go back to our last campsite, that hill with the shallow cave. I'll meet you there." Micajah then fetched Wiley's loyal, yet undersized steed named Lady. He worked his way north through the forest.

Left to deal with the sudden crisis on their own, Betsy led Sally into the forest. Susan followed with the two boys.

As they burrowed into the forest's darker regions Susan asked, "Why don't we wait for the posse and give ourselves up? You keep saying we need to get away. Wouldn't that do it?"

"Not anymore. Remember us talkin' about those men who wanted to string us up when we stopped for supplies? I 'spect most folks feel that way," Betsy explained.

"But, we ain't done nothin' wrong," Susan complained.

"Don't matter. We'll get blamed just as much as they will, just because we traveled with them. Bein' their women makes it even worse, especially if they get away. People's mad, and somebody's got to pay. No, we need to find someone we can trust, someone who will speak up for us. We need a hero," Betsy replied.

Susan added, "Like Samson?"

"Like Samson!" Betsy said without emotion.

Chapter Thirty-Three:
Big Harpe and the Posse

Leiper, clearly the best shot of them all, and his posse of five dealt with considerable frustration while trying to bring Big and Little Harpe to justice. They hoped that this time they'd have a far better opportunity.

One of the women who recently attended a revival service met a young woman who didn't seem like a normal churchgoer. After hearing the description, Leiper decided they would look over the place. This lead could bear fruit if they hurried.

In addition to Leiper, the posse consisted of Moses Stegall, two of Moses' relatives, Mr. Tompkins- an affable man who felt in over his head, and a young fella named John Huffstutler. Huffstutler had joined just a couple of days before.

Stegall received word that the Harpe brothers had murdered his wife and child as punishment for him chasing them in the first place. Since then, Stegall's desire for revenge rose to a fever pitch, just as it did for relatives who accompanied him. Tompkins felt duty bound to bring Micajah and Wiley to justice. He'd survived a chance meeting with the brothers and felt guilty over not doing something to end the Harpe Brothers' rampage at that time.

John, new to the region, and anxious to make a good name for himself, hounded Leiper for a chance to join the posse. Leiper almost turned him down because he felt John needed more seasoning before tackling such a challenging task. John never gave up. He repeatedly volunteered, promising to do whatever Leiper expected of him. Leiper finally gave in because he needed the help.

Six horses galloped toward Campground. At one point, Leiper waved his arm, signaling for the men to split off from the main posse. Huffstutler pulled away to cover the northern flank and Thompkins headed south. The plan was for them to come in when they heard a shot and come through the forest on those different sides.

When Leiper and the men with him reached the clearing, they found a deserted campsite. He knew they didn't miss them by much. Leiper shot his rifle into the air. The four men dismounted and searched for clues. Moses stopped cold when he heard a distant cry from a baby.

He turned toward the forest- trying to locate the source of the sound, but when Tompkins rode up making a lot of racket, he lost the lead and never heard the sound again. One of the men found a knife on the ground. Tompkins thought it might have belonged to Big Harpe, but he had his doubts.

John rushed back to the posse yelling, "A big fella just broke out of the forest, and he's headin' west. Don't have too much of a lead on us, neither."

"He alone?" Leiper asked. Huffstutler's description about the man's size provided a sufficient reason to pursue him.

"As far as I could tell," John replied. Each man wondered about the whereabouts of Wiley. They all saddled up to continue the chase.

The likelihood of a casualty or two ran high during a death struggle like this. John Huffstutler became the first, well actually, his horse did. It came up lame, and because of it, the horse unceremoniously dumped John on his hindquarters. Since the horse decided nobody would ride him for a while, John had to drop out of the chase. He wouldn't receive the glory he hoped to receive for restoring peace throughout the land. His dreams of heroism would have to wait.

Leiper pulled up and turned around while the remaining four pressed forward. He rode back as John got to his feet. Leiper said, "Keep your eyes and ears open, just in case. We'll come back for you later." He then galloped off to rejoin the chase.

Further ahead, Micajah knew he had to stretch out the posse and demoralize them from continuing if he had any chance of escaping. Wave after wave of rolling hills favored him in his effort. No one could get a clear shot at Micajah because he was always on the other side of the next hill. This pattern continued for quite a while.

Once the men gained ground on Micajah, he added another wrinkle to the chase, just to frustrate them. Since he was out of sight, he often changed directions- left or right down in the valleys. This maneuver forced the posse to stop each time and decide which way Micajah went before charging forward. One time, Micajah nearly escaped using this maneuver. Afterwards, Leiper had Moses Stegall stay behind by a hill or two just in case Big Harpe escaped and circled around behind them.

So far, the cat and mouse game belonged to Big Harpe; but just as Micajah anticipated, riding on the smaller of the two horses eventually betrayed him. The horse put up a valiant effort but she "tuckered out", just as Big Harpe knew she would. The posse reached the top of a hill while Micajah slowly rode his horse across the ridge of another. They finally had their chance. Micajah sat atop the horse. He was well within range of their long rifles. It looked as though he barely moved.

In rapid succession, the sound of three gunshots rang out. Two shots missed Micajah completely. The third, Leiper's shot, hit Big Harpe in the leg. Micajah considered it a waste of gunpowder for it did little to slow him down. The shot may have done little harm to Big Harpe, but when the bullet tore into the horse's underbelly after glancing off Micajah, it caused considerable misery to the horse.

Big Harpe believed he had won the fight. Finish it, that's all he had to do. He had already identified the man in charge. He needed to shoot that man down before anyone reloaded.

Not a posse, not an infant, not a brother, nor an insect, nothing, NOTHING would ever get the better of him. He was invincible, or so he thought.

Big Harpe figured that if he shot and killed Leiper, the posse would lose interest in continuing. He aimed at the leader of the posse and pulled the trigger. It jammed. His rifle jammed! He cursed the world as he swung the wounded mount around.

Tompkins, who for some reason refused to shoot earlier, said, "Here, You're a much better shot than I am." He tossed his rifle to Leiper. Leiper grabbed it, swung around, aimed and fired. The lead ball ripped through Micajah's spine. Big Harpe fell off the horse who staggered away out of Micajah's reach.

Micajah, still determined to fight on, swung his tomahawk at the men who drew near, but had lost his ability to aim. The posse had doggedly chased him all day and wanted to see the man called Big Harpe before he died. Leiper came up and kicked the tomahawk away. A couple of others pulled Big Harpe by his shirt. They dragged him over to a spot underneath a solitary tree with twisting and turning branches and leaned him up against it. Micajah asked for some water. Tompkins pulled off Micajah's boot, filled it, and gave him what he requested.

The men stood around waiting, for what Big Harpe didn't know. Therefore, as the center of attention, Micajah recalled what these men didn't want to hear.

"Me and Wiley, we dun in some fella by Johnson, I think. He was the first. We cut him open and pulled out his guts." Micajah had to stop and take several breaths. "Then we filled 'im with rocks and dumped 'im in the river. Worked pretty good 'til that Brit floated away. We dun a bunch like that."

He went on and on.

"I Killed Wiley's baby last night. Shouldn'ta done that," His voice trailed off. "That was wrong. Bashed her head against a crazy old Jesus tree... Huh." Micajah's moment of remorse lasted only a moment. He chuckled, which turned into him spitting up blood.

"Wiley and me, we caught these two brothers. Well, one got away so we killed the other." Big Harpe chuckled again. "We waited around for the other one to come back. We knew he would. That's when we..."

A lot of people, when they face death, recall their accomplishments with satisfaction, but seek forgiveness for their failings. How strange it felt to listen to a man recall all his ghastly murders as achievements - a morbid, heinous list of accomplishments. Except for one, he showed no remorse for what he'd done.

With great effort, Micajah turned his head toward the horse galloping up. He leaned his head back against the tree. Then he saw Moses dismount. Stegall, with his knife already out and ready to use, walked toward Micajah. All the men stepped aside.

Micajah knew what to expect, so he looked at Moses with hatred in his eyes and said, "You're a damned rough butcher, but cut on and be damned." No one said a word. Nobody protested over the legality of doing such an act. Moses knelt by Micajah, took him by his hair, and twisted his head to the side. Moses began sawing away. With his pupils enlarged, and his chest heaving up and down, Micajah tried to look at Stegall, but couldn't. His hands clenched the ground. Death finally came to Micajah when the knife pierced his jugular vein. Blood spewed forth. Big Harpe's body shook spasmodically, just as a chicken did when it lost its head.

Moses Stegall, as if participating in some obscene ritual, raised Micajah's head high into the air. The blood poured out. After a few moments, he put Big Harpe's head in his saddle bag. Moses, awash in blood, felt satisfied for the moment.

When the men walked back toward their horses, someone asked, "What should we do with the body?"

Leiper responded, "Let the dogs and worms have him. That's all he deserves. Nobody here's gonna dig a grave for him."

Forever after, in the fields of western Kentucky, an unimposing mound of dirt bears the name Harpe's Hill in remembrance of an evil man. A man who lived a violent life, and on that hill, he died a violent death.

PART THREE - Chapter One: An Unexpected Future

"Ugh!" Betsy sighed as the women saw the cave they hoped to never see again.

"Come on," Susan said, encouraging her sister to follow. "At least we know where we can find some berries." Betsy took Sally by the hand. They settled in and waited, but they didn't know for whom they waited, nor for how long they should wait.

They could wait for Big Harpe just as he instructed, or Wiley might surprise them and return, or the posse might find them. None of the options warmed their hearts. However, there was one prospect that nobody spoke of. What would they do if nobody came?

Susan asked, "Where do you think Wiley went?"

"Dunno." Betsy replied.

Susan asked again, "Do you think he's comin' back?"

"No! Not after last night." Betsy said with a sense of finality. It had become clear over the last week that Wiley, in his odd way, acted as a buffer between Micajah and the women and babies. With Wiley no longer there, both Susan and Betsy felt quite concerned about staying with Micajah.

Betsy joined the others in resting beneath the shade the cave provided. She laid her head down, closed her eyes and waited. Waiting made Betsy worry.

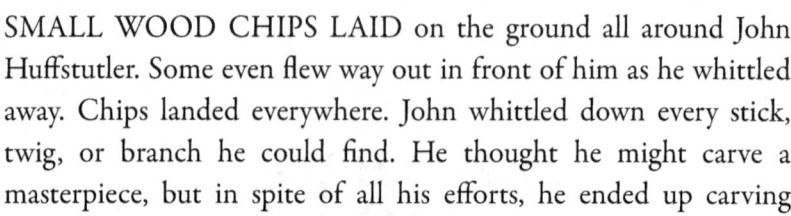

SMALL WOOD CHIPS LAID on the ground all around John Huffstutler. Some even flew way out in front of him as he whittled away. Chips landed everywhere. John whittled down every stick, twig, or branch he could find. He thought he might carve a masterpiece, but in spite of all his efforts, he ended up carving toothpicks, various sized toothpicks.

At first, John followed Leiper's command to keep his eyes and ears open. He inspected every detail of the clump of trees to make sure no one hid out of sight. That lasted all of thirty minutes. John thought of inspecting his horse to see why it came up lame. He found nothing. He even mounted his horse. The horse, in no time at all, bucked him off again. That's when John decided to carve his masterpiece.

With his, so called, pile of masterpieces completed, John stood up, stretched, walked out about twenty feet from the tree and yelled, "I hate this!" John really wanted to capture somebody. He returned to the tree, sat down and closed his eyes.

Betsy sat up with a start. She wondered, *Did I dream it, or did someone just yell?* Betsy shook her sister. Susan didn't appreciate Betsy interrupting her dream.

Betsy asked. "Did you hear somebody yell?"

"No, I was asleep," Susan responded. "What'd they yell?"

"It sounded like, 'I hate this.'" Betsy replied.

"So do I. It's a dream. Go back to sleep," Susan muttered as she settled back down.

Betsy figured Susan knew best and once again closed her eyes. Her eyes popped open when she heard, "I'm tired of this."

She was drowsy, and without thinking about the consequences of her actions, Susan yelled, "So am I!" The "I" of "So am I" sounded muffled. It took that long for Betsy to reach Susan and put her hand over Susan's mouth.

John scrambled to his feet. His mind raced as he fumbled with his rifle. *What? Somebody's here. What'd they say?* John didn't mean for anyone to hear him. Out of frustration, he simply stated how he felt. That's all. Suddenly, he had to face the danger of an unknown quantity all by himself. He wished his horse had not pulled up lame. A posse provided the comfort he wished he had at that moment. John heard a baby crying. The sound came from over yonder, beyond that distant hill.

Betsy's sudden move to muffle Susan upset everything. First, one baby started crying, and that set the other one to join in. The noise from the infants finally became too much for Sally, and she began to rock back and forth. Even with all the chaos around her, Betsy sensed someone approaching.

John tenuously walked toward the hill where the noise emanated. He crouched down as low as possible to reduce his size as a potential target.

"Did you hear that?" Betsy asked.

"Hear what?" Susan responded. A twig broke, then another. Betsy put her finger to her lips to warn Susan. Betsy then looked for anything she might use as a weapon. She found a partially burnt branch from the unlit campfire. With her weapon resting on her shoulder, she slid along the wall of the cave in the direction where she would do battle. Set in place, Betsy wound up, ready to swing a mighty blow. She mouthed, "One, two, three."

John cringed when he stepped on not one, but two twigs. He could not believe he'd made such a stupid mistake. He cursed himself for losing the element of surprise. He regretted facing an opponent who expected him. With grim determination, he slowly crept along the side of a large boulder until he reached his destination. He raised his rifle and prepared to do battle. He mouthed, "One, two, three."

John swung around. So did Betsy. The two adversaries stood face-to-face with mere inches between them. John looked into her eyes. How could he not, they mesmerized him. Betsy's notion of a posse, something she decided to avoid at all costs, dissipated when she saw John. *He's not scary at all.* John lowered his rifle.

John thought, *There's no danger here, My God, she's beautiful.* He smiled.

Betsy thought, *Oh my, he's so innocent looking. He's smiling at me. How dare he smile at me!* Betsy swung.

The brittle wood cracked when she hit him on his side. It knocked him over and he hit his head on a stump. His smile had turned to a look of confusion, and he lay on the ground, unconscious, with his rifle beneath him.

By then, Susan had shown up. "What happened?" She asked.

"I hit'im" Betsy responded.

Susan asked, "Is he dead?"

Betsy leaned in close to see if he was still breathing. When she did, she noticed he had quite a gentle-looking face.

She told her sister, "No, thank goodness, but he'll have a headache when he wakes up.

"You hit 'im? Why didya' do that?" Susan asked again.

Betsy answered her sister saying, "He smiled at me."

"He what?" asked the surprised Susan.

Betsy repeated her answer "He smiled at me." This time, she realized how foolish her answer sounded.

Seeking more clarification, Susan repeated her question, "You hit 'im 'cause he smiled at you?"

Betsy replied, "Uh huh."

"Remind me not to smile at you," quipped Susan. Betsy ignored Susan's comment.

"Here, give me his rifle," Susan insisted.

Betsy asked, "Why?"

"Cause, when he smiled at you, you hit 'im. You'll probably shoot 'im when he says, 'Good day.' Now, give me the gun," Susan repeated.

Flustered, but knowing Susan had a point, Betsy tugged at John's rifle until she successfully freed it from underneath him. Thankfully, the rifle didn't discharge by mistake. Betsy then gave the rifle to her sister. Betsy pulled John by his arms to a shady area.

Susan leaned over and examined the side of John's head. She felt his forehead.

"At least he's still alive. He has a horse somewhere, don't he? Go look for it," Susan suggested. Betsy rose and then took a long look at John.

"Whatya' thinkin? Susan asked.

With a voice that sounded deep in thought, Betsy replied, "Oh, nothin.'" She then went searching for the young man's mount.

The first time John regained consciousness he thought everything around him had the makings of a strange dream. His world spun around - sometimes moving one way, and then in an instant, it would spin in the opposite direction. It sped up or slowed down based on whether he moved or not, and if he moved, how quickly.

His visual focus, fuzzy at first, slowly regained its accuracy, just as did his ability to hear. The right side of his head throbbed with pain, but he didn't know why. He didn't know how he ended up here, or where "here" was. He remembered whittling wood beneath a tree. He wondered how far he got on his masterpiece. That's the last thing he remembered.

John assumed the crying he heard woke him up. He hoped the crying came from human babies. He didn't know for sure, since he hadn't seen any babies yet. All he had seen, that he could make sense of, appeared as large angular rocks. He didn't remember any large rocks while whittling.

He opened his left eye. There sat a young woman rocking back and forth for no reason at all. He heard a woman's voice saying something to someone, but he couldn't make out what the voice said.

He peered over toward the voice. Moving made his head spin even more. The crying stopped. He wondered why. His eyes focused to see a young woman sitting, not far from him. He saw two babies suckling, one to each breast. John faded back to sleep.

When he woke up the second time, he felt a cool wet cloth on the side of his throbbing head. Somebody tended to his wound, and it felt comforting.

Barely above a whisper, John strained to ask. "Where am I?'

Betsy responded, "You're in a cave, in Kentucky." The source of the voice came from someone just outside his line of sight.

John moved so he could see her. He felt the wound on the side of his head and grimaced. He also felt his dizziness return, although not nearly disruptively as before. "What happened to me?"

Betsy hesitated to respond, "Somebody hit you."

"Who?" asked John.

"I did." Betsy gave him one of those, "Please don't hold it against me" looks.

"Why did you do that?" John asked, and for the second time. He didn't remember the first time. He looked at her mesmerizing eyes.

"You smiled at me," Betsy replied.

Startled by her answer, he winced. "Remind me not to smile at you."

"That's what I said," Susan interjected. She had purposely remained quiet up to that point. John looked at Susan. Somewhere in the recesses of his mind, he knew he had recently seen that woman, but he didn't know where.

Susan asked, "Are you with that posse chasin' the Harpe Brothers?"

"Supposed to be. That's until my horse came up lame. Why?" John asked.

Susan said, "We want to be your prisoners."

"Prisoners! What for?" John asked.

Susan answered, "Cause I'm Susan Harpe. She's Sally Harpe" pointing to Sally, "And, she's..."

Betsy jumped in before Susan could finish, "I'm Betsy Roberts."

John said, "Nice to meet you ladi...Oh! Harpe, like in Big and Little." Both Susan and Betsy slightly nodded their heads.

John said, "Well, if you're gonna be my prisoners, don't you think you ought to give me back my...um...?" He pointed to his rifle.

"Oh," Susan exclaimed. She began to give the rifle back, but hesitated before doing so. "You're not gonna shoot us, are you?" she asked.

"No, of course not. I'm supposed to protect you," John responded. He was hurt that someone would ask him such a question.

"Why?" Susan asked. John took a few moments to think about what he wanted to say.

He replied, "Because you don't act like murderers, least ways, most of you don't." Betsy tilted her head as if a bit confused by his comment.

Slowly, the conversation waned as John grew weaker. Betsy helped John move so he continued to rest in the shifting shade. In fact, John fell asleep with his head resting in Betsy's lap. She gently applied a cool cloth to his wound. It felt comfortable to the one receiving care as well as to the one giving it.

Susan looked at Betsy and mouthed, "Samson?'

Betsy shrugged and mouthed back, "I hope so." She then looked down at John, who slept. She smiled.

SOME HOURS LATER SUSAN said, "There's some horses comin.'" She waved her arms to gain the riders' attention as the three came closer. Leiper and Tompkins stayed back to find and put down the wounded horse that Micajah rode. The riders didn't know what to expect when they rode up. Sensing a trap of some kind, they felt relieved when John walked around the corner of the cave with a sturdy branch helping him to stand and walk.

Moses spoke first, "John, it looks like you've had a busy day. What's with the stick?"

John then went on to tell a white lie about him trying mount his horse. He told them that his horse threw him and, in the process, he hit his head. Then he told a bigger lie about how he captured the women who traveled with the Harpe Brothers. Moses and his relatives doubted John's story, but they didn't press the point. Before anyone could ask, John identified the women.

"The one over there is Sally. She's Little Harpe's wife. She's not right in the head. This one is Betsy Roberts, and that there is Big Harpe's wife, Susan," John said.

"You mean Big Harpe's widow, don't you?" Moses boasted.

Betsy asked, "He's dead? You sure?"

"I've got his head in my saddlebag if you wanna take a little peek," Moses replied.

In spite of all the abuse, Susan had mixed emotions about her husband's death. It felt awkward to have someone recognize her as a widow, even though one could hardly call what they had as a real marriage. At the same time, an emotional feeling of relief rushed in. She could not deny her feelings of relief.

When Betsy heard the news, she couldn't help but think, *That Reverend Talent got it right after all. Too bad he missed his prediction by a day.*

Moses asked, "What happened to Wiley?"

Susan went on to describe how Micajah murdered Wiley's baby, how the brothers fought, and how Wiley rode off after warning Micajah of the approaching posse. She told Moses about Sally's peculiar behavior ever since they woke up that day. Susan refused to share details about Sally's rape, or the circumstances surrounding it.

Stegall, missing a large chunk of vital information, stated, "Let me get this. You said that Wiley was gone before anybody woke up except for Sally." So, you don't know if the two talked or not. Right?" Susan nodded her head.

"And, you say, beginnin' today, she's not right in the head. Right?" Moses continued, "That don't fit. I bet them two are in cahoots with each other. Wiley never left his brother's side. Ever!" Pointing to Sally, he said. "If'n you ask me, I bet she's done pulled the wool over your eyes. She's pretendin."

Moses called out, "Hey you, Mrs, Wiley." He then stepped in the direction of Sally. Fearing danger, Susan, who already stood in between Moses and Sally, positioned herself in Stegall's path and planted her feet. Once again, she overcame her personal fear for the safety of another.

Moses yelled, "Get outa my way" as he threw Susan aside.

Susan yelled, "Betsy, help." Little more than seconds passed before Betsy jumped on his back.

She clawed away at his face when he yelled, "Get 'em off of me." Stegall's relatives grabbed both Susan and Betsy, and struggled to keep the two women contained. Moses felt confident that he'd pull a truthful answer out of Sally if he had the chance, even if he had to beat it out of her. Once the fighting began, Sally's shrill screams would not stop. Moses reached out to Sally. John chose to not let that happen. John swept the branch he'd used as a makeshift crutch across the back of Segall's legs. It forced Stegall to trip and fall.

Stegall cursed, "What the he..." As Stegall got back to his feet, he asked. "What are you doin' boy?"

John yelled, "Leave her alone. I told you she's not in her right mind. Now, leave her alone. Leave them all alone."

Moses asked, "She's done' fooled you, too?" Stegall fully intended to go after Sally again, when he noticed John reaching for his rifle. Stegall dove for the rifle at the same time as John. In the scuffle that ensued, the rifle ended up out of reach of both men. John fought a good fight, even though he had already suffered a wound earlier in the day. His limited ability didn't limit his determination. Nonetheless, Moses got the better of John as the two rolled about on the ground- scuffling, yanking, squeezing, biting, clawing, and occasionally landing a punch or two. No matter what it took, John refused to give up. That's why Stegall never touched Sally, that, and the return of John Leiper.

Leiper stepped out from behind where he snuck up on them unnoticed and yelled, "Moses, that's enough. We ain't hurtin' no women, nor babies neither. Not when I be in charge. Get offa him."

Leiper looked at Betsy and Susan struggling to break free and said, "You boys let go of them two." They did. Susan scrambled back to the babies. At the same time, Betsy pushed past the one who restrained her to be by John's side.

John turned to Betsy and said. "I'll be fine. Go take care of your friend. She needs you."

Betsy squeezed his hand, got up, and went to Sally. Eventually she calmed Sally down enough so she would stop her incessant high-pitched screams. Sally returned to rocking back and forth.

Moses stood before Leiper and pleaded his case. He said he should have free rein to do whatever he wanted to do to Sally. based on the Old Testament scripture that says, "An eye for an eye, a tooth for a tooth."

"But them's their women. That one," Stegall pointed to Sally, "That one there is Little Harpe's wife. She's pretendin' that there's somethin' wrong with 'er. Give me an hour alone with 'er, and I guarantee she'd tell us where to find her man."

Leiper responded, "I heard you before, but I don't believe you. We'll bring 'em back to Henderson. If she's a lyin' we'll find out. They's gonna git a fair trial. I'm not lettin' 'em go. You can trust me on that."

"Great! Until then, you're gonna' let Little Harpe get away, just like that, aren't you?" Stegall responded. He had taken about all he would take of John Leiper's leadership. In disgust, Moses walked away, muttering to himself.

Leiper would not budge from his original position. No matter how hard anyone tried, He knew Sally would not talk, let alone divulge Little Harpe's whereabouts, even if she did know, which Leiper believed she did not.

Later that day, Betsy approached John to express her gratitude. She said, "Thank you for defending us back there. My sister and I agree that you're a hero. You're our Samson.

John replied, "Hero? Your Samson? Oh no, I'm no Samson. Look at me. I don't even have the hair for it."

Betsy jumped in saying, "No, no, no, no, not that Samson. Our Samson. Our dog Samson."

With his ego bruised John responded, "What? You're comparing me with a dog?"

Betsy realized that she had said the wrong thing, so she set out to make things right when she offered, "He was a very good dog." She waited for a response. None came. Betsy feared that she may have ruined everything when she stated, matter of factly, "You don't look at all like our Samson either.

"Thanks," John replied. A broad smile broke out across his face. He thoroughly enjoyed watching Betsy dig a hole for herself with every passing comment she made.

Chapter Two: The Little White Church

Those who got to know John recognized him as a finagler, in a good way that is. He finagled his way onto the posse that brought down Big Harpe. He finagled his way in with the sheriff so he could serve as Betsy's, Susan's, and Sally's jailor. There he successfully protected the community from the three hardened criminals and their babies. He'd also finagled his way into Betsy's heart.

John fell in love with Betsy the moment he saw her, just before she walloped him. He knew he would marry her, but marrying a girl with a noose around her neck didn't bode well for their future together, a home and family. He wanted children with her, and he wanted a quiver full. That's why he did what he did to sway the trial in the girl's favor.

Right from the beginning, John knew the girl's trial would depend on whether a jury saw the three as victims or willing participants. He rightfully feared that innuendos, hearsay, and rumors would stand in as evidence if no real evidence was found. He knew somebody needed to challenge the veracity of each of those lies. John would do his part to fight against it.

With the eagerness of a man in love, John pigeonholed almost every woman in the community, encouraging them to take pity on the girls. Many women took him up on his offer to come and talk to Betsy, Susan, and Sally for themselves. John knew that these visitors would make their own first impression of the girls based on what they saw.

Therefore, each day John brought bucket after bucket of hot water to the girls to make sure they, and the jail, were scrubbed up nice and clean. He enjoyed flexing the biceps he gained due to all that lifting. Most of all, John had a surprise for the day of the trial. He just needed some help to make his plan work.

THE SHOPKEEPER'S WIFE took a look around to see if any other customers were approaching the store. So did John. It was all clear.

"I think you're looking for something you don't usually buy, am I right?"

He nervously scratched behind his ear, and said, "Yes Ma'am."

"Well, don't worry about it none. You're not the first embarrassed man to come in here. Won't be the last neither. Why don't you tell me what you're looking for, and it'll be a secret between the two of us. Alright?" She made John feel much better. He then went on to describe what he wanted to do and why he wanted to do it.

The storekeeper's wife, thrilled by his idea, did what she could to help. In her estimation, chivalry still lived. John stood out as her shining example. She apologized for only having few remnants of cloth left. Most were scraps of varying colors. She bundled everything up in brown wrapping paper so nobody would question him, and charged him a fraction of the total cost. She wondered how she would explain it to her parsimonious husband, later.

John finally felt his idea would actually work, and it showed on his face until the woman asked, "You do know how to do this, don't you?"

His heart sank, and the smile on his face disappeared.

"No," he replied.

The shopkeeper's wife recommended that he contact an elderly woman who was known for her congeniality, skill, and ability to keep her mouth shut. "She can show you what to do." John left the store with a brown, wrapped package in one hand, and a letter of introduction in the other.

He had to work quickly because the trial date was only weeks away.

Chapter Three: The Trial

Where does somebody hold the trial of trials? At the little white church, of course. There's no place more fitting. People came from all about to see the Harpe Brother's women. Only a small portion of those who attended could fit inside the building. The number of people who came to the trial steadily grew beyond what the church could accommodate. The little white church quickly filled up. It creaked and groaned, and the elders of the church feared it might collapse. Still, no one dared leave for fear they'd not find their way back in again.

An enterprising young man who stood on the porch near the entrance rolled up a large piece of paper into the shape of a bullhorn. His makeshift public address system drew a crowd around the entrance of the church.

Finally, younger boys and girls ran as messengers to those who preferred the comfort of sitting under a shade tree, catching a fresh breeze, sharing, and hearing the most recent gossip about friends and neighbors.

The trial took on an air of excitement, so much so that it felt akin to a carnival or a holiday celebration. The trial gave most everybody a chance to set aside their own personal miseries so they could watch the misery of others, all laid out in an orderly fashion.

Yep, they came from all around. Each one came looking for something. Some had questions that needed answering. Others had imaginations that needed stroking. Fears needed calming and rumors needed fueling. The people demanded it, and they would accept nothing less to quench their voyeuristic souls. Therefore, their tiny corner of Kentucky became the center of a region's attention.

THE DAY OF THE TRIAL opened with a visit from the girl's lawyer, Mr. Spencer. He stopped by to discuss strategies. Afterwards, John brought in three sets of leg irons. He also had three pairs of stockings, all three poorly constructed and very colorful. Susan cackled when she saw them. She gave John a hug and thanked him for his gift. John put a pair of leg irons on Susan first and then escorted her out to the wagon. With Betsy's help, they did the same for Sally.

That left Betsy and John alone in the jail, actually a rented barn located near the center of town.

John patted a chair and said, "Here, come sit."

As Betsy sat, she asked, "Do we havta' wear these?"

"I'm afraid so," replied John. He despised causing the girls any discomfort.

"Why?" She asked.

John replied, "The Sheriff said so."

When John reached over for the stockings, Betsy asked, "Did you make these?"

"Yes."

"Why?"

"So the leg irons won't scrape your ankles up." He answered. Betsy tilted her head to watch John slide one sock on and then the other. She liked what he did, but didn't know what to make of his kindness. John then bent over and kissed the top of each of her feet. He cradled them in his hands for the longest time. All misty-eyed, John stammered, "For luck." He turned away without looking at her face. He couldn't let her see him this way, not this day - the day of the trial.

Betsy blushed a deep red.

No one said much while riding to the church. A young teenage boy with several pebbles in his hand ran alongside the wagon and occasionally threw one or two of the rocks at the girls just to taunt them. John scolded the boy, and warned him to move on. The boy did too, when he ran to the front of the church and proclaimed, "They're here!" Excitement grew in and around the church.

It took some time to transfer everyone from the wagon to the building, but once completed, the sound of leg irons scraping on the church's wood plank floor kept everybody's attention. When, oh when would they pull the curtain aside?

Betsy stepped out first. She led Sally by the hand. Mr. Spencer greeted them and showed Betsy where to sit. The people in the sanctuary sat stunned at first. They didn't know what to think. The mood changed by the time John escorted Susan past the curtain.

Some folks pointed and laughed, others smiled, mostly they snickered. Their snickering didn't bother John one bit, for people don't snicker at murderers. Their buoyant response gave proof that the community didn't see the prisoners as evil personified. No, they saw the three as people, just like them. The garish looking stockings made for a perfect first impression. John had done his job well.

THE TRIAL OPENED LIKE most trials, with someone saying, "All rise." It didn't stay similar to other trials for long. First, both lawyers gave their opening remarks. Afterwards, the prosecutor, William Tomlinson, took the floor. Tomlinson, an experienced lawyer who sent many a man to the gallows over the length of his career, spun a damning story of guilt on the part of the three women. He had little evidence to support his claims other than a woman's bloody footprint alongside that of Wiley and Micajah's at the Stegall homestead, but that didn't matter much. He knew he would win or lose his case, not based on facts, but on how well he painted Betsy, Susan, and Sally as willing followers of the Harpe Brothers- As participants, not as victims trapped in their own personal nightmare.

When Tomlinson called Moses Stegall to testify, Moses told of the first time he met Betsy, Susan, and Sally. According to Stegall's testimony, a one-sided account, he claimed that Sally faked an illness in order to conceal the whereabouts of her husband. The prosecutor couldn't have asked for more, especially when Mr. Spencer, an upstart lawyer, failed to cross-examine Stegall, or challenge the highly respected prosecuting attorney for his use of fictional bits of information as actual evidence.

At the end of Stegall's testimony, the prosecutor asked, "If not to protect Wiley, why do you think Betsy and Susan, those Jezebels, struggled so to keep you from asking Wiley's wife about her husband's whereabouts?"

Stegall replied, "I can't think of any."

The defense attorney remained quiet. Judge McClellan winced after hearing nothing from the defense.

However, it was Leiper's testimony, not Stegall's, that did the most to place a noose around each woman's neck. Tomlinson had Leiper recall the time when Big Harpe described the various murders he and Wiley committed before he, too, died. The prosecutor purposely ignored baby Abigail's death.

At the end of his questioning, he asked, "Mr. Leiper, Can you explain why these three women," the word 'women' rolled off his lips with disdain, "followed Micajah, even though they knew you chased him with the intent to capture or kill the man?"

Leiper responded, "No."

"If you were in their shoes, what would you have done?" the attorney asked.

"In their shoes?... I'd run away, I reckon." Leiper responded. Once again, Mr. Spencer didn't challenge or cross-examine the witness.

Judge McClellan asked, "Young man, do you have any questions for this man?

"No, Your Honor." Spencer replied. Judge McClellan fumed.

When Mr. Tomlinson said, "The prosecution rests, your honor". He felt the trial was well within his grasp to win. So did Mr. Spencer. The defensive strategy he'd mapped out looked more and more impossible every time he reviewed it. John, situated between the curtain and the backdoor of the church to make sure nobody came in that way, slumped in a chair, aimlessly looking out a window. His dreams had already started evaporating. Even Judge McClellan felt the process wobbling out of control. At that point, the Judge knew that he alone would have to make sure that justice was served, no matter what it took.

And Betsy? Well, Betsy worried about Susan taking the stand. *Would she falter? Would she whither under Mr. Tomlinson intense questioning?* Mr. Spencer led Susan through the past, going all the way back to when Big and Little Harpe arrived at their cabin door. Susan told the story well.

When Spencer said, "Your witness" Tomlinson attacked. He challenged Susan at every point imaginable. Surprisingly, Susan held her own, in spite of the prosecutor using every lawyer's trick he could remember.

Tomlinson asked, "Why didn't you run away when you first met them?"

"I was scared," Susan answered.

"Yet, you married him. You made a choice, an important decision. You willingly followed him. Why?"

Susan answered, "If you think I said, 'I do' to a justice of the peace 'cause I wanted to, then you don't know nothin' 'bout nothin!"

A howl erupted throughout the room. The prosecutor failed to appreciate the humor, especially when it was at his expense—neither did the judge. He rapped his gavel to quiet the crowd.

Susan continued, "Big Harpe had to have things his way no matter what. If you didn't do what he wanted, when he wanted, and HOW he wanted, then you got beat. If you fought back, you, or one of yours would die."

Susan looked toward Sally when she said that. Sally had already started rocking. Betsy tried to calm her, but nothing seemed to work. Both the jury and those who watched noticed the poignant interplay between Susan and Sally. Soon thereafter, Tomlinson concluded his cross-examination. The young woman who, at one time in her life lived from one panic attack to the next, returned to her seat. She dared not show it, but she had just won a war of words with someone who excelled at debating. Most people concluded that she bore no guilt. They broke for lunch.

The afternoon session promised to build to a climatic ending. It didn't disappoint.

Spencer called Betsy to the witness chair. Betsy said her "I do" on a Bible and sat. Mr. Spencer asked about her well-being, then it happened.

A disheveled man that no one had ever seen before stood in the doorway of the church. By the look of him, he had obviously traveled a long distance in a minimal amount of time. In spite of his present condition, he had a way about him. People seemed to defer to him, and he'd grown accustomed to it. That probably explained how he reached the church door without a lot of jostling about or pushing.

Barely above a whisper, the man said, "Excuse me," and the people in front of him parted so he could look inside. A cluster of clouds that blocked the sun's rays passed over at that moment, so a splash of light shown behind the man. From inside the church, his outline was the only defining feature anyone noticed.

Sally had said nothing but a few random words since that horrendous night beneath the Jesus tree. She also paid little attention to what went on around her during the trial. Nobody could ever explain how she heard the man's simple comment, but because of it, she turned her head toward the door. In an instant, Sally reconnected with something from her past. She slowly stood up, and with great difficulty said, "Daddy?"

Everybody stopped whatever they did to watch Sally. A collective gasp rose when she spoke for the first time. A second gasp, even louder this time, filled the church when the disheveled man walked to Sally and hugged her. No one stopped him, even though she was one of the defendants. The place was silent for a few seconds, and then pandemonium broke out.

Sally gleefully exclaimed, "Daddy!" as she snuggled into the arms of her father. The Judge rapped his gavel to quiet the crowd. They did, but not because of his gavel. Everybody waited for what would happen next and didn't want to miss a moment of it. Peeved, McClellan asked, "Excuse me Sir, who might you be?"

Without any hesitation and in a matter-of-fact manner, Sally answered, "Daddy."

A blurt of laughter mushroomed into the rafters above. Once again, the Judge rapped his gavel, but once again to no avail. The judge waved for the man to approach. The man gently broke away from Sally.

She let out an urgent, "Daddy!" The man returned to Sally and put a finger to his lips to keep her quiet. He then turned to the judge's bench. Sally faced the crowd and boasted, "Daddy." She did so more than once. The judge gave up trying to control the crowd.

"Explain yourself, sir. The judge sternly demanded.

"Your Honor, I am the Reverend Paul Rice, and Sally there," he pointed, "Is my daughter."

Judge McClellan said "daughter" at the same time as Reverend Rice. "Yes, that relationship has already been clarified many times," Judge McClellan chuckled.

"I hurried across the state as soon as I heard about the trial. I came to apologize for acting like such a fool to my Sally. I hope she will forgive me?" Rice said.

"Oh, I have no doubt about that." The judge offered. He continued, "Please be seated."

As he sat, Sally protested, "Daddy?"

"Reverend, could you sit?" Judge McClellan nodded his head toward Sally.

"Certainly sir," replied Reverend Rice. He moved to a bench that somebody gave up and placed behind his daughter. Sally leaned back against him and contently murmured, "Daddy."

Betsy and Sally looked at each other. Sally whispered, "Daddy?" and Betsy slightly smiled.

Betsy thought to herself *Why couldn't her pa act like that man?* She knew that would never happen. Sally's performance proved to everyone that she was incapable of killing anyone. Only Betsy remained.

For a second time Mr. Spencer spoke. It took a moment before Betsy realized he addressed her.

"Betsy, since this trial is officially about the murder of Mrs. Stegall and her infant son, can you take us back to when you entered the Stegall cabin?"

Betsy proceeded to tell of the carving on the door, the half-burnt cabin, the footprints on the floor, and how she accidentally stepped in a pool of blood which made for her footprints to appear along with the others. She even told of the critters on the baby blanket.

"Did you see how Mrs. Stegall and her child died?" Mr. Spencer asked.

Betsy replied, "Yes." Her answer piqued everyone's attention, especially Mr. Tomlinson. He leaned forward to hear every word.

"Wait a minute. You have me at a loss. You testified that you reached the cabin after the Harpe Brothers left. Now, you say you saw how they died. How could you have done both? Mr. Spencer questioned.

"I can't explain it. All I can say is that when something stung me near my eye, I fainted, When I woke up again, I could only see outta my bad eye. I could see and hear 'em talkin', but they couldn't see nor hear me. Like I was there but not there at the same time," Betsy said.

Mr. Tomlinson rose immediately and yelled, "I object. Your Honor. This is nothing more than an outlandish fairy tale. Nobody can see what already happened once it happened. That's impossible. You have to be there when something happens for you to see it," Tomlinson argued.

"Bill, I tend to agree with you, but since I gave you a lot of rope, let's give the Defense some rope too. I'll allow it for the time being, and I can always change my ruling later. Go ahead counselor, but watch your step," McClellan finished. The prosecutor muttered to himself as he sat.

Mr. Spencer turned back to Betsy and asked, "So, Miss Roberts, what did you notice first when you saw only through your left eye?"

Betsy answered, "Mrs. Stegall stood over her fire fixing breakfast. Her baby, still in the cradle, wouldn't stop cryin'. The momma had a hard time cookin' what with the baby cryin'."

The lawyer asked, "You said that you called out to her, Is that right?"

"Yes sir, I called out, but she didn't hear me. I could hear her, but she didn't hear me, 'specially when Wiley and Micajah entered," Betsy replied.

"So, you warned her?" he asked.

"Yes sir, I tried," she answered. Betsy went on to describe how Mrs. Stegall apologized for the food taking so long and asked if Major Love was coming.

"Micajah told her, 'No, he's still asleep.' They both complained 'bout that fella snorin'. We didn't know 'bout him bein' dead at the time. What with the barn burnt down and all," answered Betsy.

Mr. Spencer asked, "What happened next?"

"Wiley offered to help." Betsy stopped and looked around, obviously looking for something. She also used the time to gather herself. "May I have some water?" Someone appeared with a cup.

Betsy continued, "Wiley said, Why don't you let me hush your youngun. I'm good at hushin' 'em down." Betsy haltingly took another swallow of water. "She didn't see him take out his knife."

"You did though didn't you? What did you do?" Spencer asked.

"I screamed. Didn't help none. Wiley, he cut the baby's throat open. You could hear the child gurgling for a bit. It finally stopped. Some... some of the blood. . ." Betsy cleared her throat. "Some of the blood seeped through the bottom of the cradle and dripped to the floor. It made a tiny puddle." Betsy answered. Some of the more squeamish ones in the crowd squirmed in their seats. Those with fans either picked up their pace due to nervousness or stopped waving them altogether. A sniffle or two punctuated the otherwise quiet courtroom.

"And?" Spencer urged.

"And Mrs. Stegall, she said, 'I say, you sure do have a way with babies' when she no longer heard her baby cryin',"

Once again, Spencer urged, "Go on."

"I yelled 'No, No!" That's when she went to look at her baby." Betsy had gotten softer in her speech. The judge instructed her to speak up.

With more vigor, not enthusiasm, Betsy continued, "She screamed when she saw her dead baby." Betsy looked over to Sally,

Sally had wrapped herself in her daddy's arms and tried rocking once again. Her father's embrace kept her from doing so.

Mr. Spencer asked, "Do you need to stop for a moment? Betsy shook her head and continued. "I think that's when Susie and Sally heard me yell, 'No, no, no!' when Mrs. Stegall screamed. She kept screamin' as she tried to run, but Mickey. . .Micajah, he caught her and swung her 'round toward Wiley. She pleaded, oh, she pleaded, but Wiley cut HER throat, too. Micajah let go of her, and she plopped down on the floor waitin' for death. A tear rolling down her cheek."

"There's more isn't there?" Mr. Spencer asked? Betsy nodded. He nodded back, urging her to continue.

"She wasn't quite dead when Wiley asked Micajah, 'Hungry?'" Betsy then went on to describe how they got themselves some food. Micajah kicked the woman's body over and used it as a foot-rest. They kept talking to the corpse like she could hear them.

"I don't remember nothin' else. That's when Susie and Sally pulled me out, I reckon." Exhausted, Betsy finished.

Mr. Spencer said, "Your wit....Oh. just one more question. You said something stung you, and that made it possible to see through time. What stung you?

Betsy answered, "A bumblebee, a big one, somehow it got stuck under the blanket I s'pose. It flew right at me once I moved the blanket.

The moment Mr. Spencer said your witness the second time, Mr. Tomlinson protested again.

Judge McClellan responded, "Sit down, Bill, and take it easy. I'm going to disallow the testimony. In fact, this whole trial was a sham, a travesty to Kentucky's rule of law, and we all bear some responsibility for it. I, for one, apologize for taking part in it. That's why I declare these proceedings a mistrial." He rapped the gavel and said, "This court is adjourned."

And, never again, before they met their maker, would Sally, Susan, or Betsy stand before a judge.

With the pounding of his gavel, he ended the proceedings. Judge McClellan gathered his things with the intention of traveling to the next stop on the circuit. John, who quickly came out from behind the curtain, whispered something in McClellan's ear and the judge sat back down. Clearly, his plans had changed.

John Huffstutler knew he had a duty to perform, and that he should not show any emotion one way or the other, but he just couldn't help himself.

He unlocked the leg irons and said to all three, "You're free!" John kept glancing at Betsy the entire time he spoke to them all.

"Excuse me, I have some matters to attend to, but I hope I will see you soon."

John looked at Betsy intensely when he said that final phrase. He turned and left. Betsy felt an emptiness when he left. It bothered her.

With the sweltering heat making the church almost unbearable, everybody cleared out and moved toward the nearby apple orchard, thankful for the fresh air. Numerous well-wishers offered congratulations. Some Susan and Betsy recognized from earlier visits to the jail. They didn't know most of the well-wishers.

Chapter Four: Sally's Goodbye

Reverend Rice, anxious to mend fences with his congregation back in Knoxville, left Sally with Betsy while he made preparations for the journey home. It took considerable promising on his part to his daughter that he would return as quickly as possible before she would let him go. Sally finally agreed on the condition that she could stay with Betsy.

Sally, refusing to let go of Betsy's hand as people approached, seemed especially quiet. She worked over in her mind something final, something important that needed saying before she parted. She knew she'd never see Susan or Betsy again. Reverend Rice returned. Susan offered to tell him what led to Sally's current condition, but he refused to listen.

"Thank you, but no. God already knows. I don't need to know. God, not I, will restore Sally if that is his will. I'm just thankful to have her with me again."

Sally pulled away from her father as he led her to a newly purchased wagon. On her own, and with tears in her eyes, Sally walked to Susan, hugged her, and slowly said, "Friend." Sally then turned to Betsy

Sally slowly pointed to herself. She stammered as she worked out the word, "I forgive." She then pointed to Betsy. "The... they," Sally pointed to the church, "forgive."

Sally then looked directly at Betsy and with great effort said, "You m... m... must forgive you... too." The two hugged, and with that, Sally and her daddy disappeared from sight.

Chapter Five: A Vow Fulfilled

At long last, only Betsy and Susan remained under the shade of the apple trees. Betsy said, "I guess we better go. Any ideas?" Susan shook her head. Betsy sensed something bothered her sister, but it didn't seem to be the right time to ask her about it.

"I wish there were some place we could cook us up some food. I'm hungry," Betsy stated. Immediately, Susan fell to her knees and blubbered gut-wrenching sobs. Betsy didn't know what to make of Susan's outburst. Had her nervousness finally caught up with her once the trial finished, or did something else bother her?

Betsy found it difficult deciphering what Susan said, what with her crying and all, but it sounded something akin to, "I can't ...I can't do it."

Betsy asked. "What, what can't you do?"

"Leave you," stammered Susan. Although it took a lot on Susan's part to explain herself, Betsy learned how one of the women, who regularly visited, tasted some of Susan's cooking. Because of that, the woman mentioned how she and her husband planned to open an inn, and they needed somebody to run the inn's eating establishment. They agreed that Susan could claim the restaurant as her own in a few years if everything went as planned.

Hearing that, Betsy felt deserted. It angered her, but she couldn't adequately display her displeasure. Instead, nobody said a word for a bit. Susan finally broke the silence.

She asked, "Do you think mama knew we was gonna suffer like we did?"

Betsy replied, "Yes."

"Me too." Susan added, "I always felt mama watched over us the whole time."

"So did I. She had to keep us together so she could watch over us both at the same time," Betsy offered.

It got quiet again until Betsy asked, "What did you say you were gonna call your place?"

"Doodles," Susan answered.

Betsy repeated, "Doodles," and responded with a quiet "huh." and a smile. After an awkward pause, Betsy couldn't wait to ask, "Alright, I gotta to know..."

Susan cut her short by confirming, "Doodles, alright?"

Betsy nodded. She wanted to beat her sister up and she wanted to laugh, all at the same time. She mustered a "huh...That's it... huh?"

During their time of silence, Betsy thought about everything moving so quickly, *How can I hold her back when she growed up so? She's even gonna use the nickname she hated as a name for her place. If that ain't proof of growin' up, what is?*

With considerable hesitation and a faltering voice, Betsy said, "You know you have to do it. You have to open your "Doodles." We can't use what kept us alive as a weapon to keep us from livin' now that things are settled some. It wouldn't be right."

Susan nodded her head and walked over to an apple tree where a branch hung low. She broke it off and brought the branch back to Betsy. "It's time we declare the vow complete," Susan said.

Each sister grabbed an end of the branch, and together they snapped it in half. Susan gave the half she held in her hand to Betsy. Betsy did likewise. They both felt ill at ease over the impromptu ceremony, for they had grown accustomed to the sense of security the promise provided. Nonetheless, they both knew the time had come for each of them to stand on her own.

Like partings between life-long friends or loved ones, theirs stacked high with sadness. Thankfully, knowing that Susan had a bright future ahead of her made their separation bearable.

That left Betsy standing alone and lonely.

Chapter Six: The Proposal

Betsy turned to look when she heard a wagon approaching. John sat atop it. She wanted to jump into his arms and show how happy she felt when she saw him again, but she couldn't seem to do it. She thought she had lost him forever and rejoiced within herself when he returned. She mustered a slight smile, that's all, when John pulled up beside her with a wagon full of household goods.

"I'm glad you're still here. I wanted to say goodbye," John said.

Confused, Betsy asked, "Goodbye?"

"Yep, even though I don't know much about it, I'm a farmer at heart, not a jailer. People say there's good land in Illinois. I thought I'd get me some while the gettin's good," John replied. "What are you going to do?"

She shrugged her shoulders. That's all she could manage.

"Well, goodbye," John said. He then rode off sitting atop his wagon.

Every turn of his wagon wheels was agonizing. Suddenly, she wanted to die. *Had John finished what the Harpe Brothers began?* She wondered.

For some reason, John stopped. Betsy didn't know what to think when John climbed down, tied the horses to a nearby tree, and started walking back. He stopped again and motioned for her to stay there. He went back to his wagon, loosened a chair, and with a chair in hand once again walked back toward Betsy.

"What are you..." Before she could finish her sentence, John put a finger to her lips to quiet her.

John then said, "Sit." She almost protested, but the look on his face convinced her to sit. As she sat, John knelt down in front of her. She didn't notice that he dropped to his knee while she sat. It startled her when she turned back to face him.

John began before she could say a word, "I don't know about you, but I know some strange twist of fate has brought us together. How a lonely boy from Pennsylvania with an unhappy past and no future had to travel to a jail in western Kentucky to find the love of his life is beyond me. I knew you were the one for me when I saw your face for the first time, just before you walloped me, and I know it now. I love you Betsy, and I always will. I would never forgive myself if I didn't do this, so here goes."

John said, "I vow..."

For the first time, Betsy responded to his proposal. She said, "No, no, no vows, please no vows." Hearing the word "no" spoken so forcefully temporarily left him crestfallen.

A second after she said it, Betsy realized what she had done.

With all the emotional expressiveness she could command, she tenderly reached out to John and said, "You don't need to make a vow. You've already proven that you're an honorable man. See?"

Betsy stuck out one of her multi-colored socks as evidence, "Just say you love me."

John took a hold of her hands, and said, "I love you. Will you marry me?"

Betsy smiled in spite of herself and said, "Yes."

In one sweeping motion, John rose and brought Betsy to her feet. He embraced and kissed his future wife.

A small crowd of well-wishers, those who Betsy said fond farewells to earlier, watched from inside the church's sanctuary. They had been eagerly waiting for this moment. The onlookers poured out of the church to share in the celebration when they saw the two hug.

Judge McClellan, standing on the stairs leading to the church, called out, "Well come on. I've got a wedding to perform."

LATER, WITH BETSY'S boy asleep in her arms, the newlyweds rode down the only road leading to Illinois. Unfortunately, the road required that they pass by the tree where the head of Big Harpe hung. He had been hanged there with a great deal of local pride and as a way of announcing that the threat was over.

John pulled up to the tree and stopped. He knew he would have never met his wife if Micajah had not died that day. John looked at the head and thought of how strange it was that Big Harpe's death brought John hope. He looked over to his bride. He was ready to say something important but hesitated when he saw the tense muscles in her face and the tightly squeezed white knuckles of his bride's hands. He waited for a few seconds. Betsy never looked up. Betsy never made a sound.

"Hyah," John called out. The wagon rolled forward.

And what, you may ask, became of the head of Micajah? For the next sixty years or so, Big Harpe's head hung in that tree as a warning to those who would do evil. Nature's forces rotted away everything but the skull.

Then, in the dead of night one night, a self-avowed witch stole the skull. She boiled it down for the makings of a witches' brew. The witch's act fulfilled John Robert's prophesy. Big Harpe's remains would never be laid to rest.

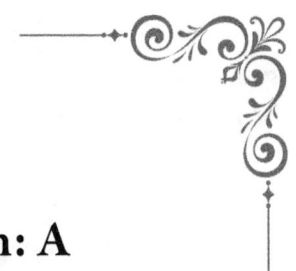

Chapter Seven: A Ribbon to Humanity

For Betsy, the day started like most days. Her life of running a home and sharing in the management of a farm provided the sense of security she craved. Her husband always included her in the decision-making about the farm. Close to three years had passed since they moved to Hamilton County in southern Illinois.

At first, John depended on Betsy's expertise, but over time, he'd learned how to run a farm to a point where their farm thrived. Her know-how made everything possible, so he figured keeping his wife involved could only help. However, he did question the building of a chicken coop that looked a lot like a castle.

Just as John learned how to farm after years of growing up nowhere near one, Betsy learned how to run a home. Unfortunately for Betsy, it was Susie who had done most of the household chores while growing up. Betsy considered herself a novice at cleaning and cooking, just as John had considered himself a novice at farming.

Cooking confounded Betsy the most. She always thought of Susan when she prepared a meal. What would Susan do this time, or how did Susie make it so tasty? She remembered how Susie could concoct something spectacular out of barely nothing. She couldn't.

For fear of John dying of malnutrition, Betsy asked a neighbor for help on how to cook. She learned how to make a tasty fried chicken. John appreciated it. However, fried chicken at almost every meal left his taste buds wishing for more. He never complained. He dared not complain. That is, if he ever wanted to eat fried chicken again. She knew she'd never win any ribbons for cooking, but she didn't mind, just as long as she satisfied her husband.

Betsy missed Susan, a lot, but when the trial was finished, both sisters knew the time had come for them to part ways. She and her sister had almost always been the best of friends. The last time she heard anything about Susan was when Susan wrote a letter. The letter spoke of her finally opening her eating establishment down south. Betsy chuckled that after all the years of drama, Susan did indeed use "Doodles" as the name of her place. She wrote that she still kept an eye out for Mr. Biegler. Betsy hoped Susan would one day have that family she always dreamed about. Susie's baby, Tom, already carried the man's name.

When Betsy was a little girl people visited quite often. Few stopped by the Huffstutler homestead. She missed that. This place wasn't as near a town as her childhood home had been. When they did, receiving a guest often turned out to be the highlight of the day. Those who did stop by were usually local folks.

So far, the only visitor of note had been the county sheriff. He would stop by unexpectedly in hopes of finding Wiley lurking about. His last visit differed from all the others. The sheriff pulled John aside and told him that the law had finally caught up with Wiley in a place called Natchez Trace. There, they stuck Wiley's head on a pike as a warning to other criminals - just as they had with Micajah. Betsy didn't know it yet, but this day the number of noteworthy visitors would increase to two.

Betsy knew good fortune smiled down on her the day John proposed. Just as important, John claimed her son Johnny as his own. John and Johnny did everything together.

Recently, she observed her little Johnny, close to four years old, first watched and then imitated walking exactly like her husband walked. Those two were like a stamp on an envelope. They both fulfilled an important need for the other. With the men of the family chumming around together, Betsy had more time to care for her new baby girl, who she named Anne, in memory of her mother.

Betsy knew she had much to be thankful for after her ungodly ordeal. With the help of time, she could once again function as a person. However, time didn't completely heal her pain, heal her haunting, or restore her to an earlier point. As she feared, Betsy lived a half-death life. She could not shake free of the demons that the Harpe brothers had placed within her.

It took a considerable amount of patience, but her husband waited for the real Betsy to reappear. He'd seen glimpses of the real Betsy before. He loved his wife no matter how she reacted to the world around her, but the warm, vibrant personality she showed on occasion still laid buried within her. That person enthralled him. However, he had no clue about how to help her deal with her pain. She couldn't let it go.

The collective weight of all the evil she bore was like a large jar of stones. She somehow traced it all back to her pa, whether it should have properly been attributed to him or not. The weight of it all sometimes became unbearable. Specific memories may have disappeared; but her anger toward her pa as the reason for all the hurt, all the pain, all the... For Betsy, John Roberts, her pa, caused all that had gone wrong in her life.

At breakfast, John and Betsy talked about how he and little Johnny would go down to the creek and bundle together some branches from the nearby trees. Illinois, noted for its flatland, had a few hills around where they lived. A large oak tree, the only one for as far as anyone could see, stood tall and off to the side of their cabin. It provided a welcome relief from the blistering summer sun. Another tree had fallen a couple of years earlier, most likely during a storm. They'd cut it up and used the wood for cooking and keeping warm during the winter. A stump remained. It served as a platform for chopping wood and beheading chickens. The rest of the wood they needed, they gathered from the stand of trees near the creek. Tall grasses, the kind a person could get lost in, originally covered the land they now called home.

A narrow, rutted road, passable only when the weather allowed, acted as a single ribbon connecting their farm to the next, and to the rest of humanity. Without that ribbon, wide enough for only one wagon at a time, all that the Huffstutlers and their neighbors worked to achieve would be for nothing. The road meant everything. There, on the road, Betsy first spotted the tiny figure of a man.

Her husband and young boy left close to an hour before, and Jacks, the family dog, had chased after them. The relationship, her son and Jacks had reminded her of the closeness her brother once had with their dog Samson. Betsy remembered *Samson. He was a good dog.* She didn't mean the opposite about Jacks. She only meant that she and Samson shared some important times together. She'd always been thankful that Samson watched over her when she watched over her mother's grave that lonely night.

Betsy brought out a couple of clay bowls from inside their home - one full of peapods and the other empty. Her baby had fallen asleep after filling her tiny tummy and Betsy didn't want to wake her, so she decided to work outside. She could keep an eye on things from the porch if anything important happened,

Sometimes living on a farm can rattle the eardrums. Other times the subtle farm sounds can even lull the industrious ants to sleep. That morning fit the latter. Betsy sat in the rocking chair on the porch and snapped peas. Each time she broke open a pod it sounded like a firecracker had gone off.

A distant woodpecker drilled away on the side of a far-off tree. A rooster felt the need to crow, "I'm here, I'm here!" He went back to foraging for something to eat. A slight breeze ruffled the oak leaves. If one listened closely, one could hear the garden's cornstalks stretching another inch taller under the heat of the summer sun. Betsy looked for the figure walking on the road. She had lost sight of the man and thought little of it. She went back to snapping peas.

If a person considers a road as a ribbon, then the path from each homestead to the road should qualify as one of the threads that make it up. The next time Betsy looked up she saw the individual walking along the narrow thread toward their home.

Betsy, now much more attentive, watched as the man came closer. She still couldn't see him clearly, nor identify any defining characteristics. Betsy felt it wise to prepare for anything, nonetheless. She picked up the bowls, one-half full, the other half empty, and took them inside. When she returned to the porch, she had a rifle in her arms. She didn't want to seem inhospitable, so she leaned it up against the cabin. She could retrieve it in a second if needed. Her husband made a special point of teaching Betsy how to shoot, just for moments like this.

Betsy looked intently at the man. He looked vaguely familiar, yet different. His most defining trait had to be the stooped-over walk of his. The man kept walking forward. She'd seen that walk before...*It's him!* Betsy grabbed the rifle and took aim.

"Stop right there. You can turn around and go back to where you came from. I don't want you here," Betsy yelled out curtly.

John Roberts, her pa replied, "And good morning to you, Betsy, or should I call you Mrs. Huffstutler?"

"Call me whatever you want. Just go away, and don't ever come back," Betsy responded. Every time Betsy's pa spoke, he slowly inched closer. She noticed it. She raised the family rifle and aimed it toward him. Seeing the wrong end of the rifle facing him made John falter for only a moment. He did not intend to walk away, not until he'd said and done what he came to do.

Betsy asked, "What do you want?" John noticed that his daughter had opened the door for more conversation.

"I came to see you," John answered.

"Well, you've seen me. Now go away," Betsy replied. She waved him off with her rifle to emphasize her desire for her pa to leave. Instead, John inched closer.

John asked, "Are you happily married?"

"Why do YOU care?" Betsy responded, irritated by his question.

"I was just askin' if you were happy, that's all. I want you to be happy," John said.

"Don't do that," Betsy complained.

"Don't do what?" John asked.

"Don't be wishin' things for me, worryin' 'bout me, or even thinkin' 'bout me. I want you to go away!" Betsy exclaimed. Ever so slowly, John edged his way forward to a point near the tree stump. It seemed like the perfect place to sit down.

John ignored his daughter's repeated demands for him to disappear.

He asked, "Do you mind if I sit?" Betsy grimaced at her pa's request, but she remained quiet. John took her silence as some form of permission. He hobbled over to the stump and pulled free the axe wedged into the top of it. Betsy, fearing danger, raised her rifle and took aim.

John, with a sense of urgency, said, "Whoa, whoa. I'm just gonna' set the axe down, See?" Betsy watched closely as he did what he said he would do. John sat.

"Aah! That feels good. The back's not as good as it used to be," he exclaimed, happy to take the pressure off his lower back.

John could trace his back problems to when Gentleman Jim's thugs gave him a brutal thrashing. It left him with permanent nerve damage. He never let Betsy know, nor did he blame her for ruining the man's fine silk coat in the first place. Although she assumed her act of vengeance to be fair and just, it had led to Gentleman Jim's act of vengeance, and so on and on it went.

Since that time, John had learned a different lesson, and he came to share that lesson with his daughter Betsy.

After waiting for her pa to settle in, and with the rifle still in her arms, Betsy asked, "What do you want?"

She had always remembered her pa, good or bad, as a strong, lanky man. His muscles didn't ripple like others, nor did he command attention when he walked into a room, but he possessed the type of heft one needed to complete any job. At least he used to.

He looked more like a grandpa than a pa, now. His stooped walk seemed more pronounced. A few extra pounds around his mid-section had decided to stay put. Even his beard, once a single color that matched the hair on the top of his head, presently displayed a cluster of colors including a pronounced shade of gray.

John answered, "I came to thank you."

Betsy, even in the little time they spoke, noticed a change in how he behaved. He seemed calmer, less imposing. It felt to her that her pa no longer had that haughty mentality she remembered. Somewhere along the way, the "you-should-take-note-of-me-because-I'm-smarter-than-you" attitude had fallen by the wayside.

"You came all this way to thank me. For what? You wasted your time," Betsy replied. She continued, "If I listen, will you go away?"

John ignored her request, "Three years ago, you sent a preacher to see me. Why, I don't know. I certainly didn't deserve it. I didn't deserve you even thinking of me at all.

Talent was his name. Yep, Reverend Talent. He took some time with me. He sobered me up, preached over me, and prayed over me. We read some from the good book and talked some. No, talked a lot. I found out that what I knew about religion, I only knew in my head. It never reached my heart. That's why a hole inside me always left me dissatisfied. I got saved. As evil as I've been, God forgave me for all I'd done, and that's saying a lot."

"Why are you telling me this?" Betsy asked, irritated by all his rambling.

John continued, "I even had to learn how to forgive myself before I could stop drinking. That's right, I haven't had a drink since. I've missed too much of my life because of drinking, Betsy. I'm a changed man."

Again, Betsy asked, "Why are you telling me this?"

"Because I came to ask you for your forgiveness over what I did to you," John answered.

Astonished by his request, Betsy said, "What? After you nearly ruined my life, you ask me to forgive you? Why? So, you can walk away from here feeling good about yourself? I'd just as soon shoot you than forgive you," Betsy retorted.

"No! It's you I'm concerned about. I can see you're hurting. Forgiving me will free YOU from the past, not me," John argued. He stood up and slowly moved closer.

"Oh, I see. Just like when you felt concerned for us when we left with Mickey and Wiley. You never came lookin' for us," Betsy complained.

"I'm sorry," John calmly stated.

Betsy could feel her anger rising, Ready to burst, she could do nothing to show it. "Stop it!" Betsy begged.

"I should have protected you from those two. I knew they were trouble. I'm sorry," John repeated.

"Stop it. Just stop it!" Betsy complained much louder. John had finally moved as close to the cabin as he dared.

Neither one said anything for a long time, then Betsy said in a quiet, yet fervent voice, "I needed you the day ma died. We all did. Whatja do? Made a vow to watch over us, then broke it within hours 'cause you done likkered yourself up. I had to finish buryin' ma that night, not you. All you did was boss us around like some pompous fool, and stole back what ma gave us to remember her by. You left it all to ME. Twelve! All alone I dun it. I was just twelve years old!" Betsy left the crucial barrier out there for her pa to hear.

Remembering that day broke John's heart just as much as it did hers. He slowly whispered, "I'm sorry."

A coldness came over Betsy. She pulled her rifle in a shooting position and said, "You've said your peace, now get."

"No. I'm not going to make it easy for you. Shoot me, and let hate rule your life, or forgive me and free yourself from all the pain. It's your choice." John then stood in front of his daughter with his arms stretched out in the shape of a cross and waited.

Furious at her pa for placing her in such a situation, Betsy's hands shook as she took aim. Even if she forgave him, she had so little physical control over the weapon that she might have shot him by mistake. There he stood, the one who instigated it all. All the bad that happened - right or wrong, she blamed on him.

She could get even. Betsy knew he deserved punishing, but time had passed and the intensity of her pain had been buried, along with some of her memories. *Why do I have to do this? Is he forcing me to shoot him for me, or for his benefit?* Betsy wondered. *Why can't he just go away and let me make do with the rest of my life as best I can? Does everything need setting straight? Why can't it just be?* Betsy tightened her grip. *Is pa saying 'I'm sorry' enough evidence that he really repented? Do I need something more? Of course, I do. That man of words can twist anything. Damn it, Pa, JUST LEAVE ME ALONE!*

Betsy shot. The lead ball flew over his head.

Her pa released a "Phew" as his muscles loosened. "I knew revenge hadn't taken control of your life. I'm glad you knew it too."

The gunshot startled Anne. Betsy heard her baby cry but did nothing to console her. Instead, she waited for some miraculous transformation to take place within herself. She felt relieved knowing she could let go of her anger, let go of her blame, and choose a peaceful remedy- instead of acting on her vengeance and resentment. She had tried avoidance. That had left things unresolved. Now, she could begin to let go of those poisonous feelings that had kept her from happiness.

Betsy looked at her pa. He looked back. Neither knew what to say.

Betsy finally said, "If you go lookin' for Susan, she moved down south and opened a place to eat. She named it 'Doodles.'"

Her pa looked up at her with a surprised look. She acknowledged his surprise and nodded her head slightly.

"Thank you," He replied.

The silence that followed left them both feeling uncomfortable. With nothing more to say, Betsy turned and entered the cabin so she could care for Anne.

Her pa quickly pulled an item from his pocket, took it out of a cloth bag, and set it on the stump. He then scurried around behind the elaborate chicken coop. John Roberts remained there, hidden until he felt he could safely return to the ribbon road unnoticed.

When Betsy returned, she stood alone. Her pa had disappeared. Even though she wanted him to leave, she felt a twinge of remorse that he actually had. She peered off into the distance in all directions. She wondered how someone could magically appear and then disappear so quickly again? How could someone say so little and yet say so much? She also wondered if she had dreamt it.

HER HUSBAND HURRIED back as quickly as he possibly could, but with the boy in one arm, and a rifle in the other, hurrying took time. He filled that time with worry.

"I heard a gunshot. What happened? John asked, as he set the young boy down by the stump.

"Pa, look," Johnny spotted the sparkling object right off, and grabbed it off the stump. He gave it to his pa.

John, confused and looking for answers asked, "Honey, what..." He showed her what the boy had found. Betsy rushed forward.

Betsy knew exactly what he held- her mother's brooch. She could not put it in her hands quickly enough. When she held it, all the locked chambers in her mind let go. Memory after memory competed for its time of remembrance. Her promise to her ma, standing guard with Samson over her open grave, her first kiss, watching The General soar high for his last time. All of those memories rushed back. Like pages in a book, each memory anxiously waiting for Betsy to turn to it. Plunging a knife into a dead man's chest. That came back too. The Stegall cabin, the heroic boy on a horse, nearing death on the Ohio River, even the dreadful screams of, "Kill me, kill me!" underneath the Jesus tree. They all came back.

She sobbed. She sobbed as she'd never done before. Her tears flowed for each memory, happy or sad. The blue brooch that matched the color of her eyes acted as the key to once again open them wide.

Betsy whispered, "I forgive you, Pa. I forgive you."

AS SHE REMEMBERED HER past, Betsy had to face the reality that she had no lasting memories of her life as a wife and mother - a new life grounded in love, peace, and consistency. She would change that. She would gather all the memories she could of her new life and not let a single one escape. She would share that legacy with her children, and hopefully her children's children. She'd show the power of compassion, not hate, forgiveness, not vengeance. Betsy felt alive, able to laugh and able to cry. She was fully alive once again.

And, for the second time in her life, Betsy made a vow.

ROBERT G. HUFFSTUTLER

The Second Vow

When a young one asked for a grandma's story,
Something fine, tales of old men's glory,
Betsy would not speak of her time in hell.
That, she vowed, she would never tell.
She spoke of love, not just man's, but God's.
Odes of peace and joy, they'd remember well.
But on tales of the Harpes she would not dwell.
That, she vowed, she would never tell.

The End

Don't miss out!

Visit the website below and you can sign up to receive emails whenever Robert G. Huffstutler publishes a new book. There's no charge and no obligation.

https://books2read.com/r/B-A-GAMCB-MTATC

BOOKS 2 READ

Connecting independent readers to independent writers.

About the Author

While other children went to bed listening to fairy tales of heroes like Peter Pan and Aslan from Narnia, Robert G. Huffstutler grew up on stories from the bible, but it was the stories that were passed from generation to generation in the family that really captured his attention.

Traditions like buttering your nose every birthday and tales of his ancestor surviving the Trail of Tears grew from small seedlings to a forest of sagas that the young boy would impart to his daughters as an adult.

Robert G. Huffstutler didn't share these legends with others outside his family until retiring as an Internship Coordinator at Northern Illinois University. As a retiree, he chose to start a new career as an author instead of playing golf and wrote his first historical fiction novel. The story of Susan and Betsy Roberts is the first book written and published by this author, but not the end of the library of exciting narratives inside his mind.

www.ingramcontent.com/pod-product-compliance
Lightning Source LLC
Chambersburg PA
CBHW072117020726
47501CB00003B/859